THIS
WICKED
FATE

Also by Kalynn Bayron
Cinderella Is Dead
This Poison Heart

THIS
WICKED
FATE

KALYNN BAYRON

BLOOMSBURY

NEW YORK LONDON OXFORD NEW DELHI SYDNEY

BLOOMSBURY YA
Bloomsbury Publishing Inc., part of Bloomsbury Publishing Plc
1385 Broadway, New York, NY 10018

BLOOMSBURY and the Diana logo are trademarks of Bloomsbury Publishing Plc

First published in the United States of America in June 2022 by Bloomsbury YA

Bloomsbury books may be purchased for business or promotional use. For information on bulk purchases please contact Macmillan Corporate and Premium Sales Department at specialmarkets@macmillan.com

Library of Congress Cataloging-in-Publication Data
Names: Bayron, Kalynn, author.
Title: This wicked fate / by Kalynn Bayron.
Description: New York : Bloomsbury Children's Books, 2022.
Summary: Briseis races to save her family even as she discovers more about their ties to ancient goddesses and deadly curses.
Identifiers: LCCN 2021045068 (print) | LCCN 2021045069 (e-book)
ISBN 978-1-5476-0920-8 (hardcover) • ISBN 978-1-5476-1069-3 (e-book)
Subjects: CYAC: Supernatural—Fiction. | Ability—Fiction. | Goddesses—Fiction. | Blessing and cursing—Fiction. | Plants—Fiction. | African Americans—Fiction. | LCGFT: Novels.
Classification: LCC PZ7.1.B386 Tj 2022 (print) | LCC PZ7.1.B386 (e-book) | DDC [Fic]—dc23
LC record available at https://lccn.loc.gov/2021045068
LC e-book record available at https://lccn.loc.gov/2021045069

Book design by Jeanette Levy
Typeset by Westchester Publishing Services
Printed and bound in the U.S.A.
2 4 6 8 10 9 7 5 3 1

To find out more about our authors and books visit
www.bloomsbury.com and sign up for our newsletters.

THIS
WICKED
FATE

CHAPTER 1

Chrysanthemum sinense. Common name, mum.

White mums symbolized grief, death, bottomless unending sorrow. The house at 307 Old Post Road was festooned with them. They twisted themselves around the exterior like a cocoon. Tendrils of mulberry purple bougainvillea writhed like snakes, intertwining with arms of Devil's Pet, crimson thorns bared like teeth, leaves so deep purple as to be black. Inside, rumbling groans from the wooden frame protesting the worried embrace of the foliage echoed through the darkened halls. The plants had come to shelter me from the agony of grief. But that was like holding back the tide—pointless and, ultimately, impossible.

Mom was dead and the goddess Hecate herself was holding her somewhere in the underworld for one full cycle of the moon. I could get her back but only if I could do the thing that had never been done—bring the six pieces of the Absyrtus Heart back together. It was an impossible task. At least it had felt impossible until I walked in on the scene unfolding in the front room.

Circe, my birth mother's sister, a relative I'd thought to

be dead until that very moment, stood in front of me like a ghost. But she wasn't spectral, she was living, breathing, and full of confusion if the pained expression on her face was any indication of what she was feeling inside. Tears clouded my vision and made a hazy outline of her frame.

I couldn't make sense of her. She looked like me—same deep brown skin, dark brown eyes; she even wore a pair of oversized glasses like me. I hadn't been in the presence of someone I was related to by blood since I was a toddler, and I had no clear memory of that time anyway.

Circe's gaze swept over me and her lips parted then closed again, like she was struggling to find the right words. "You're not supposed to be here," she said, her voice choked with emotion. "How—why—I don't understand. What is going on here?"

Dr. Grant, the head of Rhinebeck's Public Safety department, stepped forward and straightened out her blazer. She spoke gently to Circe, as if she was worried about how she'd react. "We knew something wasn't right but we didn't know exactly what. I've been here trying to piece it all together."

Circe bristled, like Dr. Grant's voice irritated every fiber of her being. She didn't turn to face her but instead kept her eyes locked on me.

Mo put her arm firmly around my shoulder. "I think we need some introductions."

Circe glanced at Mo and her expression softened immediately. "Of course. I'm sorry—I—I'm Circe Colchis. That's Persephone Colchis." She gestured to the tall woman with the braids next to Marie, and her—well I still wasn't sure what Nyx's title might be, but "bodyguard" seemed like the right thing.

Persephone.

That was a name I knew, and even in the midst of a million complicated feelings my mouth opened into a little o.

Circe blinked a few times and took a deep breath. "Not *that* Persephone." She smiled a little, but it was all nerves. "She's your—" She stopped herself. "She's a distant relative."

"This is my mom, Angie," I said, gripping Mo around the waist. "I'm Briseis Greene."

"You are," Circe almost sighed. "You really are. Briseis. Standing right here in front of me." She opened her mouth then closed it. Words seemed to fail her.

I glanced at the two padlocked cages sitting in the front entryway. The pulse emanating from them rattled me, literally. I could feel the slow steady rhythm reverberating in my bones. "You have other pieces of the Heart? How many? Two?"

Circe nodded. I tallied up the pieces in their various forms. We had the Living Elixir, the two new pieces in their cages, and we had Marie, who had been transformed by the Heart's power. I didn't know if that counted anymore, but that's where we were at, and that only gave us four pieces in total. We needed all six if we had any hope of bringing my mom back from whatever in-between place Hecate was holding her in.

Circe turned to Dr. Grant. "I think you should leave."

Dr. Grant shook her head.

"She's been helping us," I said.

"Helping?" Circe asked. She took a step toward Dr. Grant. "Just how have you been helping, Khadijah?"

Dr. Grant patted the air in front of her. "Circe, please. I have been busting my ass to figure out what was happening here.

3

I knew there was no way you could be involved, but I couldn't put it together until it was too late."

Circe turned away from her, her eyes brimming with angry tears.

"Please don't shut me out again," Dr. Grant said. Her tone was pleading, like her heart was breaking. "You know I tried to help Selene. I'd give anything to bring her back to you."

"You got one more time to say her name in front of me," Circe warned with a kind of sharpness in her tone that sent a stab of fear through me. This woman was not to be messed with. "I'm not saying we won't speak, but it's not gonna be right now and it's not gonna be with you pretending you've been doing me a favor. I need you to leave."

Dr. Grant nodded and slowly edged past Circe. She put her hand on my shoulder. "I'm so sorry, Briseis. But if anybody can help you right now, it's Circe." She nodded at Mo, then left without another word.

We stood in silence for a moment as Dr. Grant's car pulled out of the driveway.

"Khadijah said someone came after you," Circe said. "She said you showed up here under the impression that I wanted you to come."

Her voice set off something deep in my memory, something I couldn't quite retrieve. It was familiar and not at the same time. Did I know her? Was there some image of her locked away in my mind? Some memory of her voice? "There was a woman," I said. "She was calling herself Melissa Redmond, but her real name was Katrina Valek. She said she was the one who killed Selene."

Mo gasped. I didn't understand her reaction at first, but it

4

only took me a second to fit it together. While I was running around lying to my parents, something I'd never been good at or had reason to do too often, I realized I'd left out that very important piece of information. Mo had only come into the apothecary after Karter's mother had admitted out loud that she'd murdered my birth mother, Selene, in an attempt to force Circe to retrieve the piece of the Heart locked in the Poison Garden.

"Bri," Mo sobbed as tears welled in her eyes. "My god. Why didn't you tell me? How long have you been keeping that from us?"

"She told me right before she—right before—" I bit the inside of my lip until the coppery taste of blood filled my mouth. I didn't want to say the words "right before she killed Mom" aloud. It was too much.

The vines encasing the house crept through the crack under the front door, pulling themselves toward me. Circe's jaw tightened and made hard angles of her chin as she watched the plants react to the surge of grief coursing through me. She suddenly wobbled on her feet and her legs folded under her. The woman she'd called Persephone was there before I could blink. She'd crossed the room at an inhuman speed and caught Circe as she nearly collapsed. I exchanged glances with Marie, and she nodded once, confirming what I suspected. Here was another person changed by the Heart. Another living piece of it. Our total had come to five.

Mo let her gaze drop to the floor, and she shook her head in silent confusion. She must've been struggling with all the things she was seeing and learning about for the first time. She hadn't seen Marie's speed and superhuman strength yet either. We were going to have to have a serious conversation about that at some point, and soon. I squeezed her hand.

Persephone eased Circe onto the couch, and she leaned forward, cradling her head in her hands. She was clearly still grieving her sister, Selene, and my heart ached for her. I was grieving her, too, and in a way I'd never expected to. I was processing so many things at once I worried how much more I could actually take.

"Where is she now?" Circe asked through clenched teeth, her dark eyes narrow. Her entire frame trembled. "The Redmond woman—where is she?"

A shudder moved through me as images of her wild, terrified eyes flashed in my mind. "She's dead."

Circe glanced up. The dark brown headscarf she had twisted around her head brought out the brown in her eyes—eyes that were so much like mine. "Dead?"

Outside, there was a rustling, and a tangle of vines crowded the window. The red fangs of the coiling Devil's Pet scraped against the glass like fingernails. Circe lifted her hand and without even looking toward the window, flicked her wrist. The vines shrank away from the glass. She was in complete control of her power—a power that appeared to be the same as my own.

"After all this time," Circe said, more to herself than to anyone else. "I thought I'd left it in the past, moved on but—" She stopped short, then leaned forward. "How much do you know? I don't want to do or say anything that's gonna upset you, but there is so much."

I steered Mo, who seemed to be drifting in and out of a daze, to the couch opposite Circe, and we sat down.

"I'll tell you what I know," I said. "Then maybe you can fill in the blanks?" Circe nodded and I tried to think in a straight line. "Mrs. Redmond found out about me. I don't know exactly when or how, but a few weeks ago she came to our apartment in Brooklyn. She said you'd died and left me the house and the keys. She also said you left me a set of letters that were only for me to read." I pulled the lanyard that held all the keys I'd collected from around my neck and set it on the coffee table. "She lied about everything, and now I don't know what I'm supposed to do."

Circe shook her head and pushed the keys back toward me. "You can keep the house, Briseis. You can have everything I own. I don't care about any of that. I walked away from this place many, many years ago." She sighed heavily. "I don't know how to say this, and I hope it doesn't come across the wrong way, but I didn't leave the house to you or anyone else. I'm clearly not dead and I didn't write the letters."

"I know," I said. "I figured all that out. Well, most of it. I didn't expect you to show up, that's for damn sure. I thought I was seeing a ghost."

Mo squeezed her eyes shut. "Please, Lord, don't let her be a ghost."

Circe pressed her lips together and pushed her glasses up the bridge of her nose. "Don't worry. I'm not." The way she said it wasn't like she didn't believe in ghosts, just that she wasn't one. I had to stop myself from thinking too deeply about what that meant. After everything I'd seen, nothing was impossible. "What did the letters say?" she continued.

"They were instructions. Like a scavenger hunt." I realized

7

Mrs. Redmond really had no clue as to what I could or couldn't do. She assumed I'd inherited my gifts from my birth mom, but she didn't know that for sure. Walking into the Poison Garden could have killed me if I wasn't immune, and she had treated it like it was a game. The thought made me hate her even more than I already did. I gripped my hands together in front of me until my knuckles ached. "You—I mean Mrs. Redmond—said there was a place on the grounds where I'd find the answers I was looking for. I followed her instructions and found the garden and everything hidden inside it."

Circe sat back and ran her hand over her mouth, then crossed and uncrossed her legs. She angled her head toward the apothecary. "And did you find the answers you were looking for?"

I hesitated. What I found was a place that made me feel like I wasn't alone—a place to stretch, a purpose for these extraordinary gifts, and a little bit of stability for my moms. But I'd also discovered a secret so profound that even the threat of its revelation had caused a living, breathing goddess to intervene.

"I found the Heart." I took out the vial of Living Elixir and held it up to the light. The viscous red liquid stuck to the inside of the glass like honey. Both Circe's and Persephone's expressions twisted into masks of complete and utter shock. Marie closed her eyes and shook her head.

Circe got up and came over to the couch, where she crouched in front of me. As she eyed the glass vial, I took in all the little details about her. She looked like she was only a little older than Mo, even though the date of birth on her gravestone would make her a full decade her senior. A set of matching smile lines framed her mouth, and a few of the coils of hair escaping her head wrap were a mix of black and gray. She had the look of someone who knew what it meant to be exhausted. I gently set the elixir in her outstretched hand.

"Mrs. Redmond, Katrina Valek, whatever her name was, forced me at knife point to get the Heart." Saying her name was like speaking a curse, like it might conjure her from the dead to hurt me and my family even more than she already had. "She cut open my hand and I bled on it. It started to beat." I held up my bandaged hand. Blood had begun to ooze through the dressing. The physical sensation of what the Heart had done to me as Mrs. Redmond forced me to touch it with my bare hands lingered in my bones. It ached. "I brought it back here, transfigured it, and then she—she killed my mom." The words sounded like somebody else said them. They didn't feel real. I didn't want them to be.

Circe looked to Mo and then back to me. "I—I am so sorry." She wept, wrapping her arms around her waist, rocking back and forth like she was trying to soothe herself. "It leaves nothing untouched—the Heart. It affects everything and everyone it comes in contact with. It brings death but not always as a result of the poison pumping through it." She wiped away her tears. "I can't count the number of deaths in this twisted family tree that were a result of other people trying to get their hands on the Heart. They are relentless in their pursuit of it."

We sat for a moment as I tried to claw my way up from a descending spiral of pain and grief. I struggled to put into words what had happened after that, but I couldn't think straight. "Hecate was here," was all I managed to say. I hoped it made sense to her because it still didn't make sense to me.

Circe met my gaze, and I knew right away that while she

might have been shocked, she believed me. Her wide brown eyes glinted in the dim light. She gently put her hand on my knee. "She revealed herself to you? You saw her?"

Persephone leaned against the wall like she might fall over without its support.

I nodded. "She had a giant black dog with her. She told me she was Medea's mother, that we come from her. And she took my mom."

Circe's fingertips pressed into my knee. "What do you mean, she took her?"

"I asked Hecate if we could use the Living Elixir to bring my mom back, but she said that wouldn't work. She said she would keep my mom, and if we could find a way to do the thing that has never been done—"

Circe's lips parted just enough for her to whisper in a tone that was like the rustling of dead leaves in the wind. "She wants you to bring all the pieces of Absyrtus back together."

She already had a deeper understanding of all the things I was just learning about, and she still said it in a way that made me feel like it was going to be impossible to do.

I leaned closer to her. "Can we do that?" A knot made its way to my throat. I didn't know if I could handle any more disappointments. It took me a second to understand that her hesitation wasn't because she thought it was impossible, but maybe because she was thinking of how we could do it. "It's possible, isn't it? Please tell me there's something we can do."

Circe and Persephone exchanged glances, and Circe proceeded carefully. "Absyrtus, whole, would be the master of death. It can be done, but it's not as simple as that."

"And it's not without sacrifice," Persephone interjected bluntly. "We've lost so much already. The Heart takes and takes, but what does it give?"

"This isn't the time, Seph," Circe said.

Persephone twisted one of her braids around her finger and sighed, nodding.

"We have a full cycle of the moon to do whatever it is we're gonna do," I said. "That's what Hecate said."

Persephone huffed and looked away. "A catch. Why does everything have to be so complicated? That's simply not enough time."

I felt like I was falling back into hopelessness again. Marie moved to my side and sat on the arm of the couch. She gently touched my shoulder.

"I'm surprised to see you here," said Circe, standing up.

Mo sat up straight, glancing back and forth between Marie and Circe. "Y'all know each other?"

"Surprised?" Marie asked, avoiding Mo's question as she kept her gaze locked on Circe. "Why?"

"I don't know what you've shared with everyone else, but let's not act like you haven't been wrecked by this place, too," Circe said. "I thought when you got a chance, you'd have run as far away from here as you could."

"Not everything here is terrible," Marie said. She glanced at me and smiled warmly. It made me feel something other than grief for just a split second, and I was thankful for that. I rested my head against her.

Circe glanced at me and then Marie and then me again before returning to her seat on the couch.

"Marie. What are you—" Persephone began, but Circe cut her off.

"Just stop," Circe said. "We have questions. I'm sure you all have more questions too, but I've been awake for almost two days. I can barely keep my eyes open." She turned to me. "Can you give me a few hours to rest?"

I wanted to say no. We didn't have time to sleep. We needed to find out where the last piece of the Heart was so we could get Mom back.

Circe seemed to sense my hesitation. "You look like you could use some rest, too," she said.

"I don't think I could sleep if I wanted to," I said. "Not after everything that just happened." Karter's blood—spilled as Hecate's dog gripped his shin in its mouth—was probably still damp on the broken floor of the apothecary. The oleander leaves were probably beginning to curl. I wanted to throw up.

"I understand," Circe said. "More than you can possibly know." She took off her glasses and wiped her eyes, then replaced them and turned to Mo. "I can make sure sleep finds you. Just sleep. No dreams. Just rest. I can offer you that, if you'll allow it."

Mo wept silently. "Please," she said. If she wanted a break from the agony, she should be able to have it. It wasn't going anywhere. It was so raw, like an exposed nerve, and every brush against it sent us reeling.

I clung to Mo, with Marie, Nyx, and Persephone trailing behind. We led a procession of tears and shattered hearts down the hall into what was left of the apothecary.

Inside, Circe looked around but said nothing. Mo didn't look at the spot on the floor where Mom had died, but I couldn't look away. The oleander lay scattered around where she fell. An ache coiled itself around my chest so tight it took my breath away.

Circe touched the splintered remains of the ladder. Several of the rungs had been split right down the middle, and the entire thing was off its track. "Persephone, would you please get me the belladonna?"

Persephone nodded, planted her foot, and leaped to the small walkway that circled the top of the room, landing with a soft thud.

Mo grabbed my arm and yanked me behind her.

Circe pushed her glasses up. "Sorry. I should have said something."

"So say it!" Mo yelped. "How did she do that? What is happening?"

"It's the Heart," I said, trying my hardest to calm her but remembering how jarring it had been to see Marie use her power for the first time. I'd almost jumped from a moving vehicle after the incident in the cemetery. "The Heart changes them."

Mo's eyes grew wide. "Them?"

I had to be honest with her. "Persephone and Marie." I glanced at Circe, who nodded. "They've both been changed by the Living Elixir made from other pieces of the Heart."

"'Changed' means what exactly?" Mo asked.

"They're stronger, faster, more . . . resilient than they were before," Circe said.

Resilient. I guess that was one way to describe immortality.

"Like—like superheroes?" Mo asked.

"I'm definitely a villain," Marie said.

She was trying to lighten the mood, but Mo looked like she was gonna pass out.

Marie grimaced. "I'm joking. I'm not a bad guy, Mo. Promise."

Mo didn't say anything, and I was a little worried she was in some kind of shock. I didn't know Persephone's backstory, and Marie's was gonna require more than just a passing mention. But we didn't have time for that.

I patted Mo's arm. "It's okay."

"Definitely not okay," she muttered under her breath.

Persephone slid open the small door hiding the shelves stocked with the dried pieces of the deadliest plants in the garden, removed one of the jars, and hopped down as easily as she'd gone up. She tossed the jar to Circe, who set it on the disjointed remains of the counter.

"Need some hot water," Circe said.

Persephone disappeared down the hall in the direction of the kitchen.

Circe slipped off her jacket and tossed it on the floor. She rummaged through the rubble and seemed to find what she was looking for—one of the small copper dishes Dr. Grant's father had asked me to provide for him when he stopped by.

Nyx and Marie hung back as I watched Circe move with the kind of assuredness that told me she knew exactly what she was doing. Her long slender fingers worked to turn the dried parts of the belladonna out into the dish. She covered the pieces with her hand and closed her eyes. The hair stood up on the back of my neck. I wasn't the one handling the poison, but I knew what that felt like. She didn't grimace or wince. She breathed in and out slowly, rhythmically.

"Do you think you are immune?" Circe asked suddenly.

"What?" I replied, confused.

"The first poisonous plant I ever came in contact with was belladonna. My mama gave it to me in an old coffee can when I was little. She made me swear to never let any of my friends touch it. I'm sorry to say I was not the most obedient child." Her eyes became glassy in the dark of the broken apothecary. "I could grow the plant, and there was a connection there that I didn't fully understand. I thought it was just another facet of my gift—control plants and be unaffected by the poisonous ones."

"They don't affect me at all," I said. "I'm definitely immune."

Circe smiled warmly, but there was sadness there. "It looks that way on the surface, but you feel the cold, don't you? You feel the tingle to varying degrees when you come in contact with something toxic."

I nodded.

"If you were immune it wouldn't have any effect on you at all, right? You'd feel nothing."

I hadn't thought of it like that at all, but I guess she was right. "So what are you saying? Because I've had the sap of a hemlock plant go directly into my bloodstream. I held the Heart with my bare hands and I felt like I was dying." Sharp flare of pain and sadness in the pit of my belly.

Circe pressed her palm flat against the belladonna. "When you come in contact with the poisonous plants, your body leaches the poison. You take it into yourself, in essence becoming so much like the plant itself that you cannot be harmed by it. The more poisonous the plant, the more painful it is. Medea was the most talented poisonist in existence for two reasons—she studied under her aunt Circe, arguably the most gifted sorceress ever, and secondly, because she inherited the same gifts we now possess from Hecate. It's what allowed Medea to do her work with such precision. It's why people sought her out." Circe exhaled sharply as she pulled her hand back and wriggled her fingers. "I've drawn out enough of the poison in the belladonna so that it won't be fatal, but the sleep will be as close to death as you can safely get without going to meet Hades himself."

Persephone returned with a kettle and four mugs on a silver tray. She set it on the counter, and Circe dropped a few pinches of the belladonna into each cup, then covered it with steaming water. I reached for it, but Mo caught my wrist.

"Wait," she said. "I'm not tryna be rude, but we don't know you." She eyed Circe carefully. "I mean, we just met. Now you want to give us some kind of potion that's going to knock us out? This is . . . a lot, especially for Bri." She turned to me. "Love, you're in charge of what's happening here. We don't do anything you're not comfortable with. Nothing has changed about that."

For a split second my thoughts wandered to what Mom was gonna say and the realization that she wasn't there fell on me all over again. Mo gathered me to her and swayed with me in her arms as the tears came in a rush.

Circe batted at her eyes again and reached out to put her hand on Mo's arm. "Maybe you and I could talk?"

Mo gripped me tight. "Sure. But anything you need to say

can be done right here in front of Bri." She gently touched the side of my face. "You good with that, love?"

I nodded.

Circe chewed at her bottom lip, then took off her glasses and set them on the counter. "I don't know what to say to either of you. I truly didn't believe I'd see Briseis ever again. Selene never intended for her to come back here. She tried very hard to spare her all of this."

"It wasn't like Bri chose it," Mo said. "That woman, Redmond, she's the reason we're here. Bri didn't even want to come up at first, but—" Mo stopped for a moment. She cleared her throat and continued. "But it's been good for her up till now. She's been more herself, her true self, and that's all I've ever wanted for her. Clearly you know what she can do, and we—me and . . . and Thandie—we did everything we could to let her be exactly who she is. Gifts and all. We got a flower shop back home."

Circe's eyes brimmed with tears. Persephone turned away from us and busied herself gathering up jars from the floor and setting them back on a few of the unbroken shelves. Nyx just stared down at the floor. It was clear they didn't want to intrude on what felt like a very private conversation. Marie, however, didn't even try to pretend like she wasn't listening.

"I don't want to make either of you uncomfortable," Circe said, her voice tight. "I meant what I said. The house is yours if you want it. The issue of me being back from the dead might be a roadblock so maybe we just pretend I'm still dead."

"I don't know how that's gonna work," said Mo. "But listen. I let Bri know she doesn't have to choose. She can learn more about where she comes from without having to feel like she's stepping on my toes. I'm with her no matter what. But I need you to promise me that you'll respect that. Be honest with her, because I've seen things since we've been here that tell me this is way beyond me, but don't force it on her. I don't know you from Adam, but I can tell you're not gonna try to hurt her. Long as it stays that way, we won't have a problem."

I smiled. When I thought I could never do that again, I smiled. Mo still didn't play when it came to me. That hadn't changed.

Circe forced a quick laugh. "God, this kid is lucky to have you. And I'm sorry you have to be here now, under these circumstances, but I'm on your side and I'm going to do everything I can to help you both. It will not be easy. What we have to do is something I believed until very recently to be impossible."

"I've seen a lot of impossible things lately," Mo said.

Circe handed me and Mo the cups of tea.

"Drink up," she said. "Rest. Then we'll regroup."

Mo took a cup and drank it in three big gulps. She turned to me and opened her mouth to speak, but her eyes closed and she rocked to the side like she'd forgotten how to stand. Persephone caught her before she fell.

"That was quick," Circe said. "The brew is strong." She put her fingers on Mo's wrist as she glanced at her watch. "She'll be just fine. Try not to worry."

I took a cup and brought it to my lips, but Circe gently put her hand across the top.

"It won't work for you," she said. "It won't affect you at all."

"I guess it wouldn't, right?" I set the cup back down. "What do I do?"

Circe sighed. "Not much you *can* do. I have tried every botanical sleep aid known to man and still haven't found one that works."

Marie moved closer to me and nudged my shoulder. "I'll stay with you. As long as you want me to. I can call Alec and make him talk to you. That should put you right to sleep."

I took the still-piping hot cup of tea and drank it in three gulps. Maybe it wouldn't help, but I thought I should at least try. I waited for sleep to fall on me like it had for Mo, but just like Circe said, I didn't feel a thing.

"It was worth a try," I said.

Circe gave me a quick smile. "You should still try to sleep, if you can."

Persephone turned, still cradling Mo, and I followed them out to the hallway. She ascended the stairs, and as I climbed up behind her, the painting of the black dog on the wall stared out at me. The eyes of generations of the Colchis family followed me as Persephone deposited Mo in my bed. Circe lingered at the bottom of the stairs and did not follow us up.

I took off Mo's shoes and pulled the covers up around her. Marie slumped into the rocker by the fireplace, and I went to the window as Persephone left us alone. A figure moved in the dark, around the side of the house. My heart cartwheeled in my chest before I realized it was just Circe, two iron cages in hand. I squinted into the night and watched as she cut a path straight to the trailhead that led to the garden.

I kicked off my sneakers and lay across the end of my bed as Mo remained completely knocked out.

"Circe is going to help you, Briseis," Marie said as she gathered her cloud of white coils behind her neck and secured it with a hair tie she had on her wrist. "I know she will."

"What if we can't find the last piece?" I didn't want to allow such a negative, terrible thought to take hold of me, but I couldn't get it out of my head.

Marie didn't answer. It felt like a silent acknowledgment that this might not go the way we wanted it to.

I might be forced to live the rest of my life without Mom.

That thought brought the tears again. Marie was suddenly there, lifting me up so I could rest my head in her lap. Her fingers traced the tracks of my tears. There wasn't much else to say or do. I closed my eyes.

CHAPTER 2

I opened my eyes the following morning. At least I thought it was morning until I realized the sun was slanting through my curtains at full strength. A rustle near my feet almost made me jump out of my skin. The plants sitting on the hearth had knitted together in the night and were now twisted around the four posts of my bed. My hand was rebandaged, and the aroma of sweet almond oil and menthol wafted from it. Mrs. Redmond had sliced open my palm, but whatever this balm was made the pain barely noticeable.

Mo still slept, her face relaxed, her breathing slow and steady. I couldn't believe I'd managed to sleep, but as I awoke, the horrors of the previous day and night crashed over me again. If Mo could just stay asleep, she wouldn't have to feel what I was feeling. The weight of this grief held me to the bed, made it hard to breathe. I thought if I didn't get up I might lie there forever.

I forced myself to stand and slipped out of the room to let Mo rest as long as she could. I wandered through the hall and down the stairs like a ghost, like my body was just going through the motions. I rounded the corner and almost bumped into

Persephone. She had the coffee table tucked under her arm. Me and Mo had tried to move it when we first got here and couldn't because it was solid as a rock. It was made of oak and must've weighed a hundred pounds. Persephone was slinging it around like dollhouse furniture.

"Were you able to rest at all?" she asked.

"I—yeah." It actually felt like my body had completely shut down. I didn't even remember falling asleep. "What time is it?"

"It's almost one in the afternoon."

My heart sputtered. A whole morning gone. "Where is everybody?"

"Marie and Nyx left a little while ago. Marie asked me to tell you she'd be back soon. They had some business to attend to." Persephone readjusted the table. "I'm clearing out this front room. We thought maybe we could bring in a big table and lay everything out. We've done so much work, Briseis. We've spent so much time searching for the other pieces already, it might be good for us all to be on the same page."

"How did the other pieces of the Heart get split up in the first place?" I asked. I needed to put my mind somewhere else, and it seemed like a good place to start. "They were all together at some point, right in the beginning when Medea buried the pieces of her brother."

Persephone winced.

"I—I'm sorry," I said quickly, putting my hand on her arm. I had to remind myself that these weren't just stories. They were a family history—*my* family history.

Persephone shook her head. "It's all right. I'm always just a little shaken by the cruelty of what was done to Absyrtus. I've seen so much in my life, and still, his death stands among the most violent I've ever heard of."

"It's awful," I said. "I hope Jason got what was coming to him."

"He got to grow old, which feels unfair. But I take comfort knowing he was unhappy and hated by the gods for what he did to Medea. When he was an old man he fell asleep under the mast of the *Argo* as it rotted away in a shipyard, and it crushed his skull."

I paused. "Well, damn."

Persephone smiled like the thought of it was the best thing she'd ever heard of. "I like to imagine he was in agony for some period of time before he actually died." She shrugged. "Anyway, I'm not entirely sure how all the pieces of the Heart were separated. I know that soon after Medea buried Absyrtus, a piece was taken by a demigod on orders from Jason himself."

I thought of who in their right mind would or could do something like that. "Who'd he get to do it?"

"You've heard of the twelve labors of Hercules?" Persephone asked.

"Um, not really. Is that in the Disney movie?"

Persephone chuckled. "I haven't seen it. But you're familiar with Hercules?"

"Yeah."

"He was given twelve tasks to complete after he killed his wife and children."

"Hold up," I said. "He did what now? That's definitely not in the Disney version."

Persephone pushed a heavy side table out of the way with her foot like it was nothing. "I can see why they may have left that part out. But yes. He killed his wife and their children and, as punishment, was given twelve impossible tasks, things like slaying the hydra monster or capturing Cerberus, the three-headed beast that guarded the entrance to the underworld."

"Yikes," I said.

"When he completed the twelve labors he hopped on a ship and sailed the world. Want to guess what ship it was?"

I already knew. If Jason had given the order it could only be one ship in particular. "The *Argo*."

Persephone nodded. "And who was on that ship accompanying her husband as he pursued the Golden Fleece?"

I stared up at Persephone. "Medea."

"Precisely," she said. "Hercules had a front row seat to the chaos that ensued, and after everything was done and Absyrtus was dead in the ground, Jason asked him to do something more absurd than anything he'd done before—steal a piece of another demigod's body from its final resting place."

I thought I was over being shocked by the history of this family, but I was wrong.

"And he did it?"

"I'm assuming he did," Persephone said. "I don't know how. As for the other pieces, I'm not sure how they came to be separated."

"But you and Circe found two more of them."

"It took us years," Persephone said. "It cost us more than we thought it would."

I looked into her face and saw the same weariness I'd seen in Circe, but magnified a dozen times over.

"There's only one piece left now, right?" I asked. "After all this time, we only have one more piece to find."

"The Mother."

"The Mother? What's that?"

"Your mom said you all run a flower shop?" Persephone asked as she walked across the hall.

I tagged along behind her. "Yeah, we do."

"Do you ever take cuttings from plants to seed others?"

I thought for a moment. "Not really. I mean, I do that on my own sometimes. I can make another plant from any part of the original one."

She nodded and walked back across the hall and scooped up the chaise. "When Absyrtus went into the ground, his heart, his actual heart, still nestled in his chest, was the first to bloom and produce the heart-shaped plant. It seeded the other parts of his body with that magic, giving us the original six pieces. The Mother is the last and most powerful piece. You've seen what the piece we kept here could do. Imagine something a hundred times deadlier."

I couldn't. I could not fathom that another plant existed that was deadlier than the piece of the Absyrtus Heart I had held in my own hands. Persephone set the chaise down in the next room.

I glanced down the hall. "Where's Circe?"

"She's in the garden. She took the other pieces out there last night." She reached into her pocket and pulled out the vial of Living Elixir. "I saw someone installed a safe in the turret. Was that you?"

"No," I said. It had to have been Mrs. Redmond. "But I know the combination. Do you want me to put that in there?"

"If you don't mind," Persephone said. "It's already been transfigured, and it's so potent in this liquid form. Best to keep it locked up for now."

She handed me the vial, and I went up to the little door at the end of the upstairs hallway. I climbed the stairs and turned on the single light in the center of the room, removed the painting of Medea to reveal the safe and turned the dial, 7-22-99. After I set the elixir inside I rehung the painting and took a minute to catch my breath. My family tree was intertwined with the fates of gods and demigods alike. It was a lot to take in.

Dust hung in the shafts of sunlight streaming through the window, illuminating the pages of the big book sitting on the pedestal in the middle of the cramped room. I flipped through its heavy pages to find the illustration of the Absyrtus Heart Selene had drawn in meticulous detail. The velvety black leaves, the pink lobes, the artery-like stalk. She'd perfectly captured how strange and impossible the plant was, and still the drawing didn't do it justice. In the flesh, it was beautiful but equally terrifying.

I padded back down the stairs and peeked in on Mo. She was still asleep, and I didn't want to bother Persephone anymore while she was moving furniture around, so I went downstairs, grabbed my sneakers, and left out the front door.

I circled around the house and cut through the sloping, overgrown rear yard. As I approached the lush curtain of ivy and stinging nettle that guarded the path to the Poison Garden, it pulled back and I ducked onto the hidden path.

I trudged through the forest as the plants rippled along the ground on either side of me. They seemed hyperaware of my presence. Ever since I'd called to them to help me wring the life from Mrs. Redmond as she threatened everyone I'd ever loved or cared about, it was like I couldn't turn it off. I tried to push those thoughts aside and focus on what we had to do. The events of the days before were impossible to wrap my head around, and whatever was coming next felt equally unreal. I didn't know what I was supposed to do other than make it through the next hour, the next minute, the next second, and still that felt like I wasn't doing enough.

The path led to the glade of black bat flowers, which all perked up as I walked through. The trees guarding the iron gate on the opposite side of the meadow leaned away, and the bougainvillea pulled the metal bars open, allowing me to pass through. I entered the garden, holding my breath, feeling the ache of what had happened there the same way I felt the sting of toxins when I entered the Poison Garden, only I wasn't immune to this pain. Mrs. Redmond had tainted this beautiful place, but the garden was already working hard to erase any sign that she had ever been there.

The acacia tree stood like a sentinel guarding the overflowing beds of everyday plants.

Hecate's Garden had overtaken its wooden walls. Hellebore and velvet petunias climbed the wall closest to the plot. The hellebore's yellow centers reminded me of watchful, protective eyes.

Calla lilies and dahlias spilled out and covered the patch of earth where my mom had lain unconscious. Her blood was spilled there. I couldn't see it, but I knew it was there, and I felt an overwhelming rush of gratitude to the flowers who'd hid it from me. Did they know I wouldn't be able to handle that?

That seeing the patch of darkened earth might have been my breaking point?

Knowing I probably wouldn't find Circe in the front part of the garden, I cut a path straight back to the moon gate and entered the Poison Garden with only the faintest flicker of cold in my throat as the airborne toxins invaded my nose and mouth. Circe wasn't there either, but the hidden door in the back wall was sitting ajar and the rhythmic thumping of a heart echoed in my ears. My own pulse ticked up.

Ropes of Devil's Pet unfurled from the tops of the walls and slithered across the ground, circling my feet. Any fear or hesitation I'd had was gone. I had leaned into this strange power and embraced it fully and there was no going back. I reached out and drew my finger along one of the small offshoots. Cold rippled through my palm and wrist as the deadly vine sprouted a triplet of serrated fuchsia leaves.

I went to the door and pulled it all the way open.

"Uh . . . Circe? You down there?"

The was a scuffling noise, the clink of something metal, maybe glass.

"I'm here," she said, her voice rough.

I descended the stone steps into the dank space below. Sunlight filtered in from the cylindrical hole in the ceiling, but it was still mostly dark, still cold. Circe sat on the floor with her back to the wall. Her hair stuck out around her face in tight curls, her wrap halfway off her head. The two glass-paneled cages she'd brought with her stood against the opposite wall. I sat down on the floor next to her.

I looked around, unable to stop the replay of Mrs. Redmond

slicing my hand open over the Absyrtus Heart, how she'd asked if I'd fed it. I hated the stuffy little chamber, and a flicker of anger sparked inside me but I couldn't understand why. I reminded myself that it was Mrs. Redmond's deception that led me here. Circe hadn't written the letters. She didn't have anything to do with the mess Mrs. Redmond and Karter had created. But something still didn't sit right with me. After a moment I finally realized what was bothering me. If Circe hadn't brought me here, it meant that the opposite might be true—she didn't want me here, and that stung more than I expected it to.

"I know I'm not supposed to be here," I said. "That you probably don't want me here."

Circe angled her head and pushed her glasses up. "It's very hard for me to look at you. You look so much like her it's a little scary."

"You mean Selene?"

Circe nodded. "I feel like I'm talking to her."

"I'm not her," I said. It's the same thing I'd told Alec when I went to see him in the hospital. In his confusion he'd thought I was her.

"No. I know," Circe said. She bit her bottom lip and her eyebrows pushed together. I prepared myself to get my feelings hurt. "Let me be real clear about this. Did I want you here? Did Selene? Yes. Of course we did. But it was just too dangerous. Redmond wasn't the first to come after the Heart. But you're a part of this place, which is, I suspect, why fate brought you back."

"Not really fate," I said. "More like a murderous, hateful, lying-ass piece of—"

"I get it," Circe cut in. "Believe me I do." She looked thoughtful. "I'm glad she's dead. I would have liked to see it."

"I saw it."

Circe took a deep breath and let her shoulders slump down. "Gods, I wish you hadn't." She took off her glasses and sandwiched the lens between the folds of her T-shirt, cleaning off the smudges. "If I'm being honest there was a part of me that was hoping you'd come back someday when it was safe."

"Is that why you left the map?"

Circe let the air hiss out between her teeth. "I was careless, but I was also tired. Hell, I'm still tired. I drew a map, left the key. I thought if you came back someday and I was gone maybe you'd stumble on it."

"You were gonna let me stumble on the Heart?"

Circe pressed the back of her head into the wall. "I don't know what I was thinking. It's my responsibility. I knew it wasn't right to try and pass it off on you, but I wanted to put the burden down, Briseis. You have no idea how badly I wanted that." She stretched her legs out in front of her and pulled her wrap forward, tucking her stray coils under it. "The pressure of continuing a tradition that's been going on for thousands of years. I'm supposed to give up my life, people I love—"

"Like Dr. Grant?" I asked.

Circe's eyebrows arched up. "What? Hold on. What did she say to you?"

"Nothing," I said quickly. "She didn't say anything but it's kind of obvious." The way Circe had spoken to Dr. Grant—people only do that when there's a history there, when feelings are still involved.

30

Circe shrugged. "Yes. Like Khadijah. She was—is— brilliant. I loved her. I still do. But after Selene died I just kind of cut myself off from everybody. The grief was so heavy. You can't understand."

"I do understand."

She turned and looked me dead in the face. "I'm sorry. I wish you didn't. I wish for that more than anything."

We sat in silence for a minute before I worked up the nerve to ask the only real question I had. "I'd like to know why she chose adoption," I said. "Why, if this is our responsibility, the task only we can do, why try to keep me from it?"

She sighed and let her arms flop to her sides. A glass half-full of red wine tipped over and splashed across the floor. She looked at it and laughed.

"You're sixteen and a few months," Circe said. "You probably don't even know that you can't get drunk yet."

"Huh?"

She laughed lightly. "A very unwelcome side effect of this power. You take something intoxicating into yourself and neutralize its effect. Alcohol is a byproduct of plants, and we are immune to its effect."

My ex–best friend, Gabby, and I had shared a wine cooler once, and she was so tipsy she couldn't stand up. I was sure she was faking it because I didn't feel anything at all, but maybe there was more to it.

"I still try." Circe tapped the wineglass. "But it's just expensive grape juice to me." She sighed and tipped her head back. "Selene was funny. She had a comeback for everything. She loved music. She was stubborn and beautiful and I miss her so much it hurts." She clutched her chest like her heart was breaking all over again. "She chose adoption because she understood fully that what we do, what we are, has brought so much loss, so much pain, she wanted to try and keep you from it. I think we both understood that you had gifts and no matter where you were they'd probably manifest themselves. But it was your safety that concerned Selene most. She wanted you to be far from here so that the people who've been trying to get their hands on the Heart wouldn't hurt you." She laughed drily. "I didn't know she'd allowed you to keep the name she gave you. I didn't know it was an open adoption." Tears streamed down her face. "Maybe there was a part of her that hoped you'd find your way back here someday, too. But I know she wouldn't have wanted it to be like this."

"You don't want me to stay?" I asked. It was just a question, but in that moment I realized that I wanted her to tell me she wanted me to stay.

Circe turned to me. "I don't know if that's what I want."

Her bluntness stunned me. I leaned away from her. "Right."

I moved to get up, and she gently pulled me back to sitting. "If staying here means you can't be safe or happy, then no. I don't want you to stay. But if it can be a haven for you, then I want you to stay forever." She looked down into her lap like she was embarrassed. "Have you seen pictures of her?"

"I found an album in the house. She was pregnant with me in a couple photos."

"She made me take those pictures like she was modeling for a magazine or something." Circe smiled in a way that told me she had that specific memory in her mind's eye. "She was everything to me." She shook her head and climbed to her feet, holding out her hand to me. I took it and she pulled me up with the strength of a normal human being, which relieved me a little too much.

"You're here," Circe said. "Anybody ever tell you what's for you will always be for you?"

I nodded. "My grandma."

"Smart woman," said Circe. "You're here, and the Heart has already stolen something from you. Its existence has taken a mother from you, twice. I don't expect you to want anything else to do with it."

"I wish I'd never laid eyes on it." All I could see in my head was Mom's face. I swallowed the urge to cry. "But I can't go back. Like you said, I'm here. So what do we do now?"

Circe stared at the spot in the ground where the Heart had been rooted. She turned her attention to the glass enclosures. Taking a key from her pocket she opened the first small door. I didn't move as she reached in and withdrew a flat stone, red as rose petals and about as big around as her palm.

"What is that?"

Circe quickly transferred the stone to the enclosure surrounding the vacant hole in the ground. She pushed it deep into the dirt and stood back, clutching her hand.

"The resurrection stone. The philosopher's stone. It has lots of names."

"It's a piece of the Heart?" I asked. "I thought transfiguring it turned it into an elixir."

"It can be transfigured into anything. A liquid, a stone . . . a person."

Marie's face flashed in my mind.

"This stone was created by a woman named Perenelle Flamel. I don't know where she found her piece of the Heart or which of our ancestors transfigured it for her, but when she died in 1397, she was nearly two hundred years old."

"She died?" I asked. "So it didn't work for her?"

"It worked for a while." Circe moved to the second enclosure. "But the Heart, in its transfigured form, must be held within the body. That's why it's been preferred as a liquid for so long, but creating the liquid is much harder to do. Perenelle kept the stone beneath the skin of her forearm. Her husband removed it and she died. He then secreted the stone under his own skin, right in the center of his chest, and lived on for four hundred more years."

"What happened to him?"

"Persephone caught up with him in Paris many, many years ago."

I glanced at the hole in the ground where Circe had put the stone. "How did she get the stone back from him?"

Circe cleared her throat. "A knife, I imagine." She opened the second enclosure, took a halting breath, and plunged her hand inside. From it, she pulled an Absyrtus Heart, almost identical to the one I'd been forced to uproot. It was pink and supple and beat in a furious rhythm. The thick black roots dripped blood onto the stone floor. Circe quickly transferred it to the enclosure and set it on top of the stone. The roots burrowed into the dirt, writhing like worms as they anchored the plant in the ground. It immediately sprouted a half-dozen tufts of velvety black leaves as wide as a hand. Circe closed the little glass door and bent over, resting her hands on her knees.

I knew that feeling. "It's like dying," I said.

A film of sweat blanketed her forehead as she tried to catch her breath. "Like dying." She locked up the enclosure door and took a step back.

"I'm sorry I brought Mrs. Redmond—Katrina Valek—down here," I said. "I'm so sorry. I didn't understand, and I thought I could trust Karter."

"Karter?" Circe asked.

"Her son. He was—he was my friend. Or at least I thought he was."

"It's not your fault," she said. "None of this is. I wish I'd known what was happening here. I wish I'd put it together sooner. I'm so sorry, Briseis. This whole situation is a mess, and so much of it is *my* fault. We don't go into these things thinking we won't have a chance to make them right. We're just trying to survive so much of the time that I think we forget to live. I wish I could see Selene just one more time—tell her how much I love her." She ran her fingertips over her mouth as her chin trembled. "How is it that some of us have no time left and others have more than anyone could ever truly need? It's not fair."

It wasn't and I didn't have an answer to her question, only more tears. I missed Mom and I could see how much Circe missed Selene. Our pain was the same.

I took off my glasses and wiped my face. Circe reached out but let her hand hang in the air in front of me. It was her way of asking if it was okay. I met her gaze and nodded. She swept me into an embrace with all the warmth of the sun, all the tenderness of family, born out of blood or choice, it made no difference in that moment. It was she and I and all that remained of the oldest branches of our ancient family tree . . . almost.

CHAPTER 3

Back at the house I found Mo in the front room with Persephone. Mo was scratching the top of her head with the most bewildered look on her face as Persephone slid a large wooden table, plucked from one of the other rooms, into place.

Circe patted Mo on the arm. "You okay?"

Mo nodded but she was clearly not okay. I quickly wrapped my arms around her and she squeezed me tight. She brushed her fingers across my forehead and down the side of my face. "I love you."

"I love you more."

She narrowed her eyes at me. "Where you been, love?"

"In the garden," I said.

Her teeth clicked together as she clenched her jaw. "I don't even know if I can go back out there."

"You don't have to," I said. "It's okay." I leaned against her shoulder.

"I'm going to bring down all my research," Circe said. "We can start by laying it all out. Retrace where we've been and figure out where we need to go next."

She went to the mantel over the fireplace and ran her hand along the edge of the intricately carved wood. She pressed in one swirly arm of flourish, and there was a soft click. A narrow compartment, like a small drawer, fell open. Mo's entire frame tensed up, and she pulled me back a step. From the hidden space, Circe took a small object. She dusted it off with her shirt.

"Are there any other secret compartments or hidden rooms I should know about?" I asked.

Circe touched her thumb to the tips of her fingers one at a time like she was counting in her head. She raised her eyebrows and smiled. "Yes. But we'll talk about that later."

She handed me the object she'd taken from the hidden drawer. It was a heavy pocket watch with a long silver chain. The faded engraving pressed into its dull golden face was familiar, the Colchis family crest—the three faces representing the goddess Hecate. Circe reached over and pressed a small button on the side, and it popped open. Inside was a series of interconnected silver rings with notches and grooves that all fit together perfectly against a backdrop of tiny painted moons in all its waning and waxing phases. Pointed golden arrows, like the hands of a clock, moved almost imperceptibly; the longest one had just moved past the illustration of the bright, full moon.

"It's an astrological clock," Circe said. "It tracks the cycles of the moon, the rotation of the planet on its axis. Hecate and the moon are inextricably linked. This device has been in the Colchis family for at least a hundred years, maybe longer. It can help us keep track of time. If we have a full cycle of the moon, then, according to this, we have about twenty-eight more days to find the last piece of the Heart."

Persephone excused herself and came back a few moments later carrying a stack of books, papers, and a rolled-up map. She and Circe organized everything on the table.

"Do you have the parchment?" Persephone asked.

I realized she must have been talking about the crumbling document pressed between plastic I'd found in the secret office behind the fireplace in my room. I quickly went to my bag and took it out, carefully handing it over.

"Can I ask you something?" I said to Circe.

"Of course," she said.

"Did you—did you steal this from the Vatican Archives?"

Persephone's head snapped up. "You can't really steal something if it belongs to you."

"I mean, I'm on your side," I said quickly. Persephone gave me an approving grin.

Circe handled the parchment as if it were made of glass, and I felt bad I'd shoved it in my bag like some old homework. "This document was taken from our family a very long time ago," Circe continued. "It belongs to us. I wouldn't say we stole it as much as we reclaimed it. How did you know it came from the archives?"

"Mo has a friend who used to be a curator at the Brooklyn Museum," I said. "Dr. Kent. She sent me a picture of it. She's the one who told me Medea was probably a real person."

Something dark passed over Circe's face. She looked worried. She exchanged glances with Persephone, whose expression was much harder to read.

Circe turned to Mo. "Could you put me in touch with this Dr. Kent?"

A little ripple of fear traced its way down my back. "She's really nice," I said. "Like, I didn't tell her anything. I just asked some questions about Medea's story, that's all. I know y'all kept all of this within the family, but—" I pictured Marie in the cemetery—the carnage left in her wake. Persephone had the Heart's power running through her, too, and I didn't want to see Dr. Kent hurt because of something I might have said.

Circe smiled warmly. "It's okay. I actually have some questions of my own, and if she was able to glean some truths from the pages, there might be some other things she can help me with."

"Like what?" I asked.

She opened her mouth to speak when the doorbell rang. Mo went to answer it and returned a few seconds later with Nyx and Marie. Persephone had seemed distant, maybe even a little stiff, but she lit up when she saw Nyx. Nyx brushed Persephone's braids behind her shoulder, then ran a hand over her own bald head.

"Cut it all off and be like me, Seph. Free yourself."

Persephone laughed. "I like the braids. And nobody does bald quite like you. I couldn't compete."

"Stop," Nyx said playfully.

Marie came over and slipped her hand into mine. "Hey," she said. She kissed me gently on the cheek. "You doin' okay?"

"No," I said honestly. "Not even a little. But we were about to sit down and try to make a plan. Maybe that'll help me feel like we're doing something instead of just hanging around waiting for the pieces to fall into place."

Mo eyed our intertwined hands and smiled gently at me

before sitting down in the only chair Persephone had left in the room. Circe rounded the table and rested the tips of her fingers on its surface as she surveyed the vast collection of papers, maps, drawings, and books.

"The Colchis family is tasked with guarding the pieces of the Absyrtus Heart," she said. "We all know and understand this, but over hundreds of generations, the pieces have been separated as the branches of our family tree diverged. We come from Medea. She was the daughter of the goddess Hecate, niece of the legendary sorceress Circe, wife of the leader of the Argonauts, Jason. Magic—and poison—run in our veins." She took a deep breath. "Jason's line has always coveted the Heart's pieces. They have always been hunting it—and us. Just before Selene was murdered—" Circe gripped the table and I held tight to Marie's arm. "We had come to an understanding—the risk of continuing on this way just wasn't worth the pain, the loss. We thought if we could find all the pieces, we could destroy them and be done with this treacherous work. I still feel strongly that we should try to finish what Selene, Persephone, and I started, and of course now we have a reason to do it as quickly as possible." She looked at Mo. "We have to get Thandie back. I won't entertain any other options."

Mo sucked in a big breath and simply nodded.

"We have five pieces now," Persephone said.

"But I drank the liquid Astraea gave me," Marie said quietly. "That piece is gone for good."

Circe shook her head, cast me a melancholy glance, and then turned back to Marie. "*You* are the piece now."

Marie's perfectly arched right eyebrow shot up. "What?

How's that supposed to work?" She whipped around to look at Persephone. "You too?"

"We are living, breathing pieces of it now," Persephone said flatly. "Cleary neither of us read the fine print."

Marie's brows knitted together as she stared down at the floor.

"We are working against the clock, literally," Circe said. She touched a notebook stuffed to bursting with handwritten notes. "We found the other pieces by chasing down stories of people who lived unnaturally long lives: Flamel and her husband, Nicolas, St. Germaine, Merlin. Nicolas and St. Germaine turned out to be one and the same, and we now have that piece in our possession. Merlin's immortality came from another source, as does Nyx's."

I locked eyes with Nyx across the room.

"So, you just weren't going to tell me?" I knew Nyx was strong. She'd folded a grown man up like a pretzel at the cemetery, but I didn't know she was immortal.

She shrugged and the corners of her mouth pulled up into a smile. "It's not even the biggest thing I'm keeping from you at present."

"Ummm. I don't like the way that sounds." I couldn't imagine what would be a bigger secret than finding out she was immortal. "And did y'all say Merlin? Like from King Arthur?"

"The same," Persephone said. "Arthur's legend was greatly exaggerated by Merlin himself. The table wasn't even round, and his name wasn't Merlin. It was Myrddin."

"Hold up," I said. My mind raced as I thought through what

she was implying. "What are you saying to me right now? How do you know that?"

"Focus?" Circe asked impatiently. "Persephone will tell you her life stories soon, I promise."

I glanced at Mo, who had interlaced her fingers on top of her head and was slowly rocking side to side. She looked like she was about to implode.

"We tracked the pieces down," Circe said. "And now we have one more to find. The Mother. Luckily for us, I have some idea of where it might be." She ran her finger over the map and let it come to rest in the open waters of the Aegean Sea. "These waters are where Jason and his Argonauts sailed. The land surrounding them is the site of Prometheus's eternal suffering, and somewhere in these waters is the island of Aeaea. It is the last place we knew Medea to be, in the company of the eponymous Circe from Homer's *Odyssey*. It has to be there—in the place where Medea kept the original Poison Garden."

I stared at the map. There were hundreds of islands of various sizes dotting the waters to the east of Greece. Some of them had been marked by little red dots. "What are the dots for?"

"Those are the ones I've been to and have crossed off the list," Circe said.

There must have been two hundred red marks. Circe hadn't been lying when she said she'd been searching.

"And that's the issue," Circe said. "Aeaea's true location has been lost to time, and there are so many possibilities. There are thousands of islands in these waters, but because we have no idea how big or small the island actually was, we have to look at them all. People have searched for it for thousands of years. Researchers have said its location is anywhere from Paxos to Cyprus. Most of them don't think it exists at all. But I think they're all wrong. It's still out there somewhere. I can feel it."

"And we're supposed to find it in twenty-eight days when nobody has been able to find it all this time?" The little bit of hope I'd been holding on to fell away from me like leaves from the boughs of a tree in autumn.

"We need to go back over the best potential candidates for Aeaea that we haven't already checked off," Circe said. "But I'd like to touch base with Alec first." She turned to Marie. "Is he up for a visit?"

Marie nodded, shaking herself out of her own thoughts. "He's always up for showing off. You should've seen him after Bri showed him that parchment. Did y'all know he came up here when he thought the place was empty? He tried to get into the garden."

Circe's eyes grew wide. "Excuse me?" Her tone was sharp. "Why would he do that?"

"He needed the comfrey," I said.

"He pulled a machete on Briseis," Marie added.

Persephone shifted where she stood, and an entire length of Devil's Pet as thick around as my arm pressed itself against the living room window and to my utter shock, sprouted three appendage-like protrusions and lifted the unlocked window. It slithered in and coiled at Persephone's feet. I had the feeling that if Alec had been anywhere nearby, the vines would have had him in a choke hold.

"The plants almost killed him," I said quickly. "I saw it."

Persephone huffed. "Serves him right."

Marie nodded in agreement. "When I found out what he did I seriously considered killing him and burying him in the yard."

"Marie!" Nyx said, her eyes wide. "Why are you talking about him like that? He's old, and he's your—what?—your sixth great-grandnephew?"

"He was about to be six feet under the ground," Marie said. "Have you seen my house? It looks like several angry ghosts live there. Bri was scared when she came over. He put up suits of armor in the library. Why? What's the reason?"

Circe looked horrified but was also fighting back a smile. "You can't kill him because he's bad at decorating, Marie. Goodness."

Marie huffed. "Why not?"

"Please don't kill anybody, baby," Mo mumbled from the chair. "I'm trying real hard not to lose it here, just so y'all know."

Circe quickly went over and put her hand on Mo's shoulder. "I'm so sorry. This is not how I wanted to do this, and there's so much to understand. All of this has to sound ridiculous to you."

Mo patted her hand and took a deep breath. "I don't really need to understand. I don't even know if I want to. Y'all are talking about immortals and potions and gods. I—I can't get my head around any of that right now." She sighed. "But we have the same goal, right? We all agree that we gotta get Thandie back, so if y'all are vampires, or gods, or witches, or something else, that's not my business. Let's just do what we need to do to get

Bri's mama back, because I don't know what I'll do if— if—"
She clapped her hand over her mouth and squeezed her eyes shut
to try and stem the tears.

The grief washed over me again like a wave. The room was
quiet for a long time before Circe returned to the table.

"We're all on the same page," she said. "Listen, Alec is a
history buff. I'm good at the ins and outs of our own family
stories, but he's good at everything else—the wider mythology,
the stories that came before. So let's go talk to him. He might be
able to give us some insight."

"And I can get you Dr. Kent's contact info," Mo said
quietly.

I had a thought and opened my mouth to ask the question
but stopped. It sounded completely ridiculous.

"What is it?" Marie asked.

I shook my head. "Nothing. It's stupid."

"Don't say that," Circe and Mo said in unison.

Mo gave Circe a quick nod. "If you got something on your
mind," Circe said gently, "don't ever be afraid to come right out
with it. I'll answer whatever I can."

It still felt like a stupid question. "Can we ask—the gods?" I
didn't know how else to put it. "Hecate? Or one of the other
ones?"

Persephone smiled. "It's a reasonable question. But I think
you're the only person in living memory who has seen Hecate in
the flesh. My memory is long, and all I have are stories of her. I'll
never be over the fact that she revealed herself to you. I wish
I could've been here to see her."

"I don't know." I thought of the overwhelming feeling I'd

had of being in the presence of something otherworldly. "It scared the shit out of me."

"Language," Mo said.

Persephone grinned, again letting a little of her gruff exterior slip.

"Sorry," I said. Avoiding Mo's eyes.

"You were so lucky to have seen her," Circe said. "But I don't even know how or why she showed herself. I don't think calling on her would do much good."

"If Hecate can't help us what about the others?" I said. "Is there someone else who can help us?"

"There are no others," Circe said. She stared off. "Not that we know of anyway."

I thought for a moment. "Mrs. Redmond made it seem like there were others. Matter of fact she was sure there were."

Circe and Persephone stopped moving, stopped breathing.

"What do you mean?" Circe asked in a whisper. "What exactly did she say?"

Mrs. Redmond had revealed so many terrible things I had to take a second to recall what she'd said about these other gods. "She said they still lived. She made it seem like that was her main reason for going after the Heart. She wanted to take her place among them." I hooked my fingers into air quotes because I still wasn't 100 percent sure what she'd meant. "She said Jason was descended directly from Hermes. She thought if she could make herself immortal, then they, whoever *they* are, would welcome her into the fold."

Circe turned to Persephone, whose mouth was stuck in a little o. "If that's true—"

"It can't be," said Persephone.

"Briseis saw Hecate," Marie said. "You know for a fact that at least one of them is still around. If there's one, there could be more." She looked thoughtful. "You think Poseidon's still around? I'd like to beat his ass on Medusa's behalf."

Persephone joined Circe next to the table and they leaned in close to each other. Their voices barely a whisper.

"I know we've had our doubts," said Circe. "But if there's even a slight chance that what the Redmond woman said is true, it means she had information that we don't. They've probably carried bits and pieces of their own family story through the ages the same way we have. Who's to say what they may or may not know?"

Persephone nodded. "We're already two steps behind, then. Maybe more than that."

Circe sighed and pushed her hand down on her hip. "We need to go see Alec. Right now. Everybody going?"

"Nah," Mo said. "I'll stay. I need a minute to myself." She stood and I went to her, resting my head on her shoulder.

"I don't like you being here alone," I said.

"I'll stay, too," Persephone said quickly. "Have you eaten?" she asked Mo.

"I—I don't think so," Mo said. "No. I haven't. I didn't even think of that to be honest. Not much of an appetite."

Persephone looked her over. "You need food. Nothing heavy, maybe just soup." She looped her arm through Mo's and led her toward the kitchen without another word.

The gesture hit me right in my chest. Something so simple as offering to feed someone who was grieving. It reminded me of the way Mo cooked dinner for Mr. Hughes back in Brooklyn when it was clear he was just too overwhelmed by his wife's passing to feed himself. I bit the inside of my lip to hold back the torrent of tears threatening to spill over. I didn't know how to say that it moved something in the very deepest part of myself to have Persephone and Circe show such care and concern for me and for Mo. Did I expect them to be cruel? Spiteful? I didn't think so, but until two days ago I thought they were dead. I realized I didn't have an opinion about how they'd see me or my parents because I never expected to know them.

Marie slipped her hand into mine. "Persephone will take care of her."

Circe gently touched my shoulder. "You can stay, too, of course. Persephone's not a good cook, so maybe just order something for Mo?"

"Mo can't cook breakfast to save her life," I said. "Lunch, dinner—no problem. Bacon and eggs? Probably gonna be a fire."

Circe let her worried gaze wander toward the kitchen. "The two of them together might not be a good idea, then. I saw Seph burn a pot of water once."

"How'd she manage that?" Nyx asked, a grin stretched across her face.

"That's your BFF," Circe said. "You tell me."

I glanced at Nyx. "Best friend, huh? Did you know she was out there somewhere?"

"I didn't know for sure," Nyx said. "I hoped. It's hard thinking one of your closest friends might not come back."

"Why wouldn't she come back?" I asked.

Nyx pulled her bottom lip between her teeth and ran her

hand over the top of her head. "Persephone has struggled with this abnormally long life of hers. It has not always been easy."

I felt like there was more to it than that but she was probably holding back out of a sense of respect or loyalty for Persephone.

"No more secrets?" I said to Nyx. "Everything out on the table now?"

"Yes," Nyx said.

Marie cleared her throat way louder than she needed to.

Nyx rolled her eyes. "Maybe one more thing, but now is not the time." She turned and walked out the front door.

As we got out of the car and climbed the front steps of Marie's house, Nyx hung back.

"I'll meet you inside," she called. She took off her coat and set it on the hood of the car, then marched off toward the wooded area near the bluff.

"What's she doing?" I asked. "I've seen her coming and going from over there a bunch of times."

Marie paused. "She has—a pet. It makes a huge mess, so she keeps it away from the house." She opened the front door and went in.

"What kind of pet?" I asked. "Like a big dog? Like that thing Hecate had with her?"

Circe tipped her head back. "I still cannot wrap my head around the fact that you actually saw her and the dog in the flesh." The little sparkle in her big brown eyes made me smile.

"Hecate's dog is the sibling of Cerberus," said Circe. "The

50

three-headed dog that belongs to Hades and guards the underworld."

"More gods and monsters," I said.

Circe nodded.

"Nyx's pet is like a big dog," said Marie. "That's a fair comparison."

"So, it's not an actual dog?" I asked. Marie was purposely being vague and that meant she was hiding something.

"Better to have Nyx explain it to you," Marie said. She power walked down the hall toward Alec's office before I had a chance to ask any more questions, but I was not about to let it go.

Marie just about drop-kicked the door to Alec's office open, and he jumped halfway out of his chair. He clutched his chest and pounded his hand on the desk.

"Don't scare me like that! You're going to give me a heart attack!"

"Promise?" Marie asked, batting her eyes overdramatically.

I didn't know what it was between them that made them act like they were ready to square up at any moment, but it was always a little scary for me. I'd seen firsthand what Marie could do when she fully embraced the power the Heart had given her, and I just hoped she never decided to turn that power on Alec.

"Guess what?" Marie said. "I'm gonna redecorate the library and move all your haunted armor and Dorian Gray paintings into your office. Cool?"

He settled back into his chair and tilted his head. "Why?"

Marie sighed. "Because I don't like being watched by trapped souls when I'm reading, that's why."

"You're impossible," he said.

"I'd be careful," Circe said, her tone playful. "Marie is pretty upset over your decorating choices, Alec."

Alec rose from his chair like he was being lifted by an unseen hand, his eyes wide as he took in Circe, bit by bit.

"You're dead," he said.

"Am I?" Circe looked down at herself, then back to him. "Could've fooled me."

Alec caught sight of me as I trailed in behind Circe.

"Miss Briseis," he said, giving me a quick nod.

I smiled at him. "How are you?"

"I'm well," he said, still a little flustered. "You?"

I almost said "fine."

"We were hoping you could help us," Circe said quickly, saving me from having to think of an answer that wasn't a whole-ass lie. "I know you're an expert on Greek mythology, Alec."

A crooked grin spread across his face.

"Yikes," said Marie.

He didn't even acknowledge her. "How can I help? I have to say, that other document Briseis showed me has been on my mind. I would very much like to see it again. For research purposes."

"I'm sure we can arrange something," Circe said. "For now, I'd like to pick your brain about Aeaea."

Alec's brow furrowed. He sat down, and I went to stand next to Marie, who gently squeezed my hand.

"What is it you want to know?" he asked.

Circe leaned on his desk, peering down at his collection of papers. "What's your opinion on its location?"

Alec laughed. When no one else did, he stopped and readjusted his glasses. "I'm sorry. It's just that—well—it's a myth. It's not a real place."

"After everything you've seen in your life," Marie said. "You really gonna sit here and pretend like fantastical things can't be true? Sir. Stop it."

"Stop what?" he asked.

Marie slipped her hand under the edge of his desk and lifted it slightly off the floor. "I'll throw you and this raggedy desk right out the window. You don't believe in impossible things? Really, Alec?"

"Stop!" he yelled as he scrambled to keep his computer monitors and books from tumbling to the floor.

Marie set the desk back down and glared at him.

"There's a difference between what happened to you and pinpointing the location of a place that most people agree is just myth," Alec said angrily.

"Most people?" I asked. "That kind of makes it seem like there are at least a few people who think it's real."

Circe bit back a smile.

"Homer was highly inconsistent when he spoke of Odysseus's adventures," he said. "Scholars have debated its existence, with most of them agreeing that while the island wasn't a real place, it was probably based on a location off the coast of western Italy. It doesn't make much sense other than to illustrate how historians often center themselves in their research." He gestured to the map on the wall. "Notice the proximity to Rome."

"Why can't they just tell the truth or say they don't know?" Circe asked. Sarcasm dripping from every word.

"Where's the fun in that?" Alec asked. "A bunch of mostly old white men admit that they don't know everything there is to know or that something they once believed is wrong?" He raised his eyebrows. "I'd need to live a much longer life than the one I've been granted to see the day that happens." He glanced at Marie.

"So this is a dead end?" I asked. "There's no way to know if it could be possible that Aeaea actually exists?"

Alec took off his glasses and set them on his desk. "What we have is the *Odyssey*. And if we pair that with things we now know about the places mentioned there, I would say that Odysseus, traveling home from Troy, would be much more likely to have encountered the island in a 'wine-dark sea,' as Homer describes it, if he was sailing the Black Sea."

Circe's gaze swept over the map mounted on the wall behind Alec's desk. "The Black Sea?"

Alec nodded. "Let's assume some of the details are true. If Odysseus was coming from Troy, making his way home to Ithaca, why would he be off the western coast of Italy?"

Circe continued to stare at the map. "He wouldn't. He'd most likely be in the waters of the Mediterranean or the Aegean."

"The Aegean is a better candidate, but there is still the question of why," Alec said. "What is the foundation of that school of thought?"

He glanced at me, and I put my hands up in front of me. "Don't ask me. I just found out Hercules killed his entire family, and I been singing his little songs from the movie my whole life."

"Fair enough," Alec said. He turned to Circe. "Would you like to elaborate?"

Circe bit back a smile. "We believe Aeaea was in that specific area because of Heinrich Schliemann's discovery of Troy. Once he found the precise location, we had a starting point for where to look for the island."

"Right," Alec said. "Schliemann's dig site was located in the western part of what is now Turkey, but just because he, an untrained amateur archaeologist, declared it to be the Troy of legend doesn't make it true. It is a known fact that the treasure he claimed belonged to the fabled King Priam actually came from an unknown culture that had flourished over a thousand years before Troy even existed."

"You mad?" Marie asked. "Because you sound mad."

Alec waved her off. "There is, however, real archaeological, fact-based evidence to suggest the Troy of Homer's work was much farther northeast." He stood and pointed to an area of the map just south of the Black Sea, its coastline jutting out like four long fingers. "Somewhere around here."

Circe shook her head. "I've heard this theory before, but I found so little evidence to support it, I just let it go."

"You haven't seen corruption until you've seen the underbelly of the archaeology world. Disinformation is rampant." He sounded genuinely upset about it. "I've seen it with my own eyes."

I went to the map to get a better look. "So, the island could have been in the Black Sea? How many islands are there in that area?"

"Almost none," Alec said. "Which is probably why it's so easy to dismiss it as a possibility."

Marie was suddenly at my side, staring at the map like she was seeing it for the first time. She reached out and traced the coastline south of the Black Sea with her fingertips.

"What is it?" I asked.

She held her breath, running her hand over her mouth and tilting her head as she surveyed the map. "I just—I had something here." She glanced toward the door. "A piece of pottery. It was older than most of the other stuff. It had something on it that looked kind of like that." She pointed to the fingerlike protrusions of land. "And there were other things on it, but I can't remember exactly."

"What?" Circe asked. "Where? Do you still have it?"

Marie shook her head. "No. I gave it to a contact I have up in Albany. He was making a trip and said he would return it for me."

"Did he?" I asked. "Did he take it back?"

"I don't know," Marie said.

"You know how long I've been looking for something—anything—to point me in the right direction?" Circe stared at Marie. "And you had something here this whole time?"

"I didn't know what it was," Marie said stiffly. "And it's not like you've always been the most approachable person, Circe. After—"

"Don't." Circe shoved her hands in her pockets. "Just don't." She sighed and tilted her head back. "I'm gonna need you to find out if this person still has the pottery and how soon we can get a look at it."

Marie nodded. "Gimme a minute." She took out her phone and excused herself, disappearing into the next room.

"Don't get your hopes up," Alec said as he settled back into his chair. "Her contacts aren't always the most reputable people. They like to stay under the radar for a reason."

Circe patted him on the shoulder, then let her hand linger there. She leaned down, studying his face. He avoided her gaze.

"What happened to your neck?" she asked.

It had only been a few weeks since Alec got himself hemmed up by the vines surrounding the Poison Garden. The deep brown skin of his neck was crisscrossed by lines of pale pink—newly healed flesh.

"I got into something that didn't agree with me," he said.

I watched as Circe studied him closely. "You're lucky they didn't kill you."

Alec's eyes grew wide. "Marie told you, didn't she?"

Circe pushed her glasses up and smirked. "Of course she did. You're so smart, Alec. I don't know why you'd ever risk it. You know how much Marie depends on you even if the two of you live on each other's last nerve. She's bad at letting people know how she feels."

"No she's not," Alec said. "She tells me all the time how much I annoy her."

"Not those kinds of feelings," Circe said, shaking her head. "She keeps a wall up, Alec. You know what she's been through. She loves you, though. I know she does."

His eyes glazed over and he pretended to shuffle some papers around on his desk. "I love her, too. Might be good if she said it out loud sometime."

I made a note to myself—pull Marie aside and make her tell Alec she cared about him, because I was not gonna allow her to keep hurting this sweet old man's feelings.

"We can talk about that later," Circe said. "But for now, I'd really like to know what was going through your mind when you decided to try and sneak out to the garden."

He shook his head. "The ulcers."

Circe raised an eyebrow, then gave him the once-over like a concerned parent. "I'll bring you a window box. I'll start a dozen comfrey plants. Can you look after them?"

"He needs the *Symphytum uplandicum* variety," I said. "We only have *Symphytum officinale* at the house."

The corner of Circe's mouth crept up. "And the other one is better because?"

I could tell by her tone that this wasn't a question she actually needed an answer to, but she wanted to hear me say it.

"The alkaloid content is higher. It's just better."

Circe nodded in approval and then turned back to Alec. "She's right, but I'm not going to bring you a single thing unless you promise not to come up to the house without telling somebody first."

"In my defense, I thought you were dead, and I didn't know Miss Briseis and her family had moved in."

"Give me your word," Circe said. "I trust that."

He raised his right hand the same way he had when I'd visited him in the hospital. "You have my word."

Marie came back into the room. "My contact says he doesn't have it anymore."

My heart sank into the pit of my stomach.

58

"But he also won't tell me how or when he returned it to its country of origin." She crossed her arms hard over her chest. "Which means he probably sold it to a private collector."

"How very unfortunate for him," Alec said.

I looked back and forth between him and Marie. "What? Why does that matter?"

"It's against my rules," Marie said. "My contact knows that."

I turned to Circe and expected to find her as confused as I was, but instead, I found her grinning.

"What's funny?" I asked. "What did I miss?"

Circe drummed her fingers on Alec's desk, then looked at Marie. "He wronged you? Reneged on the terms of your deal?"

Marie took in Circe's expression and cracked a smile herself.

"Somebody gonna tell me what's going on or what?" I asked.

Circe patted me on the shoulder. "Marie is a stickler for rules, especially when it comes to her treasures."

"They're not treasure. They are looted history, and if I asked this mother—"

"Language!" Alec said, his eyes wide.

He sounded like Mo and it made me smile.

Marie pursed her lips and dramatically folded her hands together in front of her. "If I made a deal with this—jerk—to return something and he sold it, well . . ." She took a long deep breath and her brown eyes seemed to swim with little tendrils of black. "That's going to be a problem. For him."

Alec cleared his throat and shook his head before raising his gaze to meet Marie's. "Why are you like this?"

"Because I need to be," Marie said. She grabbed my hand

59

and pulled me toward the door. "Come on. We can get on the road and be there in an hour."

I didn't want to waste any more time than we needed to. I shot Mo a text letting her know what we were doing, leaving out the part about Marie possibly wanting to murder this contact on sight. As we walked to the car, Nyx was nowhere around and Marie reached for the driver's side handle. Circe slid into the seat as Marie opened the door.

"I can drive," Marie said.

Circe took the keys from the visor and started the car. "I know everybody thinks I'm dead, but I don't actually want to be dead."

"Are you ever gonna let that go?" Marie asked.

"Never."

"What?" I asked. "You crashed the car or something?"

"Tell her," Circe said. "Let her know who she's dealing with."

Marie huffed and lowered her gaze to the ground. "Maybe I ran over Circe's foot one time."

I looked at Circe, who was smiling smugly. "My toes ain't never gon' be right again," she said. "I love that for me."

Marie shrugged. "I'll ride in the back."

I nudged her shoulder, and she opened the rear door so I could get in.

CHAPTER 4

An hour later we pulled onto a darkened street just outside downtown Albany. The narrow street butted up to a park dotted with hearty maples and towering oaks. As I climbed out of the car, a familiar groan emanated from the green space. The trees twisted toward me, their boughs searching for me in the dark. I took a deep breath and let the air hiss out between my teeth. The trees swayed in the windless night air.

"They know we're here," Circe said.

It took me a second to remember that I wasn't alone in this anymore. I had someone who had the exact same abilities as me and who knew what it was like to live with them every day.

"They only want to be near us," Circe said. She stepped onto the grass, and a patch of canary yellow daffodils bloomed under her feet. "Has it been hard for you to keep them in check?"

"For a really long time I couldn't go anywhere without feeling like the grass and the trees were going to give it all away," I said. "And I make myself sick—headaches, nausea—all from trying to keep it bottled up."

Circe came back over to me. "How has it been since you've been in Rhinebeck? Do you think it's easier to control out there?"

"It's not so much the town," I said. "It's that I stopped trying to fight it. When I let it all go and just lean into it . . ." I wasn't sure how to describe the feeling. "It's like breathing—like I'm doing something I'm supposed to do."

"Embracing it will be the best thing you've ever done for yourself," she said. Then she raised an eyebrow and gave me a little smirk. "And with the way things are going it might be your best weapon, too."

In my head, images of roots breaking through the apothecary floor and winding themselves around Mrs. Redmond played on a loop.

"This is the place," Marie said. She had turned her attention to the brownstone directly across the street. "My contact has been living here for a few years now. He moved here from Ithaca thinking he could keep a low profile, but I showed up at his door the same day the movers were carrying his couch inside."

"He didn't want you to know he moved?" I asked.

"Guess not. But ask me if I care what he wants." She grinned. "He likes to keep things quiet. He used to deal in stolen artifacts and still has a lot of contacts in the trade. It makes him vulnerable, but it also comes in handy when I'm trying to get some of this stuff back to where it belongs. He moved because he didn't like me popping up on him and making sure he hadn't fallen back into his old ways." She gazed up at the building. "I hope he didn't do what I think he did."

I had a feeling things were about to get extremely awkward once we got inside.

The streetlights were on and cast long columns of light across the sidewalk. The narrow brick building rose up three stories and was accented with pointed arches and an intricate round portico over the front door. The shutters were drawn in the large bay window that overlooked the street, but a light was on somewhere inside, casting a muted yellow haze through the glass.

"Do we just ring the bell?" Circe asked, turning to Marie. "Something tells me this guy is not gonna be happy to see you."

"Who wouldn't be happy to see me?" Marie asked. Her voice dripped with syrupy-sweet sarcasm.

She mounted the front steps and rang the bell as Circe and I stood at her back. There were footsteps inside, a pause, and then the curtain covering the rectangular stained glass window in the door moved aside, revealing a man's face. Plastered across it was an expression that could be nothing other than absolute dread.

Marie leaned toward the glass. "Open the door before I kick it in." She gripped the handle, and the hinges groaned as if they were being pulled apart.

"Okay!" the man shouted. "All right! Just don't pull the door off! It's original to the house!"

Marie pressed her hand to the glass and a crack spread across its surface. "Sir. I have never cared less about anything in my entire life. Open the door."

The man undid the locks but before he got the chain off, Marie pushed the door in like it was made of air, scattering the broken links across the floor. She swept in and stood glowering at the man. He put his hands up in front of him—as if it would do him any good.

He was a short, balding man with a splotchy pale complexion, sweating out the pits of his pin-striped pajamas.

Circe shut the door and Marie approached him. "Well, hello, Phillip."

Nothing about this should have been funny, but I had to pretend to be fishing something out of my pocket to keep from laughing. He just didn't look to me like his name should be Phillip. A smile danced across Circe's lips, too.

"Marie," he said curtly. "Just listen to me—"

"I should snap your neck," Marie said.

"Marie! Damn!" Circe marched up and stood between her and Phillip. "Can we at least talk to him first? How is he going to answer our questions if he's dead?"

"We can have a séance," Marie said.

"Stop," said Circe. "We came here for a reason, remember?"

I slipped my hand into Marie's and pulled her back a little. "I'm not tryna tell you what to do, but maybe, if you want, just take it down a notch? At least until we talk to him?"

Marie firmly gripped my hand. "You're right." She glared but didn't approach him. "Where is it?"

Phillip looked from Marie, to me, to the door, and then back down to the floor. The damp circles under his arms grew bigger, and a glistening sheen of sweat on top of his head was reflecting the light from a lamp in his living room. He was scared out of his mind.

"I—I told you I don't have it anymore," he stammered.

Marie narrowed her eyes. "Yeah, you told me already, but you didn't explain why you don't have it or what you did with it.

Care to elaborate? We made a deal. You were to return that item to the museum in Ankara."

"I meant to," he said quietly. He took several steps back and Marie mirrored his every move. I really hoped he wasn't thinking of running. She'd be on him before he took a single step. He turned and meandered to the cramped front room of the house, where he sat down on the couch and put his head in his hands. "We've known each other for a very long time, Marie."

"You don't know me," Marie snapped. "We have a professional working relationship."

"We do," he said. "And that's exactly why I would never betray your trust."

He looked like he was about to cry.

"I need to know where it is," Marie said. "I already know you didn't do what I told you to do with it, so what happened? You sold it?"

Phillip pressed his back into the couch. "I—I wanted to."

Marie stepped toward him.

"Please!" he shrieked. "It's valuable! So incredibly valuable! And there were buyers, and they were willing to pay whatever I asked. Do you know how tempting that is?"

"Do you know how ugly you sound?" Marie shot back. "It doesn't belong to you!" I stepped away from Marie. I thought she might lose it, but instead she stared at him, her brow furrowed. "And who is 'they'?" she asked. "There was more than one buyer?"

"It was a group of three people. They wanted to purchase the pottery shard together."

"Is that weird?" I asked. I didn't know what was normal in the shadowy world of illegal antiquities trade.

"Were they the buyer's representatives?" Circe asked.

"No," Phillip said. "I think they were related. Siblings, maybe, I'm not sure."

"And you let it be known that you had the piece and waited for people to come to you with offers?" Marie asked.

Phillip sighed. "Yes. But this group was the only one who actually showed up. Everyone else who arranged to see it backed out."

Marie took a beat and then spoke in a calm monotone sort of way. "When was this?"

Phillip thought for a minute. "Three weeks ago. I arranged for a showing of the pottery shard," he continued. "I met the three people in a hotel downtown. They came to my room and then—" His eyes glazed over and he stared off.

"And then what?" Marie asked.

"I—I don't know."

Marie crossed her arms hard over her chest. "What do you mean, you don't know? Did you sell them the pottery or not?"

Phillip gave an exasperated sigh. "There was money on the table, and the shard was gone . . . after."

Circe and I exchanged glances.

"This is like pulling teeth," Marie said. "Why are you acting like this? What the hell happened to you?"

"I don't remember what happened in the room after these people showed up," Phillip said. "I think I might have been drugged. All I know is I had the pottery fragment in my suitcase. I opened the door to let in three people. We sat down at the table in my suite, and the next thing I know, I'm lying on my back in the middle of the floor, the artifact is gone, and there's a stack of money on the table."

"Were you injured?" Circe asked.

He shook his head. "No. I checked my head. I thought maybe they attacked me, but I'd know if something like that happened, right?"

I shrugged. Probably, but it still didn't make sense. He said he wasn't hurt, so clearly, someone hadn't gone upside his head.

He seemed to read the expression on my face and rolled his eyes dismissively. "I'm just as confused as you are, believe me. The pottery shard is gone. I have some money to show for it, but it's only half of what I wanted, and now . . ." He glanced up at Marie. "Are you going to kill me?"

"I'm considering it," she said.

Phillip jumped up from his seat and got down on his knees. He clasped his hands together in front of him. "Marie, please! I've always done everything you asked! I've returned hundreds of items to their rightful owners. This was one small thing."

Marie turned her back on him as he groveled at her feet. "It's not a small thing." Her voice was low and gravelly. I had no doubt that if she turned around, her eyes would be swimming with black.

"What now?" I asked. "It's gone. Can we try to track down the people from the hotel?" I turned to him. "Do you know their names? A phone number? Anything?"

"No, no, no," he said. "You think anyone uses information that can be tracked? We used burner phones to communicate, and it's not like they would have given me their real names anyway."

"Excuse me," I said, rolling my eyes. "I'm not a shady criminal so I don't know how this works."

He looked like he wanted to argue and honestly, I was ready. First thing I was gonna roast him for was his ugly-ass pajamas.

"Phillip," Marie said; her voice had returned to a singsong pitch. "What's that?" She pointed to a shelf strewn with various objects: a large gold plate, a cylindrical clay vase, several chipped and broken cups, and two identical glass jars. Marie went to the shelf and turned back to Phillip. "If this is what I think it is—"

"It's not!" he shouted way louder than was necessary.

I huffed. "I don't know what y'all are talking about, but he's lying." Anybody who hollered out an answer like that was not telling the whole truth. I'd initially felt bad for him but the only reason we were there was because we were trying to find a way to get my mom back and Phillip had sold a valuable piece of the puzzle. I was starting to lose my patience.

Circe joined Marie at the shelf and examined the twin glass jars, turning them over in her hands. "They're replicas?" she asked.

Marie held each jar, testing its weight in her hand. She held it up, allowing the overhead light to filter through it. Phillip shifted uncomfortably on the couch.

"One is real," Marie said. "And the other is a very good forgery." She swept over to Phillip, picking him up by the front of his nightshirt until his feet dangled above the ground. "You've been making and selling forgeries?"

Phillip kicked at Marie. "Put me down!"

I quickly went to Marie's side and put my hand on her

shoulder. I thought she might toss this dude right out the window, but we still needed answers. "Wait. Just hold on."

He said nothing but whimpered as Marie set him back down. She still kept a death grip on his shirt front, but she allowed him to gather himself.

"Did you sell the real pottery shard or a forgery?" I asked.

Marie tensed her arm.

"Stop! Okay! It was a forgery!"

Circe leaned close to him. "Does that mean you still have the original?"

Phillip's gaze darted around the room. "It's in the back."

Marie glanced down the hall, then back to Phillip. "I should fold you in half and put you in a suitcase. Then I should take the suitcase and run it over with my car."

"Please!" Phillip screamed. "I'm sorry!"

Circe brushed past and headed for the door at the end of the short hallway. "We're gonna get you some anger management, boo," she called over her shoulder. "I'll pay for it."

Marie grinned, but her eyes were like two empty sockets. She pushed Phillip down onto the couch and curled her hand into a fist, bringing it down right on top of his balding dome. He slumped to the side, and his eyes rolled back until only the whites showed.

"Night, night, sweet prince," Marie said.

I clapped my hand over my mouth. I knew I shouldn't laugh, but Marie was making that impossible. Phillip was doing some shady stuff, so maybe he deserved it—at least a little bit. I was just happy Marie didn't murder him right there.

"Y'all come look at this," Circe called.

Marie and I left the unconscious Phillip in the living room and went down the hall. The door to the rear room stood open, but I could see that it was made of metal and had at least three locks. Inside the back room, it was a full twenty degrees cooler than the rest of the house. The windows were boarded up with thick sheets of plywood, and the only light was coming from a lamp in the corner. Four or five tables stood all around, fitted together like puzzle pieces, and atop them lay dozens of ancient-looking artifacts and an equal number of what I assumed were identical forgeries.

I scanned the tables and finally found what we were looking for. The broken shard lay among several others that had yet to be fully copied. Circe gently lifted it up as Marie took out her phone and dialed a number.

"Alec," Marie said. "We're here. We—wait—were you asleep?"

Alec grumbled something into the phone.

Marie sighed. "Sir, if you don't wake up right now"—she rolled her eyes—"I'm going to call you on video. Just hit the green button." She switched over to a video call, and Alec's right eye appeared on the screen.

"Please back up off the camera for the love of Black baby Jesus," Marie said.

Circe carefully laid the pottery shard back down, and Marie put her phone close to it.

"Can you see it?" she asked.

"Yes," Alec said.

I stood next to Marie, staring down at the object. The

pottery itself was a faded orange color, but the images on it were painted in shiny black with accents of white and gold. It had several deep cracks running along its surface where it appeared to have been glued back together. The remnants of a painted man in a hat and winged sandals carrying a staff adorned the piece of ancient pottery. He looked on as another man holding a small stringed instrument stood aboard a ship with several other people. A rugged coastline jutted out behind them in a familiar pattern . . . four long protrusions. Directly ahead of them lay a small island and three rocky outcroppings surrounded by what I could only describe as mermaids—bare-breasted figures with tails like fish.

"This looks like the coastline on the map back at your place," I said breathlessly. Suddenly our dead end had turned into an open road.

Down the hall a loud crack, like a dish breaking, drew my attention to the door. Tendrils of an overgrown philodendron pulled their way into the room and wrapped around the legs of the table.

"Oh my god!" Phillip must have regained consciousness and was now freaking out in the front room. "Please! The plants are going to kill me. What is happening?"

"Pipe down!" Marie shouted in his general direction before returning her attention to the phone. "Alec, what is this piece showing?"

"Aside from some scant rocky formations close to the coast, there are no islands in the Black Sea," said Alec. "And this artwork clearly shows an island. This—this can't be right." He seemed at a loss. "Move the camera a little closer."

Marie did as he asked.

"The man with the staff is probably Hermes, but it's hard to tell with the amount of damage. The ship is the *Argo*. No doubt about that. And the man with the lyre is Orpheus."

Circe suddenly gripped Marie's arm as her gaze darted from the art on the pottery shard to someplace in the middle distance, her own thoughts probably. She chewed at her bottom lip.

"What's wrong?" I asked.

The philodendron sprouted another length and went to her, coiling around her leg. She waved it away. "Aeaea, the sorceress Circe's island, is beyond the Sirenum scopuli." She gently touched the mermaid figures. "The Sirens' Rocks."

CHAPTER 5

Even in the middle of grief and hopelessness and the impossible tasks piled up in front of me, hope bloomed anew. We had a solid lead. Circe's excitement was palpable, and the philodendron sprouted a dozen offshoots and braided itself between us, latching onto our arms and hands.

"I've been combing the Aegean for years," Circe said. "I went to Greece and stayed there for years, searching, basing all my research on the consensus that Aeaea had to be somewhere in those waters." She looked completely defeated. "So much time wasted."

I touched her arm. "We don't have to waste any more."

She straightened up. "You don't think Phillip happens to have Orpheus's lyre lying around here somewhere, do you, Marie?"

Marie looked around. "Probably not, but if you want to feel worse about it, it's probably in the collection of some rich asshole who'd rather hoard it than share it with anybody else."

"Thanks," Circe said.

"It's a long shot," Alec said. He'd moved his face closer to the camera again, and we were now gazing up his left nostril. "A very long shot."

"Bye," Marie said, hanging up before he could say anything else.

Circe gently wrapped the pottery shard in a sweater she found draped over the back of a chair. "He's right, but this is all we have. It might be a long shot, but it's also our best one."

We left the room and headed for the car, but as I walked into the front room, I once again had to keep myself from laughing. Phillip was caught up in a tangle of *Rhaphidophora cryptantha*, commonly known as a shingle plant. He lay by the front door, wrapped in the shingling growth of juniper-colored leaves with veins the color of bone. The only parts of him that were visible were his bare feet and his balding head. He must have been trying to escape, and the greenery had decided that wasn't gonna happen.

"I'll be back," Marie said as we headed out the door. "And you better be here. We're gonna have a little chat about your activities."

"I'll make it up to you! I swear!" he said as he struggled to free himself.

Circe waved her hand and the plant loosened its grip.

Marie nudged him with her foot and he slid across the floor and collided with the couch. He scowled at Marie and she just smiled. "See you later," she said.

As we piled into the car and headed back toward Rhinebeck, there was something I couldn't get out of my head.

"Who else would want this?" I asked as I cradled the pottery in my lap. "We have a very specific reason for needing it, but who were the people Phillip sold his forgery to? And why can't he remember exactly what happened when he met with them?"

"He's so busy lying all the time he probably got his stories mixed up," Marie said. "Probably dealers who are gonna resell it for a profit."

Circe eyed us in the rearview mirror. "Or somebody else is on the same track as us and got the shard, even if it was a fake version, before us."

All I could think of was Karter, and the respite of the little side trip to Albany evaporated. Anger poured back in. Phillip hadn't mentioned that any of his three mysterious visitors had been teenagers, but one of them might have been Karter. There was no way to know for sure.

Marie interlaced her fingers with mine. "What else do we need? Are we traveling?"

"I don't think we have a choice," Circe said. "We'll need a charter flight because we have to transport all the pieces of the Heart. I don't think we'll have time to bring them back to Rhinebeck if we somehow manage to find the last piece. Probably gonna need a boat, too, something serious, because if that painting is showing what I think it is, if the legends about Aeaea are true, we're going to need more than some dinghy."

Marie took out her phone and began texting furiously. "I'm on it."

I stared at the mermaid-like creatures painted on the ancient pottery. They had claws and pointed teeth and were dragging a man from the ship, presumably to his death. I quickly covered it back up. We were a step closer to getting my mom back, and I didn't care if I had to cross a monster-infested sea to do it.

I opened Circe's clock and watched as the dials moved in their housing. Circe and Persephone were giving us a rundown of the legends surrounding the sirens who supposedly lived in the waters off Aeaea. We weren't talking about Ariel and her lovable sidekick, Flounder, either. These creatures were murderous sea-dwelling monsters who lured people to their deaths by way of enchanting sea shanties

"I've seen a living goddess, a hellhound, a plant that beats like a human heart, but mermaids?" I asked. "I'm having a hard time with that."

"That's the sticking point for you?" Persephone asked. "I love that the mermaids are the thing that's throwing you."

"Sirens," Circe corrected. "Not mermaids."

"Sea bitches," said Marie.

Persephone let out a deep throaty laugh, and Mo actually smiled.

Nyx clapped her hand over her mouth. "Oh my god, Marie. Please try to be serious."

"I am!" Marie said. "Mer-hos. Is that better?"

Nyx threw her hands up and shook her head. "I know you use humor as a defense mechanism to hide how scared you are about the danger Bri is in and everything else that's going on, so I won't hold it against you, but try to keep it in check."

"Well, damn," Marie said as she leaned back against the wall, shoving her hands in her pockets. "Just tell all my business to everybody."

Her gaze cut to me for a split second, and I could tell that Nyx had hit a nerve.

Circe opened several different books and file folders and laid them out on the table. She was poring over them, pencil in hand. "Do you know the story of Persephone and Hades?"

I glanced at Persephone.

"We're talking about the original Persephone," she said. "I would have clawed Hades's eyes out. He would've gotten sick of me real fast."

"Let's not judge," said Circe. "You say that now, but I bet you'd be pretty powerless against the ruler of the underworld."

Persephone shrugged.

"I've seen *Hadestown*," I said. "Does that count?" I could almost hear Mom in my head complaining about the ticket prices and it put an ache in my chest.

"What's that?" Circe asked.

"A Broadway show," I said quietly. "It's a reimagining of the story of Orpheus and Eurydice."

Circe looked thoughtful. "I've been gone a long time. I guess I'm out of the loop. But it goes like this: When Persephone was abducted by Hades, Demeter—Persephone's mother—tasked her closest friends with finding her daughter. But they couldn't search the sea, so Demeter gave them tails like fish so they could look for her. That's how sirens came into existence, and over time they grew to be vengeful, dangerous creatures." She pushed an open book toward me. "The sirens on those three tiny islands we saw on the pottery are said to guard Aeaea. Their songs beckon sailors to the water. To their deaths."

"Seriously?" I asked. "If we gotta get by them to get to the island—"

"We?" Mo chimed in. She came to the table. "*We* aren't going anywhere. *I'm* gonna go get your mama. You are gonna stay your butt right here."

"What? No. I have to come with y'all." I glanced around, expecting Circe and Persephone to agree with me, but they both avoided my eyes. "You gotta be kidding me. I want to go. I want to help get Mom back."

Persephone motioned to the door, and Marie walked out of the room with Nyx trailing behind her. Persephone then left me, Mo, and Circe alone.

Mo stood in front of me. "This is too dangerous. You're talking about traveling to the other side of the world, and who knows where that kid Karter ran off to. He can't be the only one looking for the pieces. And we've seen firsthand that people are willing to kill anyone they need to in order to get to it." She clenched her teeth. "I can't lose you, too, love. I can't. I won't. I'll go get your mama. I'll bring her back."

"You can't go either," Circe said.

Mo spun around and tilted her head to the side. "Excuse me?"

"You're absolutely right," Circe said, choosing her words carefully. "This *will* be incredibly dangerous. We have to travel with the existing pieces of the Heart. The only people who can semi-safely be around them are those of us who are mostly unaffected by them. And I anticipate that the Mother, that piece that seeded the others, will be a thousand times deadlier than the pieces we already have. You can't go, Mo. It's not safe."

Mo rounded on Circe, her bottom lip trembling, her eyes wet with tears. "You don't get to tell me I can't go get my wife back. That's not up to you."

78

"Listen to me," Circe said. "I understand what it's like to lose somebody you love. Selene died in my arms." She paused, cleared her throat, then continued. "I didn't have a chance to bring her back. Nobody could have stopped me from trying, though. So, I get it."

Mo hung her head. "I'm sorry. I'm so sorry I just—"

"Don't apologize," Circe said. "I know that you're going through it right now and I wish you weren't. I can't stop you from following us out the door when it's time. All I'm saying is that if you choose to go, there's a really good chance you won't survive. And if by some chance we can't get Thandie back, then you'll be gone, too. Then what?"

Mo looked at me with tears in her eyes. "I need a minute," she said.

She turned and walked out of the room and out the front door. Not two seconds later she walked back inside, and I heard the locks click shut. She came into the front room and stood, visibly trembling, her fingers interlaced on top of her head. I rushed to her side and took her by the arm.

"What's wrong?" My heart raced. I glanced to the front door. "Mo? What happened?"

Nyx stood outside the window, peering in through the glass.

"Mo!" I shouted. "What is going on?"

"I—it's—I saw . . ." Her legs went out from under her, and if I hadn't been holding on to her arm, she would have cracked her head on the edge of the table. I tried to guide her down, but she still hit the floor with a loud thud.

"Oh my god! What happened?" I screamed, my heart cartwheeling in my chest. "Mo!"

Circe raced to the front door, and just as she reached for the handle, the room suddenly darkened as vines slithered across the windows, blotting out the light. My heart punched inside my chest. The twisted foliage pushed its way through the crack under the door. A tapestry of *Peperomia prostrata* unfurled from the second floor banister, dropping down around me and Mo like a curtain.

Circe yanked the front door open, glanced outside, and sighed. "Nyx! Come on, now! You're gonna give her mom a damn heart attack. She passed out!"

Nyx and Marie came stumbling through the front door. Persephone appeared at the top of the stairs, peering down at us.

"Oh no," Marie said, crouching down and effortlessly readjusting Mo so that she was lying on her side. "Damnit, Nyx. I thought he was hibernating or something."

"He doesn't hibernate," Nyx said. "What else was I supposed to do?"

"Tell him to stay his ass at home!" Marie shot back.

"Yeah, okay." Nyx rolled her eyes. "You know how disobedient he can be when he misses me."

"We're gonna put his funky ass on a leash and tie him to a tree or something," Marie said.

"Over my dead body," said Nyx.

"Well, we both know that isn't gonna happen, so I guess we'll have to figure something else out," Marie shot back.

"He's outside all the time," Nyx grumbled. "He doesn't mind, but maybe we could let him in—"

"In where?" Marie asked angrily. "Not in the house? Are you

serious? He can't even fit in there! And I know you've seen the size of his droppings. Ain't no way."

They were both breathing hard, and then they exchanged glances. Marie's chin wobbled, and then they both descended into a fit of cackling. My heart continued to beat out of my chest, but Marie and Nyx weren't overly concerned about whatever it was that was happening outside.

I was about to cuss them both out when a shadow engulfed the front entryway. Not the patchy darkness the vining plants had created, but a full and total eclipse of the fading evening light filtering through the windows flanking the front door and the stained glass at the top of the wall.

Something enormous was standing in front of the house.

A familiar sound split the air. The same sound I thought I heard from the bluff the other night at Marie's.

The rhythmic beating of wings.

CHAPTER 6

Mo stirred as I cradled her head in my lap. I stared out the open front door, unsure of what I was seeing. I shut my eyes and opened them again, thinking maybe I was seeing things. Maybe I wasn't immune to the poisonous plants, and their toxins had finally caught up with me. Hallucinations were a side effect of deadly nightshade, henbane, and mandrake—all of which I'd come in contact with at some point.

That didn't make any real sense, but neither did what I was seeing—a mass of black feathers, taloned feet, four heavily muscled legs extending above the roof of Marie's black sedan, slope of a fur-lined belly. Wings.

Mo's eyes fluttered open, and she sat up groggily. I scrambled to my feet as the creature folded its giant wings against its body and lay down in the driveway.

"It's a griffin," Marie said, like that was supposed to mean something to me. "He belongs to Nyx. They've been together forever."

I couldn't find the words to say how I still didn't trust what I was seeing with my own two eyes. "It's—it's your—your pet?"

Marie winced, and Nyx narrowed her eyes at her. "You've been telling people he's my pet?" She looked absolutely disgusted. "The disrespect." Nyx turned back to me. "I'm so sorry. I didn't expect him to follow me here. He's usually very good about staying put. Is Mo okay?"

Mo was sitting slack jawed on the floor. "Not okay," she mumbled. "Not okay. Not even a little."

Nyx motioned toward the door. "He's my companion. He's actually very friendly once you get to know him."

Circe grunted. "Oh. So now we're telling bold-faced lies?"

"He's protective of me," Nyx said. "And I'm protective of him. That's the way it should be." She walked out onto the front porch.

Mo stood on wobbly legs. "Bri, love, I think I'm losing my grip. I gotta sit down. This is just too much." She all but fell into the couch across the hall, but I took a step toward the door.

"It's probably safe to go out there," Marie said. "If you want a closer look."

I whipped my head around to look at her. "Probably?"

She pursed her lips. "Most likely safe. As long as you don't threaten Nyx, he's not terrible."

I nudged her toward the door. "You go out there first."

She smiled, gave me a quick kiss, and led me onto the porch. Nyx went down the steps and stood at the griffin's side. Nyx was pushing six foot two, and the griffin's shoulder was an arm's length above her head while it was lying down. Its head was half the size of our car.

"He's friendly," Nyx said. "Come here. You can pet him."

"Yeah. No. Not gonna do that," I said. The enormity of the

creature was one thing, but its strange assortment of parts made even less sense. It had the head, wings, and feathers of a bird. All these parts linked to a body that looked like it belonged to a lion, but its fur was black and shining. Its talons dug into the gravel, gouging out chunks of the ground as long as my arm.

"His name is Roscoe," Nyx said.

I readjusted my glasses like that was going to somehow help me get a grip on what I was seeing. "His name's what?" Despite the cocoon of confusion and disbelief that had wrapped itself around me, I couldn't help but laugh. "Roscoe? Like Roscoe's Chicken and Waffles?"

Nyx grinned. "It suits him."

"It sounds like somebody's grandpa's name," Marie said.

"He lives on the bluff?" I asked. "That's where you're always sneaking off to, huh?"

Nyx nodded and scratched the griffin's underbelly. A rumble echoed inside his chest—a purr. "Yes. He nests there when we're not together. He was with me when I came here from—"

"From California?" I asked. "That's where you said you were from. Is that a lie, too?"

"No," she said. "That's technically true."

I tilted my head. "You know what? I'm not even gonna ask anymore. I need to just accept that the weirdest shit is gonna happen right in front of me and all of y'all are gonna be unsurprised by it."

Marie slipped her hand around my waist. "I'll take you for a ride later if you want," she whispered against my ear.

"You ride it?"

Marie shrugged. "When he lets me. He's a jerk. Like I said."

The creature whipped its head around and stared at Marie, its big yellow eyes narrowing, the pupils big as tennis balls.

Marie stuck her finger in its face. "Don't get an attitude with me. I won't bring you any more treats."

The griffin lowered its head and huffed so hard a shower of dirt and dust from the drive flew up into the air.

"Do they sell griffin treats at the pet store?" I asked.

"He loves a live rabbit," Nyx said.

I put my hands up. "You know what? Forget I said anything." Now all I could think of was Nyx catching rabbits in the woods and tossing them to Roscoe like dog treats.

A rustling drew my attention to the tree line at the far side of the driveway. A length of Devil's Pet, as big around as a telephone pole, slithered out and coiled itself like a snake at my side.

"Looks like we all have our own sort of familiars," Nyx said.

I reached down and ran my fingers along the rough surface of the deadly plant. A chill bloomed in my palm, then dissipated. "I guess so."

"Mo went to lie down," Circe said as she came out of the house and down the front steps. "I gave her another cup of tea. Not quite as strong as what I gave her last night, just enough to get her to calm down. Mostly chamomile."

I raised an eyebrow. "That's all?"

Circe shrugged. "Maybe a little belladonna. She'll probably be out for the night."

The sun was already lying low in the sky. Exhausted as I was, I knew I wouldn't be sleeping.

"Mo gave me Dr. Kent's phone number," Circe said. "I gave her a call."

"And?" I asked. "Are you hoping she has something else we can use?"

Circe looked thoughtful. "Don't you find it coincidental that you came here to Rhinebeck, found out you're related to Medea, and then you find my document telling the true story of Medea, which just so happened to be something this Dr. Kent is familiar with? Do you know how obscure the document is? It's a one-in-a-million chance that you just happen to know someone who would even be familiar with what you're talking about."

"Dr. Kent has known my parents since before I was born," I said.

"Even stranger still," Circe said. "Was it fate that brought Dr. Kent into your circle before you even knew how useful her knowledge would be?"

"You believe in fate?" Marie asked as the arch of her brow shot toward her hairline. "I'm not saying I disagree. I'm just saying you don't really seem like the type."

"I believe in a kind of fate," Circe said. "And I have a theory about ours, but in order to test it we'll need to pay Dr. Kent a visit."

"Road trip?" Marie asked, looping her arm around my shoulder.

"Wait," I said. "What's your theory? Do we even have time to make a trip back to Brooklyn? I feel like we're wasting time."

Marie pulled me close. "I'm already trying to pull some flights together, but it's important to keep things as quiet as possible, so it might take a minute."

"We don't know where this boy Karter is or who he's been in contact with, and we don't know who those people were that were after the pottery shard," Circe said. "We have to assume they're trying to get their hands on the last piece of the Heart. While Marie is arranging things I think we have some time to follow up with Dr. Kent."

"You're not going to tell me why?" I asked.

"If I'm wrong, I'll tell you what I was thinking and we can laugh about it," Circe said. "But if I'm right, you'll see for yourself."

"When do we leave?" I asked.

"Now," said Circe.

CHAPTER 7

Persephone stayed behind while Mo slept and Nyx took off with Roscoe the rabbit-eating griffin in tow. Marie piled into the front seat of the car next to me, and Circe drove. We made the trip in a little over two hours and pulled up to the Brooklyn Museum right before midnight.

I'd been there on a few different field trips but never in the dead of night. As we crossed the plaza in front of the glass pavilion that now framed the original portico, Circe steered us to a path that ran along the eastern side of the giant marble building.

"She said the front doors wouldn't be open to the public this late," said Circe. "We have to go around."

Marie huffed.

"Are we gonna have a problem?" Circe asked as she glanced back at Marie.

"What's wrong?" I asked.

Marie gazed up at the glass awning that curved around the Brooklyn Museum's facade. "Nothing," she said.

I took her hand and pulled her toward the side entrance as Circe turned her face up to a small security camera mounted above the door. She gave a little wave, and the outer door clicked open. Circe ushered us inside, and we found ourselves in a long corridor draped in shadow.

Circe led the way, and I followed close behind as Marie trailed me. The smell of floor cleaner and recycled air was thick. The hallway ended at the side of a large rectangular courtyard, the floor of which was inlaid with squares of blue glass. Above, the glass ceiling made the starry night sky look as if it were laid on top of the building itself. It was silent except for the steady flush of the AC.

"It's beautiful," I said, taking it all in.

Marie and Circe paused and looked up.

"It is," said Circe.

"It was designed to frame the night sky," a familiar voice said.

I spun around. A figure stood in the shadows just off the courtyard. Marie grabbed my hand. I strained to see into the dark.

I knew that voice.

"Dr. Kent?" I asked.

"Hello, Briseis," Dr. Kent said.

I'd spoken to Dr. Kent on the phone. We exchanged emails. But I'd never actually seen her. The hair on the back of my neck stood up as she swept into the open space. She was tall, like Persephone. She had a mass of wavy dark hair that went down to her waist, and her dark brown skin shone in the dim starlight.

"I'm glad you could come," Dr. Kent said. She stuck out her hand, and Circe took it. "I'm Madeline Kent."

Something—a feeling I couldn't put my head around—raised goose bumps on my arms.

Dr. Kent turned to Marie and then looked away. "Would you follow me, please?"

She stepped between us and crossed the courtyard. We followed along behind her as she took us down another series of hallways. The wide legs of her linen pants obscured her feet and made it look as if she were floating. I couldn't hear her footsteps. The sense of unease I'd had as she spoke to us in the glass atrium had crept up to something much more like fear.

"I wanted to see if—" Circe began, but Dr. Kent held up her hand.

"Can we wait to discuss things until we've reached my office?"

Circe looked confused. "Oh. Sure."

I didn't understand why, if we were going to discuss some old documents, we needed to wait, but clearly Circe was holding something back. My gut was telling me it was something serious. I glanced back at Marie and her eyes were black as the night sky. In the dark she looked terrifying. I quickly checked to see if Dr. Kent had noticed anything, and when I was sure she hadn't, I let out a long shaky breath. Marie must have sensed the same thing I had—a creeping sense of dread that now sat at the nape of my neck like a heavy, cold hand.

Marie reined herself in as Dr. Kent led us down a short flight of stairs and through a set of double doors to an area off-limits to the public.

Workstations with pieces of restored art and fragmented statues dotted the floor of a room the size of a school gym. Floor-to-ceiling shelving, six or seven rows deep, held thousands of items. Dr. Kent led us through the tables and down an aisle between two rows of shelves. She paused and opened a long narrow drawer.

Inside it were dozens of gold rings adorned with jewels of all different colors and shapes. She pulled a white glove out of her pocket and slipped it onto her hand.

"Something I thought you might be interested in," she said as she gently lifted a ring from the back row and turned it toward me. It was solid gold with a leafy pattern stamped around the band. Its face was a small oval indentation where something had once been painted. I leaned in and saw a figure with three faces. The Colchis family crest.

I reached for the ring and Dr. Kent drew it back.

"I can't allow you to touch it," she said. "It's very old, and while the staff here has cataloged it as something from around 540 BCE, it is in fact much older, made from the remnants of a piece of jewelry that may have once sat on Medea's own wrist. I thought that might be of interest to you and your family."

Circe inhaled sharply. "How did you—"

"Oh yes. Descended from Medea." Dr. Kent smirked and set the ring back in the drawer. "I know. And you're already putting other things together aren't you?"

Circe took a step back.

"You should return it," Marie said.

Dr. Kent chuckled. "Excuse me?"

Marie cocked her head to the side. "The ring. It doesn't

belong to you, just like most of the other stuff in here. If you know it belongs to their family, keeping it here is theft."

"Not exactly," Dr. Kent said.

"Yeah," Marie shot back. "That's exactly what it is."

Circe cleared her throat. "Is this where we're supposed to talk? I thought you were taking us to an office or something."

Dr. Kent roughly closed the drawer and stuffed the white glove back in her pocket. She turned and walked the rest of the way down the narrow aisle until she came to the far wall. Placing her hands against it, she gave it a solid push, and a doorway opened along an invisible seam. Behind the hidden door was an elevator. She swiped her badge in front of a panel, and the doors slid open. She stepped inside. I hesitated.

"Where are we going?" I asked.

"My office," Dr. Kent said. "To talk."

Circe stepped inside the elevator. "Remember what I said, Briseis? About whether I was right or wrong?"

I nodded.

She met my gaze. "I'm right. Trust me on this."

I took a deep breath and stepped in. Marie stepped in, too, but stood directly in front of Dr. Kent. My entire body tensed as Marie's eyes darkened.

"You're a little too dramatic for my taste," Dr. Kent said. There was no fear or wonderment in her voice. She wasn't fazed by Marie's transformation at all. "What?" she asked. "I'm supposed to be intimidated by your little show? You'll have to do better than that."

The elevator doors slid shut, and we dropped farther and faster than I'd anticipated. I expected us to come to a stop quickly. We'd climbed in at ground level, and there couldn't have been more than one or two stories belowground, but the descent felt like we were going much deeper than that. My stomach lurched, and I reached for the rail. I leaned on Marie. Dr. Kent eyed me as Marie wrapped me up, faint hint of a smile on her lips.

The elevator finally came to a rest, but the doors didn't open immediately. From the wall near the buttons a panel unfolded, and Dr. Kent put her hand on top of it. A light filtered through her fingers, and the doors opened.

"This way," Dr. Kent said. "And watch your step."

The air was markedly cooler in what I assumed was some kind of subbasement. The walls along the hallway were rough-cut stone, and the distinct musty smell of dirt and dampness lingered in the air. As we approached the end of the hallway, we passed under a grand archway with two marble pillars on either side. The space beyond was cavernous, cut deep into the bedrock far below the museum. A roaring fire stoked in a deep pit illuminated the space along with dozens of half-melted candles. There were tables and chairs made of wood and stone, and a shallow pool filled to the brim with water that seemed almost luminescent. In the center of the space stood a wheel the size of a large tire mounted to a wooden stand, and wrapped around it was a skein of glowing golden thread. All around, alcoves cut into the rock were stuffed with threads that shared the same strange hue and others that were dark and frayed. I gripped Marie's jacket, and Circe pressed her shoulder into mine.

"What is this place?" I asked.

Dr. Kent lowered herself into one of the chairs and tented

her fingers under her chin. "I call it the Grotto. It is where I work."

I turned to Circe, who was trying and failing to stay calm. She kept opening her mouth like she was going to say something but she couldn't get it out. Marie was silent.

"Who are you?" I asked. "Is your name even Madeline Kent?"

"That is one of many monikers I've used over the years." She glanced to the spinning wheel. "There was a time when all I did was sit and weave together the lives of mortals. Their short, delicate threads have always been of particular fascination to me."

"I knew it," Circe whispered into the dark. "I knew it couldn't be a coincidence that you knew so much about Medea, that you just happened to be the one ready to answer Briseis's questions."

"There are very few coincidences in life," Dr. Kent said. "And you're right to assume this isn't one of them."

"Wait," I said, my heart crashing in my chest. "What are you talking about?"

"She is one of the Moirai," Circe said. "One of the Fates. Clotho, if my theory is correct."

Dr. Kent smiled wide. She laughed, and the sound echoed off the high stone walls. "You're right, but you give me too much credit. I am not the great goddess I once was. My loom gathers dust as we speak."

CHAPTER 8

What did I know about the Fates, and why was everything I could think of from Disney movies or Broadway shows? I tried to quiet my racing heart enough to think clearly. Dr. Kent studied me carefully, and as she leaned forward in her chair she seemed to grow a head taller. I stepped back. My gut had been trying to tell me something, and I was kicking myself for brushing it aside. Now we were in a cave somewhere deep underground and in the presence of another living, breathing goddess. I didn't understand how I'd missed this. Dr. Kent had been helpful, even kind. Now she seemed amused but distant. I didn't know which version of her I was supposed to believe.

Circe lifted her chin and spoke in a calm, steady voice. "You knew the Medea story. You'd seen the document. It's the real story of Medea, and no one in all the years it has existed could pinpoint where it came from."

"Maybe you hadn't figured it out, but I guarantee the Vatican knew what it was," Dr. Kent said. "Your family had been in possession of the document for a long time, my dear Circe. And then it fell into the hands of the Church. Why would they care so much about it? Why should they?"

"It's—I don't—it's very old," Circe stumbled over her words.

"They wanted it because it is written in the hand of a goddess." Dr. Kent splayed her hand out in front of her, then curled her fingers like she was holding an imaginary pen. "It was a very foolish thing for me to do. I can admit that now. But you must understand that I have found myself oddly intrigued by your family and its long memory. I gifted that parchment to Medea's eldest child, a girl called Eriopis. I wanted her to have an accurate record before mortals got their hands on it. That any part of it still remains is a miracle in and of itself."

"Briseis said that you are a friend of her mother," Circe said. "That you've known them since before Bri was born. Did you know this entire time how this would play out?"

"That Selene's life would be cut short?" Dr. Kent asked. "That Thandie's would as well?"

Hearing their names rocked me to my core. I took another step back.

Dr. Kent stood and went to her loom. She let her long fingers trace the filaments of golden thread around the wheel. "When I weave a mortal's life, I see it like a moving picture. I see how they enter the world, how they exist in it, and how they depart this mortal plane. That is the extent of my terrible gift."

She turned to me, and then her gaze flitted to the ground. I followed it and saw a network of lacy green moss had blanketed the rocks around my feet.

Dr. Kent rested her hand on the loom, and again sadness pulled the corners of her mouth down and made her shut her eyes. "I wove the thread of predetermined events, Lachesis determined the thread's length, and Atropos cut it at the appropriate time. Together my sisters and I see a hazy picture of the life we've helped usher into existence."

"You knew what would happen to my mom?" I asked. "And you knew what was gonna happen to Selene, too?" A white hot rage ripped through me. "You've known Mo since before I was even born. Why didn't you help us? Why didn't you step in?"

Dr. Kent walked toward me. The moss at my feet puffed up and began to spread out all around me.

"Do you know how often I've been asked to interfere in the lives of mortals?" she asked in a way that told me she wasn't expecting a real answer. "When some lustful god falls in love with a mortal they come to me begging for insight to their fate. How long will they live? How will they die and what can be done to keep it from happening? We knew all, my sisters and I. But we were not tasked with judging these fragile lives. We don't write their fates, only see them, and bring them into being. And we do not interfere in the lives of mortals."

"Why not?" I asked, anger still burrowing its way through my chest.

Dr. Kent returned to her chair. "I don't have an answer that you can understand. It's just the way things are. Some ancient covenant—the specifics of which have been long forgotten. What I know now is that interfering in the lives of mortals creates chaos each and every time. The potential for disaster is never greater than when a god intercedes in mortal affairs."

I didn't like her answer, and I was so tired of everything being a riddle. "So why are you interfering in my life? Why were you talking to Mo? Why were you giving me the information about Medea?"

Dr. Kent's expression darkened. "I'm not interfering. I'm assisting. There's a difference."

I crossed my arms hard over my chest. "So you *can* step in but only when it works for you?"

She smiled politely but not genuinely. "As it turns out, I owe a debt to Hecate. I've always taken up my loom for her and showed her the threads of her mortal family."

Marie stepped forward. "You say gods are forbidden to step in, so why would she bother keeping tabs on anyone?"

"To bear witness," Dr. Kent said matter-of-factly. "I cannot interfere and neither can Hecate. She cannot persuade you to move away from something that is fated for you. Imagine what it must be like to watch your family over thousands of years, hundreds of generations, and be able to do nothing in the face of their suffering." She sighed heavily. "She did turn away for a long time, but she made her way back. She watches because that's all she can do."

Marie turned back to Circe. "Why are we here?"

Circe took a deep breath and chewed at her bottom lip before speaking. "I need to know if we can get Thandie back. If it's even possible to reunite the pieces of the Absyrtus Heart. I need to know if we can survive it."

"I thought we came here to find out more about Medea," I said.

Circe nodded. "I did, but— we're here and Clotho— Dr. Kent—knows so much more than that. I need to know how this is going to go because I can't lead us into this and lose everything all over again." Her eyes filled with tears, and her breath caught in her throat. "I've lost almost everything and everyone who has ever meant anything to me. All for the sake of the Heart. I don't know if I can do that again."

I didn't know what to say. I understood. Maybe just as much as she did. The Heart had taken from me, too.

Circe clasped my hand between hers and pushed her glasses up. "I won't put you in harm's way. Especially if it leads to nothing."

Dr. Kent suddenly cleared her throat, and we all turned to look at her.

"You want a glimpse into the future?" she asked. She stood and marched up to Circe. By the time they were face-to-face, Dr. Kent loomed over Circe, glaring down at her. "Maybe I give you exactly what you're asking for, but then what? What happens when you see something you wish you hadn't? Something you can't unsee or undo?"

Marie moved to my side, and I took her hand in mine.

Circe stood tall, her chest poked out, her chin up, defiant. "Maybe I could do something about it since you won't—or can't."

The silence that followed was awkward and uncomfortable as the two women stared at each other. Then, in one quick motion Dr. Kent swept over to the spinning wheel and grabbed it by the spoke, yanking it down. It spun so fast the shape of it was lost in a blur and the gold thread began to shimmer, making long shadows in the dim light.

"Please have a seat," Dr. Kent said.

Marie moved to one of the chairs and pulled me down next to her. Circe balanced herself on the chair's armrest and watched as Dr. Kent walked to the shimmering pool in the middle of the floor. She crouched and stirred the strangely luminescent water with her fingers. When she pulled her hand back the skin hung from her exposed bones, ragged and wet.

I stifled a scream as the skin quickly re-formed around her hand. She opened and closed her fist.

"Come forth, sisters," Dr. Kent said. "We have company."

A rumble from somewhere deep under my feet shook the ground. Little bits of loose rock bounced across the tops of my sneakers. The legs of the tables and chairs rattled against the stone floor.

Dr. Kent backed away from the pool as the water inside it sloshed against the sides, spilling out across the floor. As the rumbling settled, I took a deep breath, but the relief was short lived as a skeletal hand reached up from the water and clamped down on the pool's rim.

I was on my feet without thinking. I grabbed Marie by the arm and yanked her back. She clutched Circe by the collar of her shirt, and the three of us stood frozen in absolute shock as a figure clawed its way up and over the edge of the shallow pool.

A strangled cry escaped its throat, which began to re-form from bits of naked bone and flesh.

"What is that thing?" Marie asked as her black eyes grew wide.

"Atropos," Dr. Kent said. She wasn't answering Marie. She was addressing the thing that had just emerged from the pool like a monster from a nightmare. "I have guests, and you are scaring them."

"Atropos?" Circe asked breathlessly. She was trembling so bad she could barely keep her feet under her. Marie kept her upright with one hand while keeping a death grip on me with the other.

The strange figure clambered to its feet and straightened up. The bones popped and snapped as they oriented themselves. The skin plumped up on its bones and the face became something more living than dead. She was an older woman, though she looked remarkably similar to Dr. Kent, draped in a pale yellow dress that seemed to materialize out of nowhere. She took a few steps on wobbly legs as the water dripped from her face and beaded on the mass of black coils atop her head. Her skin was the color of boat orchids, her eyes a stunning chestnut brown. She swept the water droplets from her bare arms and sighed. She leaned over the rim of the pool and took hold of something that almost pulled her off her feet. She braced herself against the pool's wall and drew something up from the water.

Another person.

This figure was more flesh than the other had been, almost fully intact as she emerged from the water, and was clothed in pale blue robes. Instead of looking like an older Dr. Kent, she looked like she might have been her younger sister.

"We haven't long, Clotho," said the younger-looking one.

Her voice sent a shiver through me.

"I won't keep you, Lachesis," Dr. Kent said. "Look who I have here."

The sisters' gaze swept over Circe and then me. Three sets of inhuman eyes watched us carefully.

"Descendants of Hecate," Lachesis said. She walked to the spinning wheel and stared at the glowing threads. "What would you have us do?"

Dr. Kent went to one of the surrounding alcoves and pulled from it a wooden chest the size of a shoebox. She handled it like it was fragile, but as she closed the gap between us and opened the top in front of me, it was only filled with more of the same string that was stuffed into the rock-cut shelves. Some strands glowing, others dull and nearly disintegrated.

"These are the threads I have spun for your family since Medea's time," Dr. Kent said.

I stared into the box, and as terrified as I was, I couldn't help but feel a swell of fascination.

"Did you know that Medea and Absyrtus were the only children Hecate ever brought into this world?" Dr. Kent asked. "They were precious to her. And Medea was so talented. Gods. She was so skilled with poisons. She could craft a concoction that would kill a man over weeks, months even—extend the suffering as long as she liked. She was much like her own mother in that way. None of the stories save the one I penned were anywhere near the truth. They only served to soften her, to make her into something broken and spiteful—murderous. It's a shame I didn't have a chance to record more, foolish as it was. I could spend a hundred pages telling you of the ways in which Medea cut down the people who betrayed her. She was ruthless when it came to the protection of her family—and her garden."

My heart ticked up. "The garden? Is it on Aeaea?"

Dr. Kent tilted her head and shrugged one shoulder. "Who's to say? But *that* would be a tale worth telling, wouldn't it?"

I wondered if part of their covenant or whatever it was that kept them from interfering with mortals also made them unable to give a straight answer to a simple question.

Dr. Kent plucked a short dull thread from the box and held it up.

"Selene Colchis," Lachesis said in a raspy exhale. "Thirty threads."

Atropos reached into the folds of her dress and took out a pair of glinting gold shears. "Gone." The blades made a gentle clicking sound as she opened and closed them.

I sucked in a breath and held it as Dr. Kent picked up another dull string.

"Thandie Greene." Lachesis pulled a length of thread from the wheel. "Forty-one threads."

Atropos opened and closed her shears but said nothing.

I thought of Hecate having to watch everything that had happened to her children, forbidden to interfere though it was clear she had at least tried. She was a goddess that these other beings seemed to have a certain reverence for, but I'd looked into her eyes and seen something familiar, something human—the unmistakable mask of grief. My chest felt like it would cave in. I struggled to find a rhythm in my breathing that wouldn't make me pass out.

"Enough," Marie said, her voice little more than an angry growl. "What's the damn point?"

Dr. Kent—Clotho—and her two sisters turned to Marie with eerily similar expressions.

Dr. Kent plucked a string from the box. It was thicker than the others. As big around as my thumb.

"Marie Morris." Lachesis eyed the string. "I continue to add threads to your unnaturally long life."

Atropos swept over and held up her shears. She positioned the string between the blades and closed them. A cry escaped me, and Marie flinched away, but the string would not be severed.

"I'd like to cut it," Atropos said. "Maybe someday soon I'll get the chance."

Marie tilted her chin up. "You been swimming around in that sewage water too long." The darkness in her eyes had bled into the skin of her eyelids and down onto the high planes of her cheeks. Atropos looked genuinely stunned.

"Why are you showing us these?" Circe asked.

"You said you wanted to know if you'd come out of your situation unscathed," Dr. Kent said. "I'm showing you what you asked to see." Her tone was cold, almost angry.

Atropos huffed. "Clotho, you are obsessed."

Dr. Kent lowered her eyes. "I'm fascinated. There is a difference."

"Not from where I'm standing, there isn't," said Lachesis as she stared at her sister. "What is it about them that enraptures you so?"

Dr. Kent's expression grew tight, and she clasped her hands together in front of her. "A great many things." She locked eyes with me. "That Hecate's line still exists. That Jason's line does as well. That even after all this time the blood of the gods is still powerful enough to give you these . . . gifts." She glanced down at my feet where a slick of green algae had spread out all around me.

"Jealousy, then?" Marie asked. "That's what it is?"

The three sisters whipped their heads in Marie's direction. She didn't look away, but instead stared Dr. Kent right in the face.

"That's exactly what it is, huh?" Marie tilted her head like she was thinking very hard about something. "You had a family once? Or maybe you never did, but you wanted one? It's gotta be something like that. And then Hecate has this family that has managed to last for so long, and all you have are these Ninja Turtles over here." She shot Atropos and Lachesis a wicked grin, and even though I was pretty sure any one of them could have killed me right then and there, I had to hold back a smile. "Y'all live in this sewer, and I'm not gonna lie, it smells like ass. I'd be bitter if I was you, too."

Circe put her hand on Marie's shoulder. "I'd really like to not die down here, so please just hush for right now."

Marie shot Dr. Kent one more dagger of a glance before moving back to my side, and I could tell by the mask of absolute rage on Dr. Kent's face that Marie had angered her. She reached into her box again, and instead of watching her pluck out the lives of the people I loved most and talk about them like they were nothing more than threads, I turned away. I couldn't stand it.

"Persephone Colchis, Circe Colchis, Angie Greene, Briseis Greene," Dr. Kent said. "And you, Marie—" The sound of the blades moving together echoed across the space. "Is this what you wanted to see?"

Circe gasped, and in a rush I was suddenly being pushed toward the grotto opening. Marie was at one elbow, Circe on the other, steering me toward the exit. The Fates cackled like hyenas in the dark behind us.

"Wait!" I dug my feet into the ground, but Marie lifted me up and pushed me forward. "Circe! What is happening?"

"This was a mistake," Circe said, her eyes brimming with tears. "We shouldn't have come here."

"Not a mistake, dear Circe," Dr. Kent called after us. "Only the truth. The River Styx is high and wide. Do you think you can survive the swim?" Her laugh reverberated through the cavern.

The elevator doors slid open, and we all but fell in. As they closed again, Circe let go of my arm and slid down against the wall.

"I'm sorry, Briseis," Circe said breathlessly. "I thought she'd have something to tell us, something we could act on, but this was a waste."

"But you saw what happened to our strings?" I asked. "Atropos—I heard the scissors—"

"She's fucking with us," Marie said. She grabbed Circe's arms and pulled her to her feet. "Circe, these old bitches don't get to determine what happens to us. You saw her—Atropos couldn't even cut my string."

"Because you have the power of the Absyrtus Heart running in your veins," Circe said. "Some of us don't have that."

"You think I don't know that?" Marie asked.

"Do you?" Circe said, her tone sharp. "You can't just pop off at the mouth like that. Not when we're dealing with people— gods—like those three. You ever stop to think about the danger you put Briseis in?"

"I'm not trying to put her in danger," Marie snapped. "If anybody put her in danger it's you."

They glared at each other, and I stepped between them. "No. We're not fighting. I'm not doing anything I don't want to do, and I don't care how much danger I'm in if it means getting my mom back. Please. We have other stuff to worry about. We gotta get home and tell everybody what happened." I turned to Circe. "What did you see? What did Dr. Kent show you?"

She crossed her arms and leaned against the elevator wall. "It doesn't matter. I'll figure it out."

I thought it did matter, but whatever she'd seen wasn't changing her mind about what we were trying to do. I wondered if it was something that might have changed my mind had I seen it with my own eyes. The sound of Atropos's scissors clanging in the dark stuck in my head, but no. Nothing would stop me from trying to get my mom back. Fates be damned.

When we pulled into the drive it was almost five in the morning. The sun was just beginning to warm the sky, and I could barely keep my eyes open, but as Marie and Circe climbed the front steps, I hung back.

"Y'all go ahead," I said. "I need a minute." I turned and headed toward the rear yard.

"Briseis," Circe called.

"I'm okay, I just need a minute."

I broke into a jog and didn't stop until I found myself alone at the high point of the rear yard, right before it sloped away into the tree line. My heart raced, and my palms were slick with sweat. I lay down in the overgrown grass, spread my arms and legs out, and stared up at the deep purple sky. The moon still hung there, like it was waiting to be crowded out by the encroaching marigold glow of dawn. Blades of grass arched toward me, and little puddles of white sprang up in the waning moonlight. *Ipomoea alba*, the moonflower. The star-shaped blossoms bloomed all around me. Another beautiful, impossible gift. I touched their velvety petals as their vining stems intertwined and made for me a crown of flowers that bloomed in the dark—like the Heart but without the numbing pain. I felt like I could breathe for the first time in hours.

I lay there until Marie's gentle steps sounded on the ground near my head. She didn't speak. She just stood watch. I realized I must have looked like I'd completely lost it, but she didn't smile or joke about it. She simply extended her hand, helped me up, and walked me to my room, where I curled up next to Mo and fell into a restless sleep.

CHAPTER 9

The next morning, as Mo went to chat with Circe, I got up and showered, washing bits of grass from my hair. I put on a clean pair of jeans and a T-shirt, doused my hair in leave-in conditioner, and pulled it into a slicked-up puff. I didn't have the energy to do much else, and I fully didn't care how busted I looked. Mo was sitting on the edge of my bed when I came out, staring at her phone.

"Circe gave me a rundown of what happened last night." She didn't look up as she spoke. "I don't even understand half of what she was talking about, but she's concerned."

"It was—a lot," I said.

"Your auntie Leti called. I let it go to voice mail, but she'll call back. She's been calling your mama's phone every few hours."

"What are we gonna do?"

"We have to tell her something. Her and Mom are so close. If we keep avoiding her, she might pop up on us. Your granny, too, and I can't deal with her right now."

I pictured my auntie and grandma showing up on the front step. I couldn't blame them if they did, but that's the last thing we needed. We'd have to come up with a convincing lie, but the harder thing to think about was what we'd have to tell them if we couldn't get Mom back. I pushed that awful thought out of my head.

"I'll figure something out," Mo said. When she looked me over, she smiled. "I guess I should probably get myself together, huh?"

I sat next to her and put my head on her shoulder. "A shower helps a little. And I know you like to keep things all natural, but maybe shave your pits? Looks like you got a German shepherd in a headlock."

"Not the look I was goin' for," she said. She was so completely worn down, and it put an ache in my chest.

I wrapped my arms around her, and we sat together in the quiet as the plants sitting on the hearth outgrew their pots and crawled their way over to me. Mo held out her hand and I willed the vining plants to braid a few of their curled tendrils together. They encircled her wrist then gently broke off, leaving her with a bracelet of folded leaves.

A chorus of angry voices carried up from downstairs.

Mo sighed. "They were arguing while you were in the shower. There's something they're not telling us, but I don't know exactly what it is." She twisted her locs up on top of her head and massaged her neck. "And I gotta be honest, love. I keep asking myself if this is all some god-awful nightmare. I've seen so many things, and it's all a little—I don't know—unbelievable?"

"I get it," I said, leaning against her shoulder. "Even with this power—" I pointed to the plants vining their way up my leg. "The stuff I'm finding out is even more unreal."

"Who you telling?" Mo huffed. "Everybody's some kind of immortal? The Heart?" She took a deep halting breath. "It feels like too much."

"I just want Mom back," I said. "Nothing else matters. I don't care what we have to do or what we have to believe."

Mo nodded and kissed the top of my head.

More angry voices cut through the air, and I went to the bedroom door to try to pull it open without making a bunch of noise. The hinges screamed and immediately silenced the heated conversation going on below. I sighed and glanced back at Mo.

"Love," Mo said. "You did see a giant winged creature sitting in the driveway yesterday, right? It wasn't just me?"

"His name's Roscoe," I said.

Mo's eyebrow arched up. "Um, what?"

"Yeah. I'm just gonna go with it."

"Right," Mo said, a vacant expression on her face. "I'm gonna shower. Love you."

"Love you more."

I went out and closed the door behind me. As I went down the stairs and into the front room, Marie and Persephone were sitting across the table from each other. If looks could kill, somebody would've been dead. The look of absolute rage plastered across both their faces made me a little wary of being in the same room as them.

Circe came in behind me. "You're up. How you feeling?"

"I'm okay. Were you guys fighting?" I asked.

"No," Persephone said.

"Yes," Marie shot back.

"I need to talk to Briseis and you two should take it outside or something," Circe said. She wasn't even trying to hide the annoyance in her tone. She turned to me. "Would you come with me for a minute. There's something I'd like to show you."

Marie and Persephone got up and headed to the front door while I trailed Circe to the apothecary. The broken floorboards had been put back in their places. The vines and branches were cut back as much as possible, but an entire black locust tree had come up through the floor and looked like it might be a permanent fixture now. Pendant clusters of dense white blooms hung between the blue-green leaves. The scattered apothecary jars had been set back on the mended shelves, the ladder fixed and put on its track.

"Persephone is exceptionally handy," Circe said. "We can worry about restocking another time. The main thing I wanted to talk to you about was . . ." She trailed off, running her hand over her mouth, and chewing at her bottom lip. "Ever since I got back I feel like all we've been talking about is how heavy the burden of guarding the Heart is—how much has been lost because of it."

"I mean, it's true," I said.

"But taking care of the Heart isn't the only thing my mother passed down to me," Circe said. "She's been gone since I was a teenager but she taught me and Selene so much about these gifts, and well, it's probably easier to just show you." She picked up a large rectangular case with a handle on top and set it on the counter. It was closed by two silver locks and had the Colchis family crest—the image of the triple-faced Hecate, her torches, the crown of poison thorns—carved into its face. "If we make this journey, as I fully expect we will, *we* will need supplies."

I stared into her face. "But you said—"

"I know," she said, lowering her voice. "I know I said you couldn't go—I just—I'm hoping I can convince Mo to let you come with us, because you are the only one who has actually seen Hecate. She spoke directly to you and that has to mean something. It's your mother she's sheltering. I don't know if we can do this without you, but I did mean what I said, it is dangerous." Worry drew her eyebrows together. "I could never forgive myself if something happened to you, and of course I would make sure you were as safe as possible, but look what we're dealing with here. Ancient goddesses, power beyond our full comprehension. There is a risk."

"A risk I can take." I moved closer to her. "What did Dr. Kent show you? I'm just gonna assume that you wouldn't let me come along if you knew I was gonna die, right?"

Circe gripped the handle of the case. "No. Of course not."

A terrible thought occurred to me. Mrs. Redmond and Karter had both been kind to me. I'd trusted Karter and even thought he was my friend. I was wrong about him in ways I couldn't stand to think about. But Karter and Circe were not the same. I could trust Circe to tell me the truth, and still, I wondered if maybe I was already too trusting. The thought grew in my mind like a ragged ugly weed.

"So, what's in the case?"

She lifted the lid. Inside, the two halves were divided into smaller compartments, each containing miniature apothecary jars closed with corks. Some were no bigger than my thumbnail, but even the biggest ones were only an inch or two. There had to be a hundred vials set inside little velvet-lined cubbies.

"My mother taught me that I should never go anywhere unprepared," Circe said.

"What do you mean? Like how my grandma is always telling me to make sure I have on clean drawers when I leave the house in case I get in a car accident?"

Circe laughed. "What is it with old folks? My grandma used to tell me the same thing. First off, who's intentionally leaving the house with dirty drawers? And second, if I get in a car accident, the state of my drawers is probably the least of my worries, right?"

"Exactly," I said, laughing along with her. I pushed my glasses up. "But I'm guessing that's not what you're talking about here."

"Not really," she said. "What she meant was that we have this power over the plants but I can't bring the garden or the apothecary with me when I go places. So my mom taught me to use this." She tapped the side of the briefcase. "She made this for me. It lets me keep everything I need close by. I can find sage and mugwort almost anywhere, but bloodroot? Blue flag? Lobelia? I can't just run to the store for those, and finding them in the wild is almost impossible. Our garden is unique in that it can sustain plants that, normally, would never even grow on the same continent much less the same plot. I keep a little of everything in these containers. I only need the smallest fraction of the plant to grow a new one no matter where I am." She plucked out a narrow jar as big around as a pencil, maybe an inch long. She pulled out the tiny cork and took my hand in hers, turning my palm up. She gently tapped the butt end of the jar and a fleck no bigger than a single flake of pepper fell into my hand.

"Make it grow, Briseis."

I squinted at the flake. "I've never—" I stopped short. In the turret at the top of the house I'd inadvertently made a plant come back from what I assumed was just dust in the bottom of its planter. It had seemed impossible, and I thought the dirt and dust in the container had been hiding a leaf or root I'd over-looked. "This is almost nothing."

"It is everything," Circe said gently. She pushed my fingers closed around the speck of plant matter. "Everything you need is right there in that tiny piece. Try it. I think you can do it."

I focused on the speck, took in a shaky breath.

Circe put her hands on my shoulders. "No need to be ner-vous or scared."

"I'm not. I just—"

"You've just been hiding this gift your whole life except from the people you trust most—your parents. And your friends might have seen bits and pieces, but it scared them a little so you hid it away."

I stared into her face and saw care and concern—but there was also a familiar sadness. She knew exactly what I'd had to deal with even if I hadn't shared all of it with her yet.

"And now you're here and I'm telling you that you don't have to be afraid, but you're not a hundred percent sure you can trust me."

"Do our abilities cover being psychic, too?"

"Not that I'm aware of," she said gently. She touched my

closed hand. "I know what it's like. And you can decide for yourself if you trust me, but right now, all you have to do is make it grow."

I steadied myself and took off my glasses, setting them on the counter. I concentrated on the fragment of plant in my hand and breathed deep. The familiar tingling started in my shoulder, then flowed down to my forearm. As the warmth entered my wrist and settled in my palm, I slowly opened my hand and the speck shifted, doubling in size and sprouting roots like whiskers. A stem pushed its way through my fingers, and small waxy green leaves unfurled alongside fleshy red berries.

"It's yew," I said. "Me and one of the girls in my third grade class ate some of these."

Circe winced. "She lived?"

"Yeah. She was jacked up for a long time, though."

"I bet." She stroked the leaves of the small plant that I held in my hand, fully grown from a single speck. The plant twisted toward her and then back to me. "The seeds are deadly if you ingest enough of them. How many did she eat?"

"Six."

Circe shook her head. "Two or three more and she would have been dead."

My stomach sank thinking about it.

"But if someone had known how," Circe continued, "they could have used the stems, leaves, berries, and seeds of that same plant to raise her from the grave."

I leveled my eyes with Circe's, waiting for her to say she was joking. Instead, she glanced around the room and smiled.

"This work is unique, and there is so much more to it than

the business of guarding the Heart. Running this shop used to be one of the greatest joys of my life. It allowed me to stay connected to my past and still serve my community, to provide them something they couldn't get anywhere else."

"That's what everyone's been saying," I said, setting the yew plant on the counter. "Dr. Grant's father came up here talking about alchemy, a woman in town who's a root worker, even Marie—they all made it seem like there was another sort of community in Rhinebeck."

"This place is like a beacon," Circe said. "People are drawn here because of the plants, because of the poison. Most of them have no idea the Heart even exists. If they do, they don't have any real interest in it. They know they could never wield its power. But yes, there is a community here whose interests are spread across all kinds of belief systems and practices, but they all require the things we provide here. The Colchis family's knowledge of plants and poisons is encyclopedic." She scanned the shelves and pulled down a jar of dried marigold. "Do you know what this is?"

"*Tagetes erecta*," I said. "Four feet tall. Native to Mexico and Central America. They can grow in almost any condition, even drought."

"And do you know what it's for?"

I tried to think. "They're edible. They repel rabbits. And you can co-plant them with tomatoes to keep away pests."

"You've already got so much knowledge." Circe set the jar down and scooped out a handful, letting the dried petals fall through her fingers and back into the jar. "Strung in a garland, straight from the garden, they ward off evil. Scattered under your bed, they'll keep you safe while you're sleeping. Walking over fresh petals with your bare feet will allow you to talk to birds. In November, we grow and stock hundreds of them for those in our community celebrating Día de los Muertos. The garden is a sea of sunset orange around that time. It's magical." She breathed deep. "We respect the practices and traditions of the people in our magical little community. That is where *my* heart lies."

I could see how much this place meant to her and how much of it had nothing at all to do with the Absyrtus Heart. There was something comforting about that. "There is so much I don't know. They don't really teach you about the magical uses of all these plants in botany workshops."

"I'll teach you," Circe said. She clasped her hands together in front of her. "If you'd like me to I can show you how to make tinctures and salves. I can show you how to harvest the plants in a way that maintains their potency, and I can show you how to hybridize them for specific purposes. There's so much." Her sentences started to string together as the tempo of her words picked up. Her excitement was contagious.

I searched her face. She believed every word, and if I was being honest, so did I. I'd just seen a giant griffin named Roscoe perched in the driveway. Walking on marigolds could let me talk to birds? Seemed like something not so impossible after everything I'd seen since I'd come to Rhinebeck. This is what Mo and I were talking about. Whatever was coming would require us to lean all the way into this.

I thought of spending my days in the garden, cultivating the plants, stocking the apothecary, and learning from Circe while

Mom and Mo played aggressive games of Uno in the front room. A stab of pain nearly knocked me over as I pictured Mom's face in my mind's eye. I picked up my glasses and put them back on.

Circe pointed at one of the small jars in her case, and I turned my attention back to it. "To raise the winds, saffron." She let her slender fingers dance over another row of vials. "Celandine to aid in escaping, euphorbia for protection, black hellebore and wolfsbane for temporary invisibility."

I tried to take in everything she was saying. "Is this why people in town think y'all are witches?"

Circe smirked. "I mean, I do siphon the life from children to keep myself young." She puckered her lips and blinked overdramatically.

I didn't smile or laugh.

"Kidding. Just a joke." She looked down at the floor. "Sorry."

I exhaled and shook my head. "I can deal with a lot but probably not that."

"Nothing like that goes on," Circe said. "But I can see why some people might think something terrible was happening up here. People are nosy as hell and if they can't get the info they want, sometimes they'll just make it up."

"Karter told me there were rumors that the women who lived here were into witchcraft." I shoved my hands in my pockets to try and stem the anger, the rage. Suddenly, the window bounced open and a tangle of vines—ivy, Devil's Pet, and stinging nettle—came slithering in. They wound themselves around my leg.

Circe's brow furrowed. "I don't know what people think witchcraft means in this day and age. And honestly, I don't care what anybody has to say about what we do here, one way or the other. Witches?" She looked thoughtful. "I'm okay with that. Especially if it means people keep their distance." She bit down on her lip like she'd said the quiet part out loud. "What do you think?"

"About being a witch? I don't really know. When I think of witches I think of crystals and incense and people always talkin' about lightwork and good vibes."

Circe laughed. "I mean, that's the image you get shown, right?" She took off her glasses and massaged her temple before putting them back on. "People get a little sage, a few crystals, and think they're Marie Laveau." Her eyes wandered to the hidden door where the altar for Hecate was hidden. "What we practice, what we believe, is something that has been passed down through the generations. It's something we have access to because it is quite literally in our blood. Other people can call it whatever they like. I'm a witch, sure, but if you ever hear me talkin' about lightwork please know I have lost my entire mind."

"My grandma knows about plants, herbs, that kind of stuff. My auntie Leti, too."

Circe smiled but it was all mouth and no creases at the corner of her eyes. I ran back over what I'd said and realized it was the auntie part that seemed to have struck her. Of course it did. Circe was my auntie, too, but I didn't know if I was ready to say that yet.

I opened my mouth to speak but she beat me to it.

"You don't owe me anything, Briseis. Not a title, not your time, not a conversation. Nothing. I'll take whatever you're willing to give."

I covered her hand with mine. "I just need a little time to adjust."

She nodded. "And we have a lot of work to do in the meantime, so don't feel like you have to rush."

The vines that had tangled themselves around my leg climbed to my waist.

Circe eyed them carefully. "This kind of thing's been happening to you forever, hasn't it? The plants sort of wake up when you're around?"

I nodded. "I used to try and ignore it but I can't do that anymore."

"It's like telling your body not to breathe. It's just not possible." She stared down at the vines. "And when you're angry or scared or sad, they'll come to you just like this. And they'll do what you ask of them. You must be cautious of that. Don't underestimate what you're capable of with them as your allies." She turned back to her case and began taking an inventory of what she had, jotting down notes on a piece of paper.

Marie's voice, and then Persephone's, carried in from somewhere outside and cut through my thoughts. The window was cracked, and I figured they must have circled around the back of the house. As I approached the window their muffled voices became clearer.

"I'm not telling you what to do," Persephone said, her voice tight, angry.

"I'd never do anything to hurt her," Marie said.

"I know. I can see you're attached. But don't you get it? That's what is going to hurt her the most."

"I can't just turn off how I feel," Marie shot back. "I know you're weary, Seph. I can see it in your face. But don't act like I'm supposed to be okay with this. It's killing me."

I leaned closer to the open window.

"Didn't you guess?" Persephone asked. "If the pieces have to be reunited—" She sighed. "You have to tell her," Persephone said sternly. "And sooner is better than later."

"You know what she's been through?" Marie asked. "Her mom died right in front of her."

My stomach twisted into a knot at the bluntness of her words. I gripped the sill to steady myself.

It must have been Persephone who sighed so heavily it carried up to where I was. "And how do you think she's going to feel when the same thing happens to you?"

"You don't know that," Marie said angrily. "What happened to you? You used to be—"

"I know what I used to be!" Persephone shouted. "I don't need a lecture from you."

I glanced at Circe, who simply shook her head and busied herself with the miniature apothecary bottles.

"I'm not going to make a guess about what's going to happen," Marie said. "And I don't give a shit about what some dusty old hag in the bowels of a museum has to say either."

"Keep on with that attitude, Marie, but let's be clear," Persephone said. "You don't have to guess at what's going to happen. We're all going to die."

CHAPTER 10

My heart dropped into the pit of my stomach. I disentangled myself from the Devil's Pet that had encircled my ankles and went to the apothecary door. "I'll be right back."

"You good?" Circe asked, peering at me over the top of her glasses.

I nodded and went to the hallway, pulled on my sneakers, and rushed out the front door. I ran directly into Marie. She didn't budge, but I bounced off her and almost crashed back through the doorway. She caught me by the wrist and pulled me back up to standing.

For a minute I forgot what I was angry about. All I cared about were her big brown eyes and her toothy smile. She ran her fingertips up the side of my neck.

I shook myself out of my own thoughts. "We need to talk."

"Yeah," Marie said. "I think we do."

I took her hand and pulled her down the front steps as Persephone brushed past us. She threw a pointed glance at Marie before disappearing inside.

I led Marie around the side of the house where the over-grown trellis groaned under the weight of thousands of tendrils of ivy. They reached out for me, and I let them curl around my arms and legs. Marie leaned in to kiss me, but I gently pressed my hands into her chest.

"I heard you talking to Persephone."

Marie's face twisted into a mask of shock. "When?"

"Just now. I was in the apothecary, and y'all were outside. She made it seem like something bad was gonna happen to us. What are you not telling me?"

Marie stepped closer. I had to focus on the center of her forehead as she spoke. Looking into her eyes or at the curve of her lips was gonna make me forget that I was extremely concerned about the secrets she was keeping from me.

"Listen," she said softly. "Do you remember how I told you Circe and Selene kept to themselves? How secretive they were even when they knew Astraea had used a piece of the Heart to heal me?"

I nodded.

"It's different now. Since Circe and Persephone have been back, they've been more open with me about certain things. They both seem like they're coming to some kind of reckoning. The pottery shard was sitting in my collection for twenty years before I had time to try and return it. If Circe hadn't been so closed off we might have found the last piece of the Heart sooner, but I guess she had her reasons. The point is, she knows that it was a mistake to close herself off and she doesn't want it to happen again."

"What does that have to do with you and me?" I asked. "I

mean, I'm glad y'all are talking, but neither of you are talking to *me* about what y'all saw in the Grotto, what Dr. Kent and her sisters did to the strings. Persephone said you needed to tell me something, so what is it? And don't tell me it's nothing. I'm not stupid."

Marie looked stunned. "I would never ever think that about you."

"Okay, then be honest with me. Tell me what you and Persephone are so concerned about." A knot grew in my throat. We had a lot of secrets between the two of us, but this couldn't be one of them. Not when it might be about her safety.

"You heard the whole conversation?" Marie asked.

"Part of it." I met her gaze, exactly the way I shouldn't have. Heat rushed to my face.

Marie stepped close and gently pressed her forehead to mine. "I'm going to do everything in my power to help you get your mom back. I don't care what it costs."

"What it costs? I don't like the way that sounds. Please just tell me what it is."

"I don't want to," she said. She interlaced her fingers with mine. "I don't want you to worry."

"It's way too late for that."

She sighed, and her sweet breath in my face sent a warm rush through me. "Persephone is worried about things that no one has any control over," she said. "You think I'm dramatic? I don't have anything on her. The truth is no one has ever reunited all the pieces of the Heart. At least that's what Circe is telling me now. So, we don't know what will happen or how. Persephone is a pessimist. She wants me to run down every single thing that could possibly go wrong and I refuse to do it. She is overly paranoid."

"She said we were going to die."

Marie rolled her eyes. "Please. You really think I'd let any of this happen if we were all fated to die? Please give me a little more credit than that."

I smiled at her and she let her gaze drift to my mouth.

"You think we actually have a chance?" I asked.

"I do," she said. "I really do. But no matter what, I'd walk through whatever fire lies ahead for a chance to make you happy."

She slipped her hands around my waist and pressed her lips against mine. The world around us melted away. Her body radiated warmth and I leaned toward her like a wilted plant to sunlight. I came alive under her touch. She smelled like roses and her lips tasted like cinnamon. I let my fingers trace along the bare skin of her neck as I breathed her in. The tangle of vines behind me shifted. Marie had her hands under my shirt, her fingers trailing over the small of my back. For all her strength, she was gentle with me—her lips soft, her touch softer.

I thought I'd been kissed before, but I realized in that moment that I never had. Not really. I pulled her closer, grabbing a handful of her shirt, feeling her frame soften against mine.

She leaned away from me, and I took the opportunity to catch my breath. My head swam; my senses were on ten. Beside me, sprigs of wisteria had intermingled with the common ivy and sprouted hundreds of pale lavender blooms along the entire length of the latticework.

Marie straightened her shirt and pushed her long braid

behind her shoulder. She reached out and readjusted my glasses, which were sitting sideways on my face.

"C'mon," she said, laughing softly. "I think we're gonna go into town."

"For what?" I asked. "I don't wanna go anywhere." I pulled her close again and she nuzzled my neck, sending a rush of warmth all through me.

She pulled back and smiled. "Guess who Circe wants to pay a visit to?"

I shrugged.

"Lou."

"For real?" My last visit to Lou's had been with Karter, and Lou had made it clear that he would probably try to fight Marie if he ever saw her again. "That dude hates you."

A wicked grin spread across her face. "I know. This is gonna be way too much fun."

"Just don't hurt him, okay? He's a creep, I get it. But if Mo's going with us, I don't think she'll be able to handle you folding Lou up like a pretzel."

"That's Nyx's thing," she said. She put her hand on her heart. "I promise I won't do anything he can't walk away from. Did you know that if you cut off someone's toe, it can be reattached as long as you keep the severed piece on ice? I mean, that's probably true for fingers, too, right?"

I blinked twice and pressed my lips together. "See? Maybe you should stay here."

"Zero chance of that happening," she said. "I'm going, and I'm gonna apologize to you in advance because I'm about to be real petty."

I sighed. "Please just answer this one question—did you seduce his grandpa?"

Marie's eyebrows arched up and she puckered her lips.

"Oh man," I said. "You did, didn't you?"

"In my defense," she said. "I'm technically seventeen and so was his grandpa at the time. He wasn't anybody's pawpaw back then. We kissed maybe two or three times."

I couldn't keep my face from twisting up.

She laughed. "That was all we did, but to hear him tell it, I was obsessed. He spread all kinds of rumors about me to try and distract everybody from the fact that he was married, which was a thing back in the day. People got married really young some-times." She shrugged. "I didn't know. I left him alone when I found out, but he tried to make my life miserable."

I grimaced. "He clearly didn't know who he was dealing with."

"He sure the hell didn't. I made a point to pop back up when he got older just to mess with him. I hadn't changed at all, and he was probably seventy the last time I saw him. He thought he was seeing a ghost and passed smooth out."

I sighed. "This should be fun."

She rubbed her hands together. "Yup."

I ran inside to check on Mo, who had showered and changed her clothes. She sat on the end of my bed looking mostly refreshed, but nothing was washing away the dead tired look from her eyes.

"We're going into town," I said. "Wanna tag along?"

"Where are y'all goin'?"

"Lou's. It's a funeral parlor."

"Why do you—you know what? I don't need to know. You taking some of the Avengers with you?"

"Just Marie and Circe," I said.

"Y'all go ahead. I'm gonna stay here. Persephone said she has a few more things to patch up in the apothecary. She don't really need my help. She asked if I knew how to run a circular saw."

The look of horror on my face must've been clear because Mo quickly put her hands up in front of her.

"Love, you don't even have to worry. Persephone saw how confused the question made me. Now she got me handing her pieces of wood that she already cut. I think I can handle that."

"Okay, good," I said. "Because I don't think anything I have in the garden or the apothecary can grow your hand back if you cut it off."

"Which is exactly why I'm on assistant duty."

I gave her a hug and went back down to join Marie and Circe in the entryway. Marie jingled the keys in front of Circe.

"I'm driving."

Circe tipped her head back and stared up at the ceiling. "Fine. Let's just go."

I slid into the front seat of the blacked-out sedan that Nyx usually drove us around in. Circe climbed into the back and slipped on her seat belt, yanking it back and forth. When she seemed satisfied it would hold, she made eye contact with Marie in the rearview mirror.

"Me and Briseis aren't immortal so please stick to the speed limit."

I glanced at Marie, and her devilish grin made me smile, but I also touched the buckle of my seat belt.

Marie drove us across town. She stayed five miles under the limit the entire time but somewhere in Rhinebeck was a jogger recovering from a near-death experience due to her insistence on hugging the curb. When we parked in front of Lou's Funeral Parlor, Circe unfastened her seat belt and leaned through the partition, yanking the keys out of the ignition and stuffing them in her pocket.

She sat back and let out a long exasperated breath. "I'll drive us home."

Marie shrugged. "Probably a good idea."

The funeral home stood quietly, set back from the road, its wide green lawn neatly trimmed.

"Why are we here again?" I asked.

Circe narrowed her eyes at the sleepy Victorian. "Lou's family has been in Rhinebeck almost as long as ours. We have a long-standing agreement, but I have a sneaking suspicion he hasn't been holding up his end of the bargain the way he should."

Marie sucked her teeth and gripped the steering wheel. "I take back what I said about not hurting him."

"Wait," I said. "What isn't he doing? The deaths have been covered up pretty good. Everybody thinks you're dead. They think Selene died of an illness. He made it seem like everything was going the way he wanted it to."

"That's true, but I have other questions." Circe crossed her arms over her chest and cocked her head to the side "How are so many of us being tracked here? How is Jason's line able to pinpoint our exact location here even after we've been so careful? Our families are linked. Medea had children with Jason, so we technically descend from him, too, but this other branch of our twisted family tree developed completely separate from us. What are the odds that they would know we're here, in this place, at this time?"

I felt like the air had been sucked out of my chest. I hadn't thought of it like that. In some twisted way me and Karter were like distant cousins a thousand times removed. It made his betrayal sting even more.

"Lou knows that we're here to protect something important and I used to trust him because that's the way it has always been," Circe said. "But things have changed. We're not doing things the same old way anymore, not when it's putting what's left of our family in danger."

"Let's go in and talk to him," Marie said. She rolled up the sleeves of her shirt and cuffed them at her elbow.

I gently touched her arm, and she only grinned wider.

"I can't ask him anything if he's dead, so keep yourself in check," Circe said. "Please."

Marie didn't respond, which I took to mean she wasn't making any promises about what she would or wouldn't do.

I followed Circe up to the front door, and we let ourselves in. The front room was again prepared for a wake, but there was no coffin perched on the platform this time. A strong vinegar smell hit the back of my throat as I breathed in. I quickly cupped my hand over my nose and mouth.

"It smells like pickle juice and hot dog water in here." I bit the side of my tongue to keep from gagging.

Marie's face twisted up. "It's formaldehyde."

Circe waved the air in front of her like that was gonna help. "Hello?" she called. "Lou?"

A door opened and closed somewhere. Footsteps echoed down the hall, and Lou appeared, in all his Lurch-like glory. A heavy plastic apron covered the front of his body, and he had a pair of blue rubber gloves pulled up to his elbows. Streaks of dark liquid were smeared across them, and as he approached us the pickle-like odor grew stronger, making my eyes water. He smiled at me as warmly as a man who looked like he'd just committed a serious crime could.

"Miss Briseis," he said stiffly. His gaze flitted to Circe and he stopped dead in his tracks. He clasped his long, sticklike fingers together in front of him. He grinned maniacally, and I had to look away because there was no reason he should've been that terrifying when he was smiling.

"Back from the dead," he said. "You know, I much prefer to deal with people who stay in their graves."

"You make it sound like I'm some sort of zombie," Circe said. "I was never actually in the ground, Lou."

"No, I suppose you weren't." He sounded deeply disappointed. He glanced at the front door. "Will you be letting the wide world of Rhinebeck know you're back, or will you remain a ghost?"

I held my breath as I waited for him to register Marie. As his gaze fixed on her, the sallow pallor of his skin actually flushed pink. The horrible expression of happiness faded away, revealing an even more disturbing mask of terror and anger mixed together.

He clenched his jaw. "You."

Marie crossed her arms over her chest and tipped her chin up. "What's good, Lucifer? Still love that your parents named you after Satan. They must've seen something special in you

132

from the beginning, huh? What was it? That little glazed look in your eye? Your penchant for dead things? Do tell."

Lou balled his gloved fists and stepped toward her. Anger rolled off him in waves. "Get out."

Marie touched her chin with one finger, her fire-engine-red nail poking into her bottom lip like she was thinking very hard. Then she shook her head and shrugged. "I think I'll stay."

The vein in Lou's forehead looked like the vine of some deadly plant had worked its way under his skin.

"Hang on," Circe said. "She's with me."

"I don't give a damn who she's with," Lou said angrily. Frothy white spittle gathered at the corners of his mouth.

The thought of him rushing Marie was ridiculous. She'd hem him up, no problem, which is probably why he hadn't attacked her already. He might've been mad, but he wasn't stupid.

I stepped back and stood next to Marie.

She leaned into me, her mouth against my ear. "This dude is somethin' else. It's all that embalming fluid he's huffing in his basement. It's rotting his brain."

"Lou, whatever Marie did, I'm sure it was petty and awful," Circe said, shooting Marie a sideways glance. "But we can all agree it was probably a very long time ago and maybe we should try to put it behind us."

"I'll never let it go," Lou said matter-of-factly. "Ever."

Marie rolled her eyes. "Oh come on. Your granddaddy's been dead for—"

"You don't speak about him!" Lou screamed, his voice cracking under the strain.

"Gods, Lou," Circe said. "Take a breath before you give yourself a heart attack."

He did as she said. But just barely.

"I'm back and I was hoping we could catch up," Circe said. Something lingered in her tone—a faint edge of anger but she was keeping it under control. "I'm very interested in what you've been up to lately. You remember the covenant between our families?"

"Of course," he snapped. He collected himself and turned to her. "Is that why you came back? To remind me of my oath?"

"Partly," Circe said.

Lou's eyebrow arched up. "Are you questioning my loyalty?"

Circe narrowed her eyes at him. "Yes."

Lou had been rude to Karter. He'd been short with me. And he clearly hated Marie, but it occurred to me that he was this way with Circe, too. There was an undercurrent of anger that ran through all his interactions with us that I hadn't really noticed before. He was weird and most of it had to be because he spent way too much time with a bunch of corpses, but there was something else there, too.

"I'm not surprised that your first order of business is to show up here to try and intimidate me," he said. "Your family has always resorted to such tactics."

I tried to gauge Circe's expression but her face remained unchanged.

"Not true," she said calmly. "It wasn't until your grandfather died and your father took over that things changed between us."

I glanced at Marie. Her right eyebrow was arched halfway up her forehead in confusion.

"I have no idea what you're talking about, you ridiculous woman."

Marie shifted her weight from one foot to the other and let her hands fall to her sides. Something stirred in the pit of my stomach—a warning. The ancient willow trees outside groaned loudly as they leaned in and dragged their long branches across the windowpanes.

"Did you pass information to the Redmond woman directly?" Circe asked. "Or did it go through someone else?"

Something shattered in the front room, and my heart leaped into my throat. The tendrils of a heart leaf philodendron crept through the doorway and sprouted hundreds of new offshoots, the shards of its broken planter still stuck between its roots. The arms of the plant branched out so fast Lou had only been able to take a single step before they caught him around his wrists and ankles.

"Oh, Briseis, that's very impressive," Circe said, beaming.

I hadn't even realized I was doing it. I hadn't just watched it happen—I'd willed it to, much the same way I had with Mrs. Redmond. I leaned into it. Lou struggled against the vines. He tore pieces of them away, but they grew back tenfold. I imagined them gripping him tighter and they responded by doing exactly that.

Circe approached Lou cautiously, then stole a glance at me.

"Can you keep hold of him?" she asked. "No matter what?" Something flashed in her eyes, like rage and fear all mixed together.

I took stock of myself. The plants obeyed me, but Circe's warnings echoed in my head. The problem used to be—could I control it? Would it slip away from me and mess something up? Now, it was the same question but with a different sort of answer. I could control it, clearly, but what would I do with it? What was I capable of?

"Briseis?" Circe repeated.

I nodded. "Yes. I can hold him."

"Stupid girl," Lou seethed.

An offshoot no bigger around than a pencil wriggled around his neck. I pictured it slithering up his left nostril, and as it started to do just that he thrashed wildly, twisting his neck around to avoid the tendrils.

Lou let out a strangled, angry roar. "Get away from me! Let me go!"

Circe lifted her chin. "No. We're going to have a little chat, and you're going to be honest with me or I am going to have Marie tear your arms out of their sockets. We clear?"

My heart galloped into a furious rhythm. Her tone was dark, serious. Circe was threatening Lou's life, and everything in me felt like she meant every word.

Marie moved to the front door, turned the dead bolt, and pulled the shade. Fear dialed my senses all the way up. Lou's breaths came in quick, frantic gasps. The branches and vines that held him creaked and popped as they gripped him tighter. Marie's wrist-full of bracelets made a soft tinkling sound as she reached up to push her braid behind her shoulder. She brushed past me and stole a glance with eyes like blackened voids.

"When did you tell this Redmond woman about Briseis?" Circe asked.

My heart thudded in my chest as Lou's gaze darted from Circe to Marie and then to me. He was terrified. "I don't know what you're—"

Before he could finish the sentence, Marie lunged forward. She grabbed him by the neck and lifted him straight up into the air. She swung him into the wall and held him there, his feet dangling off the ground.

He coughed and sputtered as the pale skin around his lips turned bluish-gray. Circe gently put her hand on Marie's shoulder. Marie loosened her grip and allowed Lou's feet to meet the ground again, but just barely, and she didn't move her hand away from his neck.

Circe leaned closer to him. "You are going to tell me everything I want to know. How did you come in contact with Redmond? Did you find her or did she find you?"

"She came to me," Lou spat. "She wanted more information about your family."

"And you gave it to her?"

Marie squeezed his neck a little tighter and he gasped. His eyes bulged.

"Not—not at first," he stammered. "I followed the covenant. I kept my word."

"Until you didn't," Circe said. "What made you do it? You've always been angry. I've always suspected you simply didn't like knowing that you aren't really in charge here, but I did expect you to fall in line. After all this time, after everything our families have seen and weathered together—"

Lou's thin dry lips peeled back over his teeth as he tried to scream in Circe's face. "Not together! We've been cleaning up your messes, sheltering you from the world, and for what? What do we have to show for it?"

Circe balled her hands at her sides and blinked repeatedly. "You've been paid. Handsomely. You've been compensated in every possible way."

Lou stuck his neck out, pressed against Marie's unrelenting grip. "Money? Material possessions? You think that's enough?"

"People have been killing us to get their hands on what we have," Circe said. "Hunting us like animals across every continent for hundreds of generations. Isn't helping to save people's lives enough of an incentive? We damn sure have saved more members of the Holt family than I can count. That's how our covenant first came into existence."

Lou stared at Circe like he couldn't comprehend what she was saying. "You think I don't know that? I do. And I don't care. Your money isn't enough. You and your family hoard everything! All the while reaping the benefits." He glared at Marie. "I would have taken another form of payment, though."

"And what form of payment would that be?" Circe asked in a way that sounded like she already knew what he would say.

"Redmond offered me more than you ever did," he said. "She offered me a chance to *be* more."

My mind was going in circles trying to comprehend the level of deception Lou was admitting to. I took a step closer to him as his words repeated in my head. *Be more.*

"She offered to use a piece of the Heart on you, didn't she?" I asked.

Lou lifted his head and stared at me with so much contempt,

so much hatred, that I had to step away from him. I didn't know why I hadn't seen it clearly before—he hated me. He hated everything associated with the Colchis family and had clearly decided that his days of being a living record for us were over.

Circe shook her head in disbelief.

"She said when she became a god she could grant me anything I could think of, anything I wanted," Lou said. "Any sort of power I could conceive of could be mine."

"She thought she would become a god?" Circe asked, turning to me.

I thought of Marie and Persephone, of what they'd become. What kind of terror would they have caused if they'd thought of themselves as gods?

Lou sneered. "I would have been a fool to turn it down."

"You're still a fool," Marie said. Her voice deep and rough, her words sharp.

"When did you tell her about Briseis?" Circe asked.

Lou tried to wriggle out of Marie's grip, and she pressed him into the wall so hard one of the wood panels splintered under his shoulder.

"A year ago," he said quickly. "When I was sure you weren't coming back. The county was preparing to declare you dead, and I thought—"

"You thought you weren't going to have to answer for your actions," Marie growled. "Coward."

"Shut up!" he screamed. "You don't know what you're talking about. She'd come around before, asking questions, and I kept up my end of our bargain."

"Until you gave into greed or cowardice," Circe said angrily.

"And did you—" She paused as she seemed to come to some kind of conclusion in her own head. "You brought her here the first time, too? You told her about Selene and me?"

He'd been in collusion with Mrs. Redmond all this time? Since Selene's murder?

"Mrs. Redmond killed Selene and my mom," I said. The branches of the philodendron tripled their length and wound themselves around him again. "We wouldn't be up here if it wasn't for her, and she wouldn't have found me if you hadn't helped her. They're dead because of her . . . because of you." The branches wrapped around his neck, taking over for Marie, who let go and stepped to my side. The dark green lobed leaves fanned out around his mouth and tucked themselves inside, muffling his terrified screams.

Circe walked up to Lou and pulled a handful of leaves from his mouth. She flexed her fingers, and the remaining tendrils curled away from his face.

"What else do you know about Redmond and her son?" she asked. "Where did they come from? Where were they planning to go after all this?"

Lou clawed at the branches encircling his neck. "I don't know where they came from but—I—I heard—"

"What did you hear?" I asked. The ropes of philodendron roots upended him, dangling him by his ankles. He squirmed like a fish on a hook.

"They were going to a lighthouse! A lighthouse!"

"Not helpful," Marie said.

Even as he was hanging by his ankles he managed to give Marie the dirtiest look. "The Great Eye."

Circe let her gaze drop to the ground and then turned around to look at me. "We need to go. Now."

She ushered me toward the door.

"Wait. What about him?" I willed the branches to let go, and Lou dropped to the floor like a sack of bricks. He groaned and rolled over on his back. I hoped he broke something.

"I got it," Marie said. She was gathering him up before I could blink. She pulled him down the steps that led to his basement workspace and returned a few seconds later . . . alone.

"Did you kill him?" Circe asked.

"No," she said. "I put him in the freezer where he keeps the bodies. I slipped his phone into his pocket. When he figures out he has it on him he can call somebody to let him out."

"Is he gonna be able to get a signal down there?" Circe asked.

Marie shrugged. "I don't know and I don't care."

There was a long silence. I thought of Lou feeding information to Mrs. Redmond. How that had led her to hunt the Colchis women down and murder Selene and my mom. If he died in that basement, I wouldn't be upset.

We piled into Marie's car, and this time Circe slid into the front seat next to me. I scooted closer to Marie.

"Were you able to get anything booked?" Circe asked Marie. "Flights? Hotel? Anything?"

"It's going to be two weeks at the earliest," Marie said.

"Two weeks?" Circe asked. She pressed the back of her head into the seat. "We don't have that kind of time."

"We're flying to Turkey," Marie said. "That means we need passports, which you can't get because technically you, me, and Persephone aren't even supposed to be alive."

"Okay?" Circe asked.

"That means I gotta find a document specialist who can arrange everything," Marie said, slight edge of annoyance in her voice. "Then we have to charter flights from people who don't care what we're up to. It's not gonna be easy and it will take time. I'm sorry. This kind of thing would normally take six months to plan, and we have to do it in a few weeks."

"You've done this kind of thing before?" I asked.

"Sort of," Marie said. "I usually use somebody like Phillip to do the traveling when I'm returning looted pieces. I have the resources to travel by myself if I need to but I've never had to arrange it for more than one or two people."

"What do we do when we actually get there?" I asked. I didn't want to think of all the ways this could go wrong before we even got started, but I couldn't help it. "Once we're there we still have to find the island. Are we positive that's where the last piece is?"

Circe hesitated. There was still doubt.

"I'm going," I said.

"We just had this conversation," Circe said.

"I know. But I'm going. You're right about Mo. She can't go, but I have to, and we can try to convince her but even if she says no, I'm going."

Circe ran her fingers over her forehead. "You understand how dangerous this will be?" She glanced out the window. "And it just got potentially more perilous. You heard what Lou said about the Great Eye?"

I nodded.

"It's a lighthouse from the myths," said Circe. "One of the

older stories that isn't as well-known as some of the others." She rubbed her temples and leaned forward in her seat. "When Zeus freed the Cyclopes from their imprisonment in the Underworld, they gifted him the lightning bolt to use in his war against the Titans. They also forged Poseidon's trident and Hades's helmet. Zeus had his weapon but he needed more than that to overthrow the Titans, and so he forged an all-seeing eye and placed it at the top of a tower—a lighthouse. It allowed him to see across land and sea, even time."

I didn't know for sure what that meant, but I was not about to question it. "And we know where it is?"

"No," Circe said flatly. "But it sounds like this Redmond woman and her son did. They were chasing the pieces of the Heart, and if her son still has that information, if he has help—like those people who were trying to get the pottery shard—they might already be making their way there. They could use it to find the location of Aeaea."

"Can they?" I asked. "Can they use the Great Eye to find it?" A new fear gripped me. They get there before us. Even if they didn't reach the last piece of the Heart they could make it impossible for me to reunite the pieces in time and get my mom back. I felt sick.

"I don't know," said Circe. "If they'd figured out where to look, then maybe. But we're talking about something lost to time. I don't even know where to start." Circe turned to me and looked me straight in the eyes. "How will we convince Mo to stay behind?"

"I'll tell her the truth, but I have to make her stay," I said. "It sounds like we've got a few days to plan. Give me a couple days to think about it. But we agree, I'm going, no matter what, right?"

Circe sighed and rested her head against the window. "I've seen you do some things that I didn't learn to do until I was much, much older. I know you're capable and Hecate showed herself to you when she hasn't done that for any of us in more generations than I can count. That has to mean something. Just make sure you're ready to go when it's time, because as soon as we have what we need, we need to roll out."

She was hesitant. I could see it all over her face, but she was setting that aside for reasons that weren't entirely clear. I didn't really care. I was going to go with her to find the last piece of the Heart, and I was going to bring my mom back from the dead.

CHAPTER 11

The next day as we sat in the front room Circe convinced Mo that she and I both would stay behind while the others went ahead to find the last piece of the Absyrtus Heart. Mo wasn't happy about it, but she kept repeating that everything would be fine. I didn't think she actually believed that, but it's how she dealt with the crushing improbability of this entire scheme actually being successful. So many impossible tasks had to be completed within a short period of time, and the final task, actually reuniting the pieces of the Heart, was something none of us had a real handle on.

Circe and Persephone pulled together every piece of information they had about the Great Eye and where it might be located. I helped them read through texts and books and obscure websites, and after three more days, we still had nothing.

As Marie made arrangements for fake passports and chartered flights we turned our attention to what would happen if we were able to actually reach Aeaea.

"How do we combine the six pieces of the Heart?" I asked.

Mo shot me a sideways glance.

"How are *y'all* going to put all the pieces back together?" I made sure to act like I was upset but resigned to the fact that I wouldn't be going.

Persephone's face was tight. She didn't like lying to Mo. The two of them had become friendly. But she stayed quiet.

"The first and most important step is finding the last piece," Circe said. "If we can't do that, nothing else even matters."

My phone buzzed in my pocket. The screen was still cracked, held together by packing tape, but through the fractured glass I could make out the name I'd saved for the number that was calling me.

Karter.

I stood up and walked out of the room. Mo called after me, but I ran to my bathroom and shut the door. I answered the call and held the phone to my ear.

"Bri?" Karter's voice called through the static.

I couldn't speak or move. I couldn't believe I was hearing his voice.

"Bri. Listen to me, please. You don't ever have to forgive me, I just—I'm sorry. I'm so sorry. I can't—I don't know what to say."

I wanted to scream at him. To curse him out, but none of the curse words in my vocabulary felt adequate.

"What do you want?" It was all I could manage.

Karter breathed into the phone. "I want to help you, but I don't know—"

"Help me?" My face flushed hot with rage. "You can't help me! You were supposed to be my friend!" That was why it hurt so bad. After having to pull away from my friends back in Brooklyn all because they couldn't accept me exactly as I was, his friendship had felt like a lifeline. It pulled me back from feeling like I'd never have another friend and then he'd let it all go—left me to drown in my grief.

"You don't understand. I can't explain. We—we're going to get the last piece of the Heart and you have to just stay away. It's the only choice."

"The Heart doesn't belong to you!"

"It doesn't even matter now. Just—just don't go after it. Hide. Please. Just go somewhere far away and wait. My family hates you. They'll come after you when they get the last piece. Please, Bri."

"I don't care about you or your family," I said. "We're going to get to it before you, and when we do you better hope I never see you again." I couldn't hold it in anymore. All I wanted was to see him held responsible for his part in all of this. The plants from my room pushed their way under the door, through the keyhole, and knitted a curtain of leaves around me.

There was a click and the phone went silent. I stared at the screen as it went dark.

A text came through from Karter. Just one word.

Abana.

The doorbell rang, and I sat in silence as someone went to answer it. I moved toward the bathroom door, and the foliage pulled it open for me. As I passed through the curtain of leafy green buds, a delicate string of *Erinus alpinus*, fairy foxglove, wound its way around my ear and bloomed into a tuft of pink, pillowy soft petals near my temple. I took a deep breath and let the anger wash away from me. That anger could be useful, I'd proven that with Lou, but it wasn't the right time.

Downstairs, Dr. Grant was in the front room. She was wearing jeans and a T-shirt, the most casual I'd seen her look since I met her. She held her car keys in one hand and a paper coffee cup in the other.

"Morning," she said.

"Morning," I said. "Everything okay?"

Circe swept into the entryway and stood so that Dr. Grant couldn't take another step inside without bumping into her. I braced myself for them to start bickering, but Circe spoke gently to her.

"Thanks for coming."

"Of course," Dr. Grant said.

Marie grinned at me from the front room and mouthed the word "awkward" to me.

Nyx and Persephone disappeared down the hall, leaving me, Mo, and Marie to witness the extremely uncomfortable situation that was Dr. Grant clearly trying to kiss and make up with Circe.

"You look beautiful, as always," Dr. Grant said.

I winced. I waited for Circe to hurl some insult or tell Dr. Grant to kick rocks, but to my surprise, the corner of her mouth lifted in a little half smile.

Dr. Grant tilted her head to the side and stared at Circe like she was the only person in the room. "I'm glad you called, because I got some information about that Karter kid. Thought it might be of interest to you."

I gripped my phone.

"What is it?" Mo asked. "Did you find him?"

Dr. Grant followed Circe into the front room and pulled out her phone.

"It looks like he was treated at a hospital in Red Hook. They wanted to keep him, but he left against doctor's orders. The address and phone number he left with them were fake. Then he pops up again on some security footage we pulled from an incident outside Red Hook."

Circe straightened up. "Incident?"

Dr. Grant nodded. "There's an airstrip out there. Doesn't get much use, but kids use it for racing. Illegally. The owner was sick of it, so he put in some cameras a few months back." She angled her phone toward Circe, and I peered over her shoulder as Dr. Grant hit play on a grainy video. "The morning after Karter left the hospital somebody landed a private plane on the strip. The security camera captured this."

Karter limped into the frame. He held his face like he was in pain, flash of white on his wrist, a hospital bracelet. He shuffled to the plane and climbed a set of steps, disappearing into the cabin.

"Whose plane is it?" Circe asked. "There's gotta be a record of it."

Dr. Grant nodded. "The flight originated in Turkey, but I'm having trouble tracking down a passenger manifest."

Circe tipped her head back and stared up at the ceiling. I tapped the screen on Dr. Grant's phone and the video played again. I watched Karter hobble to the plane over and over again.

"Karter called me," I said. They needed to know what he'd told me.

"What? When?" Mo eyed my phone.

"Just now. When I was upstairs. He said he was sorry. He said we should hide because him and his raggedy-ass family are going after the last piece of the Heart and once they get it, they'll come after us."

Circe gripped the table's edge and Marie settled into an unnaturally still posture.

"Can I have your phone?" Dr. Grant asked. "I might be able to get the department to pinpoint his last location."

"I think I already know where that is." I opened the text he sent me and showed her. "It says Abana."

"Where's that?" Marie asked.

Circe scrambled to the map and searched the area near the place where the four finger-like protrusions of land jutted out into the sea.

"Here," she said. "It's a town on the south shore of the Black Sea. It's very close to where I was thinking we should look for the Great Eye. If they're headed there, then we must be on the right track."

Anger bloomed inside me. I wanted so badly to believe there had been some part of our friendship that was real. The way we'd laughed together and shared things that neither of us had before. Tears welled in my eyes and my throat burned as I tried to swallow the white-hot anger. I hated myself for being so open with him. Look where it got me. Images of him in the apothecary helping his mother terrorize me and my parents played in my head. He really didn't care what he'd done. He used me to get his mom the information she needed, then bounced, and I was supposed to be grateful that he'd given me this clue? I shoved my phone back in my pocket and gripped my hands together in front of me.

The doorbell rang.

Circe went to answer it, and I recognized a familiar voice. Dr. Grant's father, Isaac, came in, with Lucille from the candle shop in town trailing behind him.

"Hey, Miss Briseis," he said. I tried to fix my face but I couldn't wipe the scowl off quick enough. "Uh-oh. Bad timing?"

I shook my head. "No. It's fine."

Isaac smiled warmly at me even as concern flashed in his eyes. "We came to say hello to everyone." Circe patted him on the back before embracing Lucille.

"Persephone's here, too," Circe said.

Lucille chuckled. "Are you having a family reunion?"

"Something like that." Circe winked at me.

Lucille swept over to me and took my hands in hers. She traced the lines on my palm, the same way she had when we first met. She stared into my eyes. "Oh, baby, what happened?"

I shook my head. "I don't even know where to start."

She ushered me into the front room as Persephone and Nyx rejoined us. Nyx grabbed a few chairs and we all sat down. Mo and Marie sat on either side of me, while Dr. Grant and Circe seemed to have reached some kind of shaky truce. They sat side by side on two folding chairs, their knees brushing against each other. Isaac stood in the doorway, and Nyx and Persephone stood shoulder to shoulder by the fireplace. Lucille paced in front of the table as Circe spoke.

"I'm glad we're all here together." She quickly glanced at Dr. Grant. "I have a confession to make."

I held my breath. I didn't know if I could take another revelation.

Circe massaged her temple and sighed. "I think I've done a disservice to you and, if we're being honest, to myself by not being a little more open about what has been going on here over the years. I've always been a pretty private person. I thought it was what was best. Now, I know that was the wrong thing to do." She kept her gaze on the floor. "I can't go back but I can start to try and do better."

"Nobody blames you for being so private," Lucille said. "Look what you've had to shoulder."

"The burden is heavier than you could possibly imagine," Circe said. "But I'm learning to set it down."

"Or let us help you carry it," Dr. Grant said.

Circe looked into her face, and it reminded me of the way Mom and Mo looked at each other. Circe swallowed hard and continued. "What I want to tell you all is that we have a pretty good idea about where the last piece of the Heart is and we have to go get it to try and bring Bri's mom back."

Lucille turned to me. "Was it the oleander?"

I could only nod.

"I—I didn't know," she mumbled half to herself, half to us. "I just saw that it was bad. I felt the pain but I didn't know."

"The only people to blame are this Redmond woman, her son, and anyone who was helping them along the way," Circe said. "Lou's disloyal ass was feeding them information."

"I never trusted him," Isaac said. "Not fully."

"He's so good at his job, though," Dr. Grant said. "He did the body when my aunt Nene died."

Isaac nodded. "Nene looked like she was sleeping."

All I could think of was the body I'd seen in the coffin when

Karter and I had gone to see Lou for the first time, how Lou had been so proud of the reconstruction work he'd done on that poor old lady's skull.

"He has a good cover," Circe said. "He needs to be good at his job in order to steer suspicion away from him. Nobody would have known he was betraying a sacred oath at every opportunity."

"He's been dealt with," Marie said.

Isaac raised an eyebrow, and Lucille shrugged her shoulders like she didn't care one little bit.

Mo gripped my hand. "So now what?"

"We have to go to Abana," Circe said. "We have to locate the Great Eye."

"We're not worried Karter is leading us into a trap?" Marie asked.

"We were already going to the general area," Circe said. "What I'm more concerned about is that they're already so far ahead of us."

"If they get in your way it could trip things up," I said. Circe's celestial clock sat open on the table. We were running out of time.

Lucille suddenly shuffled past Circe and approached Mo, extending her hand. Mo glanced at me and I gave her a half smile. She rested her hand in Lucille's and Lucille traced the lines on her palm.

"You stay here when they go," Lucille said. "You don't step foot outside this house when they go or you'll die, just like—"

"Okay, Lucille," Circe said. "I know your word is ironclad but ease up just a little for me, please. We have to focus here."

Mo pulled her hand into her lap. "I'm staying. So is Bri."

I stared into my lap because if I looked at her, she'd see that I was up to something. Moms just know, and I couldn't lie to her right in her face.

"I think our best course of action is to gather as much information as we can about Aeaea and then get to the last piece of the Heart before Karter and the others do," said Circe. "It's clear that Karter still has someone in his corner, probably his extended family, who ferried him away on a private jet. I don't know what resources he has, what he's told them about what happened here or if it even really matters. All I know for sure is that this is going to be extremely dangerous."

Isaac cleared his throat. "We were all so close for so long and then you up and disappeared for ten years. I hate seeing you leave again, but I understand you all have something you need to do." He reached into his pocket and took out a small vial. "I have something that may lift your spirits." He uncorked the glass container and poured a small amount of the shimmering silver liquid into his palm.

Circe's eyes grew wide. "Isaac. Is that what I think it is?"

He nodded. "Briseis transfigured this mixture for me the last time I stopped by. She is very skilled. Maybe even more than she realizes." He rubbed his hands together like he was lotioning up. His hands glistened with the substance.

Persephone stepped forward. "Briseis. You did this with no other training? No other preparation?" She seemed absolutely dumbstruck.

"I did something," I said. I remembered how afraid I'd been when he asked me to help him, but transfiguring the wolfsbane mixture had come naturally to me. "It felt like my muscles were coming off the bone." I turned to Isaac. "You never told me what it was for."

His eyes glinted in the light. "Watch."

He stretched out his hands and flexed his fingers. A haze clouded the air around them. I blinked, thinking maybe I had something in my eye. It was like looking at the space right over the sidewalk on a blistering hot day. The strange halo of rippling air enveloped his hands completely, and suddenly, they were gone. His hands disappeared.

My heart cartwheeled in my chest but I stepped closer. Isaac shifted and extended his arms toward the surface of the table. In the space where I estimated his hands were touching the table-top, the wood took on a wavy, mirage-like appearance and then disappeared, too.

Marie watched with wide eyes. Everyone, including Persephone and Circe, was struck silent.

"What you transfigured for me was an invisibility token," Isaac said. "It renders an object invisible for a set period of time." He drew his hand away from the table and it slowly reappeared. "It is very hard to manage."

"What do you even need something like that for?" Mo asked.

"I have my reasons," Isaac said.

Marie huffed. "That's not suspicious at all."

I stared at the empty space where his hands should have been.

"Wait," I said. "Could somebody do this on a larger scale?"

Isaac looked thoughtful. "I don't know. How much larger are we talking?"

I glanced at the map, at the blank space in the center of the Black Sea. "Island sized."

Circe looked at the map, too. Her lips parted but she didn't—or couldn't—speak. An improbable but intriguing thought bloomed in my mind.

"That would be next to impossible." Isaac watched as his hands continued to rematerialize. "An island, even a small one, is still a huge undertaking. This single vial is barely enough to keep me completely concealed for a solid twenty minutes. Anything I come in contact with would also be affected for roughly the same amount of time, but imagine the amount that would be needed to conceal a piece of land."

I walked over to Circe. "This has to be why nobody has been able to find Aeaea. If it's the only island out there somebody should have come across it by now."

"It's been cloaked," she said in a whisper. "Hidden."

"It just isn't possible," Isaac reiterated. "The kind of skill involved, the amount of wolfsbane alone—"

"Medea *and* the original Circe were on that island," Circe said. "Together. For who knows how long. They had more than enough skill to do it."

"Why hide it at all?" Isaac asked.

"Because the island is sheltering something no one should know about." Circe's tone turned dark. "It's there. The last piece."

Lucille stood quietly by the fireplace, wringing her hands. "Must you go? There's no other way to get what you need?"

"No," Circe said sternly. "We have to go."

Lucille nodded but still looked troubled.

"But you think we have a chance?" Mo asked. "Please be

honest with me. Do you really think you can bring Thandie back?"

Circe came over and crouched in front of Mo. "I'm going to do everything I can. And I will have to do things that might look bad from the outside."

"I don't care what it looks like to anybody else," Mo said, squeezing Circe's hands. "I'm trusting you to bring Thandie back—" Her voice caught in her throat. "Please bring her back."

A terrible silence gripped the room. What we were about to attempt was impossible, and even if there was a chance we could find the island, get past whatever creatures guarded it, locate the Heart and combine the pieces, we wouldn't come out whole.

This was a hero's quest and something would have to be lost.

CHAPTER 12

Isaac ran his hands over his neatly trimmed gray beard and glanced at Circe and Dr. Grant. "If you're going to make this trip and it's as dangerous as it appears to be, then maybe it's best to let people know how you feel about them right now. Clear the air a little."

Circe returned to her seat. Her face was tight, and it reminded me of the face I made when I was trying not to cry. She was holding her emotions in and it was starting to wear on her.

Dr. Grant slowly reached out and touched Circe's knee. "Pops is always knee deep in my business," she said. "I'm forty-five this year, and he's still acting like me and you are in high school."

Isaac just shrugged.

Circe scanned the room, then took Dr. Grant by the arm and pulled her down the hall toward the apothecary.

Marie cleared her throat. "Awkward as hell."

"I think we should get going," Isaac said.

Lucille joined him in the entryway, and as she went out to

the car, Isaac tucked the small vial of invisibility elixir into my hand.

"I can't take this," I said as we walked out onto the porch. "I wouldn't even know what to do with it."

"Take it anyway," he said. "It'll make me feel better if you have it." He sighed and looked up into the sky. "Miss Briseis, I have to believe that all of this is very overwhelming for you."

"I don't think that's a strong enough word."

"Maybe not," Isaac said. "I hope that you get a chance to put things right, but so much of what you need to do is over my head. Please try to stay safe."

"I will," I said.

"I know you're not going on this trip with Circe, but I'd like to tell you that if for some reason or another you were wondering who might be here to keep Mo safe *if* you had to leave for a little while, well, Lucille and I are a couple of old farts, but we are not to be underestimated. We'll be here."

He squeezed my hand, then got in his car and pulled out of the driveway. I went back inside to find Dr. Grant and Circe emerging from the apothecary with tear-stained faces but holding hands. Dr. Grant squeezed my arm as she, too, went out to her car and left.

"Are you okay?" I asked Circe.

She nodded but didn't say anything else about it, and I decided to stay out of her business for now.

The mood had changed. The hopeful feeling I'd had as we discovered Aeaea's most likely location was being eclipsed by an encroaching dread—what were we really stepping into here? We knew where we needed to go and how we'd get there but had no clue as to how it would actually unfold. On top of that I had to think of a way to leave Mo behind, to lie to her without hating myself for it. I didn't know if she'd forgive me for leaving when she'd made it clear that she wanted me to stay. If I brought Mom home, I could see her letting it go, maybe. But if I couldn't get Mom, if something happened to me along the way . . . I pushed those thoughts away and pulled out Circe's moon clock and stared down at the dials.

Waning gibbous. Third quarter moon. Waning crescent. Six days on the calendar and three phases in Circe's moon clock had ticked by. Marie's contacts were dragging their feet, and I was pretty sure Circe had aged five years in that same time. Every morning she looked like she hadn't slept, and her interactions with Marie became more and more strained. Mo was starting to think her plans weren't going to work. She urged Circe to make a plan B, but there was no alternate plan that didn't involve missing our window to resurrect my mom.

I spent as much time in the garden as I could. It felt far from the chaos that enveloped me in the house. I lay among the overgrown beds of the Poison Garden, staring up at the scaffolding that crisscrossed high over my head. I worried about how much longer I could hide myself away. Mo was worried. So were Circe and Marie. But it was Persephone who found me in the Poison Garden early in the morning.

"Thought I'd find you here," she said as she leaned against

the curved arch of the moon gate that separated the front part of the garden from the back.

I sat crisscross on the ground as a tangle of black hellebore bloomed around me, their velvety petals unfurling by the dozens. "It's quiet out here."

Persephone had her braids piled high on top of her head and wrapped in a red scarf. She came over and sat down across from me. She stretched her legs out and rolled her head from side to side as she leaned back on her hands. "I need a favor."

I glanced up at her. "Okay?"

"I need you to let me have this place to myself tonight."

I looked around. "The Poison Garden?"

She nodded.

"Yeah, sure," I said.

She stretched out her hand and beckoned to a gathering of pale purple bell-shaped blooms sprouting from thick ovate leaves arranged in rosettes. They leaned toward her.

"*Mandragora officinarum*," I said quietly.

"Herb of Circe," Persephone said. "Sorcerer's Root. Mandrake. When I learned about these plants I didn't know them by their scientific names. I'm still a little hazy on that, but I know their folk names like I know my own."

"I thought if I studied plants I'd be able to figure out what was going on with me."

Persephone's brows pushed together. "I'm sorry you didn't have someone to guide you."

"I did, though. I had my parents. Maybe they didn't fully understand it, but they embraced it from the jump."

"I can see that," she said. She took a deep breath. "I see so much in you that I don't have. You have a life ahead of you that can be filled with learning and practice. You can build yourself up and know that you've made peace with this gift."

"You don't have that?"

"No," she said bluntly. "A long time ago, maybe. But when you live a life as long as mine you do all there is to do." There was sadness in her voice and behind her eyes. "So you'll leave me to it later tonight?" She changed the subject and masked the pain in her face with a wide smile.

I nodded and she hopped up and dusted herself off. "Just for tonight." She strode out of the garden, and I disentangled myself from the hellebore and made my way back to the house.

Circe was in the front room and waved me over as I came in. "Marie and Nyx took Mo to get some groceries."

"Oh, okay. Did Persephone come back yet? She left the garden right before me."

"We probably won't be seeing too much of her. It's a dark moon tonight."

I palmed the little moon clock in my pocket. "Is that important?"

Circe looked up from her notebook. "Will you come sit with me? We can have a little lesson."

I went over and sat on a folding chair by the table. She opened a journal to a blank page and sketched out several circles. "The moon goes through various stages. You've obviously heard of the full moon, maybe even the waxing and waning phases, right?"

"Right," I said.

"Opposite the full moon is the new moon. But the phase

that occurs the night before the new moon is called the dark moon. The moon is essentially invisible in the night sky, and it's typically when we put out offerings for Hecate. Persephone never misses the chance to offer up something to Hecate—eggs, garlic, tea cakes, black flowers."

"Crow's feet?" I asked. "That's what I saw on the altar in the back room."

Circe nodded. "Back in the day there were ritual slaughters of hundreds of black animals on the dark moon. I don't know that Hecate required those things, but the people who followed her thought she did. We don't do that anymore. Those crow's feet were harvested from birds that died in the Poison Garden."

"Persephone asked me to give her some time alone out there tonight," I said. "You think that's what she's doing? Preparing some kind of offering?"

"Sounds about right," Circe said. "She didn't say anything to me about it. I don't like her pushing you out of a space that seems to have given you some comfort in the past few days."

"No, it's okay," I said. "Maybe I've been spending too much time out there."

"Not possible," Circe said. "I used to do the same thing. It really is a special place. Selene used to give me a hard time about staying out there so long and coming home all dusty and disheveled with bracelets of flowers. So you know what I started doing?"

"What?"

"I brought the outside, in." She went to the window and opened it. A breeze wafted through the room. "Do you have a favorite flower, Briseis? Something nonlethal because we're not tryna put Mo in the hospital."

I smiled. "Peonies are—were my mom's favorite." An ache gripped my chest. I hated talking about Mom in the past tense, like we weren't going to get her back. That possibility kept pushing its way to the front of my head, and I beat it back every time.

Circe touched my shoulder, then disappeared down the hall, returning a few seconds later with the onyx peony I'd grown for Mom. It was still supple, its vibrant red center still bright even though the water had evaporated from the glass it was in.

"You grew this for her?" Circe asked.

I nodded.

"I don't know if you've noticed yet, but when you grow something for someone out of love, there is a very good possibility that it will never die." She eyed the flower. "I don't have a solid answer for why that is. It's some other aspect of this power that doesn't have any kind of rational explanation. I just know that when you put your whole heart into growing something for someone you care for, it changes the nature of the plant itself." She smiled. "I grew a dozen *Middlemist camellia* from a petrified seed for Dr. Grant twenty years ago. She still has them and they look like they were collected yesterday."

"Middlemist red?" I asked, stunned.

"The very same," Circe said.

"That's the rarest flower on the planet. There's only, like, two actually still alive."

"And a dozen more in Khadijah's living room, but, hey, who's counting?" She gently plucked a petal from the peony and held it in her hand. She took a few deep breaths and as she concentrated, little arms of ivy stretched through the open window.

Two onyx peonies sprouted from the petal in her palm, and as she gently set their exposed roots onto a tendril of the ivy, a half-dozen black blooms with red centers sprouted along its length. "You can create a hybrid of almost any kind. I liked combining roses with ivy so that they could snake into the house and I wouldn't have to keep them in pots or planters."

The newly hybridized ivy climbed the wall and wound itself around the curtain rods and attached itself to the crown molding. It made the room feel more alive, but the rare peonies reminded me of Mom, and the pain of her absence made my chest hurt.

Nyx and Marie brought Mo back, and I helped them put away groceries and make dinner. Marie, Mo, and I ate at the small table in the kitchen while Nyx, Persephone, and Circe returned to the front room.

Mo went upstairs early. It worried me that sleep seemed to be her only refuge. She slept more than she did anything else, and I was pretty sure her clothes were fitting her a little looser than they had before.

After Marie and Nyx left for the night, I joined Mo in my room, where she was already knocked out. I went into the bathroom and brushed my teeth, threw my hair in a bonnet, and changed into a pair of leggings and an oversized T-shirt. I cut out the lights and got ready to curl up next to Mo when something, a tug in the pit of my stomach, drew me to the window. The sun had long since set and the sky was a blanket of ebony dotted with twinkling stars. The moon was invisible, making the stars so much brighter. It made sense that offerings to Hecate were traditionally put out on a night like this. She was born from the night itself in a time when maybe all that existed were stars and sky. I pushed my glasses up and let my gaze wander to the tree line.

Mo had begun to snore as I tiptoed out of the room and stood in the hallway. I heard some rustling from the extra bedroom directly across from mine. The door was shut, but a faint light danced out from under it. I made my way downstairs and again, stood quietly, listening. Circe had gone up around the same time as me and Mo, but Persephone had disappeared.

I went to the kitchen and took three eggs from the fridge and a fresh bulb of garlic from a mesh sack sitting on the counter and slipped down the hall into the apothecary.

Passing under the newly sprouted black locust tree, I let my fingers dance over the hidden lever to the secret door at the rear of the room. It bounced open and I ducked inside.

I flipped on my phone's flashlight. It pitifully sputtered to life, flashing on and off. Circe and Persephone must have already found time to tend to the altar because it was completely free from dust; the triple-faced statue of the goddess herself glinted in the dark. The offering bowls had been cleaned out and the dusty pillar candle had been replaced by a taller, newer one. I set the eggs and garlic down. Circe had said something about small tea cakes, and I wondered if it'd be disrespectful to add some of the chocolate chip cookies Mo had brought home to the spread. I lit the candle and sat in the dark room for a long time before looking up at the family tree painted on the wall, the family crest emblazoned in gold paint at the very top.

It still felt surreal to see my name nestled under Selene's protective leaf right at the bottom. I wondered if she ever thought I'd be sitting here in this place that was so much a part of who she was. I couldn't find a single part of me that resented her even though a counselor had once told me that was a normal thing to feel. After everything I'd learned about her and about why she made the choices she did, all I felt was appreciation. What were the odds that she'd choose adoption and that my parents would turn out to be the most amazing people I'd ever known? Mo with all her funny tenderness, her honesty, concern, and terrible breakfasts. Mom with all her worrying, wonder, her take-no-shit attitude, and love of scented candles and old-school music. Two imperfect people finding each other, then finding me, both of them loving me like it was what they were born to do. I took off my glasses and wiped my eyes with my T-shirt.

As I gazed at the altar I saw that the flowers hadn't been replaced yet. I quickly got up and went down the hall to the entryway where I listened for any sign of Persephone. She'd asked for some time alone in the garden, but she hadn't said exactly when. It was late, but I wanted to ask her if she was done so I could grab some flowers from the garden to add to Hecate's shrine.

I slipped on my shoes and slowly pulled open the front door, trying to keep the hinges from waking up the entire house. I pushed through the knee-high grass in the rear yard and stepped onto the hidden path.

The darkness in the woods was complete, and my phone's flashlight was on its last leg. The way ahead would be free from obstacles, the foliage surrounding the path always made the way clear for me, but as I struggled with the light on my phone the underbrush on either side of the trail began to glow. I switched off the flashlight as the intensity of the soft green light grew brighter.

Tufts of *Omphalotus nidiformis*, commonly known as ghost fungus, lit up the dark. They'd made homes of fallen logs and numbered in the dozens among the rotted wood. They seemed to wake up as I pushed forward, sensing my need for a lit path.

As I emerged into the glade of black bat flowers I reached for the lanyard around my neck and realized too late that I didn't have it. I'd left it on the table in the hallway so that Persephone and Circe could have access to it if they needed it.

"Great," I said aloud. "All the way out here with no key." The flowers tilted toward me. "Don't judge me, y'all." I turned to leave when a noise caught my attention. Just a hint of a familiar voice. Persephone was speaking somewhere close by.

I slowly approached the gate and found the lock open. Persephone was still there. I hesitated but only for a second before slipping through the gate and standing still against the inner wall. I inched along until I had no choice but to step into the open square in the middle of the garden.

"I'm sorry," I said as I went around the corner. "I thought you might be done and I—"

I stopped short. A cloud of sweet-smelling smoke rolled gently out of the moon gate and covered everything in a gauzy haze. The flickering of firelight cast dancing shadows in the smoke.

I crept to the wall, peering through the opening into the Poison Garden. Persephone stood with her back to me, two blazing torches stuck in the ground on either side of a makeshift altar of black hellebore, Blacknight hollyhock, and Devil's Pet all tangled together, on top of which sat black candles whose flames held back some of the dark. Smoke from some kind of incense billowed over the rim of a large bowl and spilled down in ghostly sheets. Hundreds, maybe thousands, of black blooms had sprung up at Persephone's feet—more black hellebore, black velvet petunias, calla lilies, more hollyhock, black bat flowers, and dozens of others. New blooms burst to life all around as Persephone swayed side to side.

"It is all I ask," Persephone said, her voice wavering. "Let it be me."

A hand clamped down on my shoulder, and as I opened my mouth to scream another set of fingers pressed against my lips. I spun around to find myself caught in Circe's arms, her eyes wide. She motioned for me to keep quiet, and I swallowed my terrified scream. She moved her hand away from my mouth and peered into the Poison Garden. A look of confusion twisted her features.

I stepped back as she continued to watch Persephone. I wanted to grab the flowers I'd come for and get out when Circe stepped into the Poison Garden.

"What the hell are you doing?" Circe said, anger coloring her every word.

Persephone huffed. "Leave me alone, Circe."

"Why are you doing this?" Circe said, her voice tight, her hands balled at her sides.

"You know why," Persephone said.

I suddenly felt like I was intruding on grown folks' business and turned to leave.

"You don't think we can do this," Circe said.

I stopped and stood still.

"I actually think we might, and that's an even more terrifying thought," said Persephone. "You know what the possibilities are."

"I don't know anything anymore," Circe snapped. "I didn't think you'd be out here doing . . . this." She got right up in Persephone's face. "What are you saying to her? To Hecate?"

"I'm trying to do my part," Persephone said. "Do you know what it's like to feel so useless?"

"Useless?" Circe was sobbing. "I need you! Everybody else is gone!"

"Not everybody," Persephone said. "And this is how you'll make sure she's safe. That's all Selene and you and me ever wanted. Whatever it takes, Circe. That's what we said."

Through the moon gate I watched as Circe hung her head. I left the garden as fast as I could and made my way home in the dim light of the bioluminescent plants, the smell of incense and flames clinging to me. I didn't have black flowers as an offering, but Persephone seemed to have it covered. Circe's agonized response to witnessing whatever it was Persephone was doing stuck with me, burrowed its way into my head, and rooted itself there. As I climbed into bed next to Mo, Persephone's words echoed in my head.

Let it be me.

CHAPTER 13

I sat at the end of my bed staring down at Circe's moon clock. The golden dial had passed over the waxing crescent and was about to pass over the first quarter moon. Another seven days had gone by, and the mood in the house had plummeted from tentative hopefulness to despair.

In the early evening, I sat in the apothecary after Mo had gone upstairs without eating, without speaking other than to tell me she loved me. Circe came to join me and closed the heavy door behind her. When I looked up to meet her gaze she was smiling.

"Please tell me what there is to smile about because I really need something right now," I said.

She stood in front of me and took my hands in hers. "It's time."

I stared blankly at her. "What?"

"Everything is wrapped up. Marie got the call. We leave tonight."

I leaped from the counter and Circe wrapped me up in her arms. I hugged her tight.

"Nyx is on her way," Circe said. "How are we going to do this, Bri? You want to come. And I really believe in my heart that we need you with us, but Mo is not gonna let you go." She shook her head. "I hate lying to her. I hate it."

"So do I," I said. I meant it. We didn't keep secrets. We didn't need to, but this situation was impossible. There was no way around it.

"Say goodbye to us," Circe said. "Then I'll have Nyx pick you up in a few hours, after Mo is in bed."

I nodded and she hugged me close, then rushed off to get her things together. A half hour later Nyx was helping her load her bag into the car. Circe asked one more time if it would be possible for me to go along with them, and Mo said no in a way that made me a little worried for Circe's safety. Circe let it go, said goodbye to me, and as I walked her to the car Nyx caught me by the shoulder and pulled me into a hug.

"I don't like this at all, but I'll send transport for you at midnight. Be prepared and only bring one bag, preferably something you can wear on your person. And here"—she slipped something into my hand—"put your glasses on this or you'll regret it." Without another word she let me go and got in the car.

I joined Mo on the porch as they drove off, and she looped her arm through mine and led me inside.

"They're gonna be okay and they're gonna get your mama back," she said.

"I know," I said.

"What'd Nyx give you?" she asked.

I opened the small package and found a long chain that was

meant to keep my glasses around my neck if they weren't on my face. It was dotted with little gold stars and moons.

"Pretty," Mo said.

I hooked the ends to the arms of my glasses and put them back on my face.

"You look like a librarian," Mo said. She smiled, but she couldn't hide how exhausted she was or how heavy the burden of keeping up a front for me was.

I wrapped my arms around her. "I love you so much, Mo. More than anything."

"I love you more," she said as she buried her face in my hair. "I'm gonna go to bed. Are they gonna call us when they land?"

I nodded. "That's the plan."

"You coming to bed?" she asked.

"I don't think I can sleep," I said. "Circe said I could look at some books she's got in her room. I'll probably just stay up and read until I'm tired."

Mo looked me over and I could feel her searching for something in my movements, in my words, that told her what I was hiding. I didn't meet her gaze.

"I might stay up a little longer," she said.

My heart sank into the pit of my stomach, but I quickly collected myself. "We can watch something on my computer."

She nodded, and I followed her up to my room to set up my laptop so that we could pretend to watch a movie when really we were only going to watch each other. I'd given myself away. She'd caught onto something I did or said, and now she wasn't going to let me out of her sight until she was sure I wasn't going anywhere.

She brushed her teeth and tucked her hair under Mom's ugly red bonnet and fluffed up the pillows on my bed, where she stretched out, clearly prepared to stay all the way awake.

Panic gripped me. I had no doubt that if I wasn't outside to meet Nyx at midnight, they'd leave without me. They had to.

"I'll be right back," I said.

"Where you going?" Mo asked, avoiding my eyes.

"I'm gonna grab a book from Circe's room. I've seen all these movies already anyway."

Mo pressed her lips together. "Okay. Hurry up because I want us to pick something we can watch together."

"Give me one second," I said. I hurried across the hall. My backpack had been ready for days. I'd shoved it in the back of Circe's closet, where I knew Mo wouldn't go looking. It sat waiting with a pair of sneakers, a jacket, my ID, and a few changes of clothes stuffed inside. Most importantly, I'd transferred the vial of Living Elixir to my bag, tucked inside a padded inner pocket alongside the invisibility token Isaac had gifted me. I moved the backpack to just inside Circe's bedroom door so I could grab it the moment Mo fell asleep.

"You good?" Mo called.

"Yup," I called back. I grabbed a random book off Circe's dresser and gently closed the door.

Mo and I watched a movie and were halfway through a second one as the clock ticked past eleven thirty. I watched as Mo began to nod off, fighting her sleep. I rolled onto my side and shut my eyes, hoping I could convince her I was asleep. A few minutes later Mo turned over and after a while, began to snore.

In the dark, I took out my mangled phone and composed a note to Mo. I couldn't think of what to say that would be enough. It occurred to me that this might be the last thing she ever heard from me if things went sideways. What could I say to her to make her understand that I loved her more than anything but that I had to go?

Mo,

I don't know what to say. I just have to tell you that I love you. So much. More than anything, but I have to go help get Mom back. I can help Circe and together, we'll bring her back. We'll come back and we'll make this place a for-real home. I never want to hurt you or lie to you, but I know you, and I know you'd rather put your life on the line than let me risk mine. You're such a good mom. The best mom. I love you. Please don't be mad at me. I'll see you soon.

Love always,

Bri

I couldn't see through the tears. I kept the text open as I slipped out of bed and went across the hall, where I put on my shoes and threw my backpack on. I went down and opened the front door, glanced back up the stairs one last time, then gently closed it behind me.

I looked for a car, thinking Nyx might have been waiting in Marie's black sedan. The sky was cloudless, the color of purple-black velvet. The moon hung above me, its bright face slowly revealing itself, pushing us toward the full moon.

A sudden gust of wind knocked me back against the railing. As I scrambled to right myself, the griffin swooped down and landed in the drive almost silently. In the dark he was a hulking shadow, a ghost. He folded his wings against his body and lowered himself as close to the ground as possible.

"You gotta be kidding me," I said.

The creature squawked so loud, a high-pitched ringing lingered in my ears when he was done. There was a sudden pounding of footsteps from inside. Mo was up, and from the sound of it, barreling down the steps. The front door bounced open.

"Briseis!" she yelled, her eyes wild.

Suddenly, a tangle of ivy cloaked the doorway. Mo clawed at the vines, ripping them down, but they grew back immediately, trapping her inside.

"Don't do this!" she cried as I tripped down the front steps and sprinted toward the griffin. I grabbed a handful of feathers and tried to pull myself up. With a quick flip of his wing, he boosted me onto his back, where a makeshift harness had been looped around his neck. I wound my shaking hands through the rope.

Tears once again blurred my vision. "I love you, Mo," I called through choked sobs.

Mo's cries carried through the dark. I pressed my body to the griffin's back and shut my eyes. He took three lumbering steps, and suddenly a sinking feeling, falling. No.

Ascending.

Flying.

CHAPTER 14

I didn't dare open my eyes. The wind whipped my face and my glasses flew off. I grabbed at them as they dangled from the chain Nyx had given me. I counted the beating of the griffin's wings in my head to try and calm myself. I didn't know how long we'd been airborne before we took a sharp downward turn. My stomach did a barrel roll and I had to grit my teeth to keep from throwing up. There was a sudden drop, the rustling of leaves, and then a large thump.

"Briseis," a voice called to me. "Bri. I'm right here. Give me your hand."

I opened my eyes and lifted my head. We'd landed and Marie was there, reaching for me, but I couldn't let go of the rope. My hands were locked in position.

"Lie down, Roscoe. Damn!" Marie grumbled.

The griffin snorted and pressed himself to the ground, bringing me a little closer to Marie. She climbed up and disentangled my hands from the harness, then pulled me down in one quick move. She set me on the ground, and I promptly puked my guts up.

"Yikes," Marie said. "Couldn't we have just picked her up with the car?"

"It's a thirty-five-minute drive there and back," Nyx called from somewhere. "Roscoe got her here in ten."

"What if she fell off?" Marie shouted back. "Did you think of that?"

"Roscoe would have caught her," Nyx said. "The only person he lets fall all the way to the ground is you."

Marie shot a dagger of a glance at the griffin.

Circe jogged over and put a cold bottle of water in my hand. "Oh, Briseis, I'm so sorry. Are you gonna be okay?"

I doubled over, hand on my knee, as I rinsed my mouth out. "Yeah. Just give me a minute."

Circe patted me on the back and returned to Marie's car, where they'd begun unloading their bags. The two metal cages sat on the ground surrounded by a cocoon of thorned vines. I glanced around as I swished water through my teeth, trying to wash out the sour taste. We were at a small, seemingly abandoned, airport. A sleek black jet sat on the runway. The whole place looked familiar.

"Where are we?" I asked. I put my glasses back on and tried to place where I'd seen this airport before.

"We're outside Red Hook. The same place Karter caught his flight, only I made sure there won't be any witnesses." Marie gestured to the shattered remains of several security cameras. "You ready?"

"I think so. Mo caught me on the way out."

Marie shook her head. "Nyx is staying behind, and Circe talked to Dr. Grant. They'll keep an eye on her."

"Isaac said he'd be around, too. Do you think they'll tell her anything?"

"I don't know. Circe's concerned about Karter and whoever he's been in communication with. If they're trying to get to the last piece, too, we have to try and stay a step ahead, and that means not letting anyone know where we are or what we're doing."

I nodded. Marie leaned in to kiss me, then reared back, her nose scrunching up.

"What?"

Marie grimaced. "I care about you. A lot. But you're gonna have to brush your teeth."

My face flushed hot. "You right."

She grabbed my hand and pulled me over to the car where Persephone and Nyx were sobbing into each other's shoulders. Marie traced my knuckles with the ball of her thumb. Nyx suddenly broke free from Persephone's grasp and marched up to Marie.

"I need you to do me a favor," Nyx said.

Marie's jaw was set hard. It took me a moment to realize she wasn't angry. She was trying desperately to hold back tears.

"I don't want you to be careful," said Nyx, her voice tight, the whites of her eyes bloodshot. "I want you to use everything that cursed plant has given you to do whatever you need to do to bring your rude, disrespectful, spoiled-rotten ass right back here. I won't accept anything less than that. Do you understand?"

Marie didn't speak. She only gave Nyx a stiff nod.

"Tell me you will do it," Nyx said. She put her hand on Marie's shoulder, and Marie couldn't hold back anymore. Tears rolled down her cheeks. "I need you to say it out loud because I know you to be a person of your word."

"I don't know why you're talking to me like this is goodbye. It's not." Marie roughly wiped away her tears. "But just so you know, I never would've gotten through all these years without you." She cleared her throat and squeezed my hand. I hadn't ever seen her this upset. Marie could be abrasive, she had an attitude as big as the sky, but what she had with Nyx was special. They were family. Marie looked Nyx in the face. "Tell me you'll see me soon and walk away."

Nyx choked back a sob. "I'll see you soon." She turned on her heel, walked to the car, and drove off.

I turned to Marie. "We'll make this work." I didn't know if I was trying to convince her or myself. I'd let myself believe we could attempt this impossible task, but promising we'd make it back safe and sound still felt like too much of a lie for me to say it out loud.

We walked to the plane and climbed the short set of stairs. Inside were two rows of plush reclining seats, grouped in twos and facing each other with tables in between. There was enough room for twelve passengers, but it was only the four of us. Circe moved the cages inside and set them under a blanket near the back.

Marie fished around inside a narrow cabinet and pulled out a toothbrush wrapped in plastic and a travel-sized tube of toothpaste. She handed them to me and steered me to the rear of the cabin where I found a bathroom.

"Thanks," I said.

Marie squeezed my hand and went to help Circe and Persephone load the last of our things.

I stepped inside the bathroom, slung my backpack onto the small counter, and brushed my teeth. I glanced in the little lighted mirror. I had to smile. My wrap was still clinging to my head, but it had been pushed back by the wind during my ride on the griffin and my edges were sticking out. But my hair wasn't the issue. What was embarrassing was the little dried trails of tears that streaked from the corners of my eyes and the one trail of dried snot from my left nostril. I took a deep breath and got to work setting myself straight.

After I cleaned up I fished my phone out of my bag. There were fifty missed calls from Mo. Thirty text messages. I couldn't bear to read any of them. I hit send on the note I'd written to her and switched my phone off completely. I met Marie back in the main cabin and sat in the beige recliner across from her.

"You look . . . refreshed," she said, biting back a smile.

"You were just gonna let me walk around like that, huh?"

She reached over and put her hand on my knee. "I think you look beautiful. Snotty nose and all."

"That's messed up," I said, laughing.

"I pointed you to the bathroom, didn't I?"

I smiled at her, and she sat back in her seat as Circe and Persephone climbed aboard and the outer door clanged shut. They sat down in the two seats immediately across the narrow aisle.

"The pilot says we'll be in the air in a few minutes," Circe said. She shrugged out of her sweater and reclined her seat until it was flat enough to lie down. "Might as well get comfortable. We'll stop once to go through customs and refuel, but then it's right back in the air for the second leg of the trip. Total flying time should be about twelve hours."

"Twelve hours?" I asked. I'd never been on a plane for that long, and the cabin suddenly seemed smaller and much more cramped.

Marie pressed her head back into her seat and sighed. "I'm already bored."

"Maybe we should try to focus on what we'll do once we land," Persephone suggested. "We'll have to charter a ship to reach Aeaea, but we have to locate the Great Eye in order to find out which way to sail. We're going to Abana first."

I sat forward. "Not tryna be rude but do we know how to work a boat?"

"I'll drive the boat," Marie said, grinning.

"I would rather swim," Persephone said. "I literally can't die, and I would still not get in a boat you were steering."

Marie sank down in her seat. "Well, damn."

"The boat is actually the least of our worries," Circe said. She propped her arm under her head and stared up at the ceiling. "If we can get to the Great Eye, figure out how it works so we can locate Aeaea, there are still the sirens. And if they exist as they do in mythology, we'll have to take precautions."

I settled into my seat as the engines rumbled loudly and the plane began to maneuver into position for takeoff.

"How did people get past them in the stories? Does it say?" I asked.

"Some sailors plugged their ears with wax," Circe said. "And there's the story of Orpheus playing his lyre so loudly that it drowned out the sirens' calls."

Persephone nodded. "But since we don't have either of those things, our best bet is going to be noise-canceling headphones or something similar."

"What happens if you hear their calls?" I asked. "Can't you just . . . not go into the water?"

"I don't think it's a question of willpower," Circe said. "Every single reference to them in the texts makes it clear that the sound they emit is impossible to resist. It could be some kind of hypnosis, or maybe the sound incapacitates you completely. I really don't know."

The engine noise rose until it drowned out our conversation. The lights flickered, and then we were tearing down the runway. The plane lifted off, and the sinking feeling in the pit of my stomach reminded me of the way I felt as I clung to the griffin's back. I shut my eyes until we leveled out and my ears adjusted to the quiet, constant hum in the cabin.

The door to the cockpit slid open, and a man with a shiny bald head and round face peered out. "We've reached our cruising altitude. Feel free to get up and stretch. This'll be a long flight."

"Appreciate it, George," Marie said.

The man's eyes grew wide, and then he slid the door shut and I thought I heard the soft click of a lock.

I turned to Marie. "He looked shook. What'd you do to him?"

Marie shrugged. "Nothing. I chartered this flight."

I tilted my head to the side. "And?"

"And I had to make sure he understood that I needed him to use discretion."

"When are you going to learn that you can't just threaten people all the time?" Persephone chimed in.

"I have to use this power for something," Marie said. "Otherwise what do I get? I get made into a monster and can't act monstrous every once in a while?" Marie was confident in almost everything I'd seen her do up to that point. She was so sure of herself, but in that moment I heard something like sadness in her tone.

"I understand," Persephone said.

"I know you do," Marie said. "I can see it in your face."

Something silent passed between them, and I tried to think of what it must be like to live forever. To have to watch everyone around you die. My stomach twisted into a knot. I didn't need to be some immortal to understand that part of it, but something else Marie said bothered me.

"You're not a monster," I said. "You really feel like that?"

"Sometimes." Marie looked into her lap. "I've just been like this for so long. It's strange. In the beginning I was in awe of this power. Nothing could touch me. I had all this strength and didn't know what to do with it. Astraea tried to help me, but she could do only so much."

In a lot of ways, Marie was like most of the other seventeen-year-olds I knew. Impulsive, a little mouthy, push-and-pull relationships with the people closest to her. She was eternally seventeen, but the reality was that she had a three-hundred-

and-seventy-six-year history behind her. The mention of Astraea's name stoked a curious feeling in me. I wanted to know more, and since we were stuck on a plane for the next twelve hours, I figured it was as good a time as any to ask.

"Can you tell me about your life back then?" I asked. "With Astraea? It doesn't sound like she thought you were a monster."

"You probably have to start with the Colchis family's history first." Marie glanced at Persephone, who gave her a little nod.

"I accompanied Astraea's mother, Ariadne, and her three sisters, across the ocean in the company of Dutch merchants in 1630," Persephone began. "New York was still called New Amsterdam at that time. Only thirty land grants were given to Black people between 1643 and 1716. We were granted two in 1643 and that is the land we are now the caretakers of. The same spot where the apothecary now sits. We were one of the few free Black families in a land drenched in the blood of the enslaved."

We sat in a silence for several moments in quiet recognition of all those who had come before us.

"I met Astraea when we were young," Marie said quietly. "I don't remember much before I knew her. My family had traveled north and came to the place that would be known as Rhinebeck." She took a deep breath and continued. "We were best friends. We spent so much time together people thought we were sisters. I remember her talking about her family, about the secrets they kept. Then we got sick. My baby sister died first. She was so little, her body didn't stand a chance fighting off the illness. Then my father died."

"Gods, Marie," Circe said.

Marie stared blankly at her. "You've heard this story before."

"And it never gets any easier," said Circe. "I can't imagine. I'm so sorry, hun."

Marie nodded then went on. "I got sick and had to stay in bed. I don't think I could've gotten up if I wanted to. I was so weak. Astraea came to visit me every day, but my mother wouldn't let her inside. She didn't want her to get sick, too, so Astraea sat outside the window, where she'd grown a bunch of sunflowers that never wilted. My mother thought it was a sign that I'd recover but I knew the truth. It was Astraea, and she had that magic that all of you have. As the days dragged on, my body felt like it was on fire. It hurt to breathe, to swallow. I wanted to die, and the look on my mother's face told me I was gonna get exactly what I wanted."

A knot stuck in my throat.

"I closed my eyes one night and fully expected to never wake up. But at some point I felt someone's hand behind my head. There was a cool sensation on my lips and then in my throat, and then there was nothing. I thought I was dead until I started to hear Astraea's voice calling to me from somewhere. She just kept saying my name over and over again. When I finally opened my eyes, I was renewed, revived. I got up and my mother fainted." She laughed lightly. "I went to her and picked her straight up, like she weighed nothing. I was stronger than I'd ever been."

"Nobody questioned it?" I asked.

"They did. Even *I* questioned it. It took years for me to convince Astraea to tell me what she'd given me. She kept saying it was an elixir or a tonic but she didn't want to go into detail."

"She knew how to keep our secrets," Persephone said.

Marie rolled her eyes. "She should have been able to tell me more than she did. She used the Heart on me. Y'all could've helped me deal with what was happening." She glared at Persephone. "You knew what I would become and you didn't even try to reach out. Real neighborly of you."

"Not everything is your business," Persephone snapped.

"Kind of feels like it's my business when I'm dying and then all the sudden I'm a damn monster!"

I grabbed Marie's arm. "You gotta stop saying that. You're not a monster."

"How can you say that after the things you've seen me do?" She put her hand over her mouth and her gaze dropped to the floor.

"I've seen you rescue me from people who were probably trying to kill me," I said. "I've seen you do what you had to do to protect the people you care about. That doesn't feel monstrous to me."

"And if I didn't have this power?" she asked. "What would you think of me?"

"I don't understand," I said.

Marie sighed. "Even if I didn't ask for this. Even if I was afraid of it in the beginning . . . It's what makes me special," she said quietly. "Now it's the most interesting thing about me. Who am I without it?"

"You serious?" I asked in disbelief. "There's so much more to you than that."

Persephone turned her face to the window, and Circe pulled out a pair of headphones and stuck them in her ears.

"I'm glad you think so," Marie said.

I laced my fingers through hers. "I'd still like you if you weren't . . . this. Anyway, I think the most interesting thing about you is the way you think nobody sees how scared you are sometimes, how you kind of put up this front with Nyx and Alec even though it's clear you love them. You're not a monster. You've seen some shit. Been through a lot of things that I can't even begin to imagine, and you're still here, trying to make it work."

Marie stared into my face like she couldn't believe what I was saying.

I leaned closer, emboldened by the feeling that we were careening toward an uncertain end. "Don't look at me like you don't know how I feel about you. What the Heart has done to you doesn't even matter to me in the way you think it does. I wish you could see what I see." I took off my glasses and let them hang on the chain around my neck. "You are not a monster."

Marie sighed as she kissed the side of my face and pulled me close to her.

We landed at a small airport outside Paris, where we were asked to sit and wait while Marie and Circe spoke to officials. They checked our paperwork, our passports, and then boarded the plane to check our belongings. My heart crashed in my chest as the pair of uniformed officials walked to the back of the plane. I turned to Marie, who was completely unbothered.

The two men looked directly at the blanket covering the cage containing the Heart as it beat slow and steady. They had to have heard it but they said nothing. The men did a quick sweep of the rest of the cabin, then returned to the front of the plane, where Marie slipped them both a thick envelope. An hour later we were back in the air.

When we landed in Istanbul thirteen hours after leaving New York, I didn't want to do anything other than eat, take a nap, and get to Abana as fast as possible. I kept taking Circe's moon clock out of my pocket and glancing at the hand hovering close to the waxing gibbous. Twenty-three days had passed since Hecate had tasked us with doing the impossible, and this was as close as we'd been at any point so far. But that left us only five days to put the rest of the pieces together. It didn't feel like progress as much as it did a gasping, frenzied rush to the finish.

When we deplaned, Marie and Circe hurried off to pick up our rental car. I helped Persephone gather our things, and when they returned we loaded our bags and the two metal cages into the trunk. After we stopped at a gas station to grab water and snacks for the drive we set off down Turkey's turquoise coastline.

The winding roads cut through rolling hills and took us past a mix of ancient ruins and modern beach resorts, sleepy seaside towns, and bustling cities. The coastline dipped in and out of view, and the Black Sea, like an endless expanse of cobalt blue, shimmered under the cloudless sky.

I dozed on Marie's shoulder and woke when we stopped for gas or food. The hours slipped by, and as the sun set, the sky turned to fire—hazy oranges and copper. We arrived in the tiny town of Abana too late to do anything other than check into a small hotel and pass out from exhaustion.

Despite our travel fatigue and a mattress I was pretty sure was made out of concrete, we were up with the sun. We got ready and met in the hotel's lobby.

"Keep your eyes up," Persephone said. "We know Karter was heading here. He and whoever he's with might still be lurking around."

I nodded as Marie pulled her hair up and secured it on top of her head like she was ready to fight. I was more worried for the safety of anyone who might come at her the wrong way than I was for us.

"We have to find the Great Eye," said Circe.

"This place is small," I said. "Shouldn't be a problem to find a big-ass lighthouse, right?"

Persephone flashed me a tight smile. "I hope it's that easy, but something is telling me it won't be."

We left the hotel and piled into the car. We drove the length of the town, sticking to the coastline to see if we could spot the lighthouse. I saw a port with a bunch of ships bobbing in the water, some beachfront restaurants, but nothing that even slightly resembled a lighthouse.

"He was just messing with us?" Marie asked. "I'm gonna stomp the yard on his musty ass as soon as I see him."

"He was musty?" Persephone scrunched up her nose.

I glanced sideways at Marie. "He was not."

Marie crossed her arms over her chest. "Okay maybe not really, but I'm mad."

"Understandable," I said.

The text from Karter wasn't the only reason we were there, though. Circe's own research and what we'd seen on the pottery shard had led us to the general area, but it was possible we were in the wrong spot.

"Why don't we ask around?" I said as the afternoon started to slip away from us. "I feel stupid asking if there's a lighthouse, when obviously there's not, but it can't hurt."

Circe shrugged, and we pulled over and parked on a street near a small blue house that had been converted into a restaurant. Outside, chairs and tables draped in checkered cloths sat under gazebos lit with white fairy lights. We sat down, and a short woman in a black dress came over, handed us a menu, and poured us each a small cup of espresso that made me feel like I could hear colors. Persephone spoke to the woman in Turkish, then turned to us to relay what she'd learned.

"I asked her if there was a lighthouse here, and she said there used to be, but it has long since fallen into the sea."

I sat back in my chair and folded my arms across my chest to keep from screaming in frustration.

The woman said something that caught Persephone's ear, and after another exchange, Persephone leaned toward us.

"She's never seen the original lighthouse. It was still standing when her great-grandmother was alive, but that was many years ago."

"So another dead end?" I asked.

Persephone shook her head. "She said they put up a new one a few towns over, but that the public isn't allowed to visit. The caretaker is extremely fussy. His name is Mr. Herman, and she says if we make contact with him, she'd like for us to tell him that she doesn't appreciate him coaxing tourists to visit, knowing they can't see the lighthouse up close and in person. Apparently, we're the second group in the past month that has come around asking about it and inquiring about boat rentals."

I sat up.

Persephone swallowed the last mouthful of coffee and stood up. She thanked the woman, paid the bill, and we hurried to the car.

"People were asking about the lighthouse and about renting a ship?" I asked. "That's gotta be Karter."

Persephone pulled onto the road leading up the coast, and for the first time since we landed I felt a fragile sense of hope. As we drove in the direction of the next town, the land enfolded us. Hills rose up on either side of the road, blocking the view of the sea. Nearly an hour later as we consulted our maps, Persephone slammed on the brakes and sent me, even with my seat belt on, into the seat in front of me.

"Holy shit!" Marie said. "You tryna kill us?"

"You can't die," Persephone said.

"But I can!" Circe said angrily. "What is going on? Why'd you—"

She stopped short as she followed Persephone's gaze.

A rusted metal sign sat crooked on its stand just off the side of the road. It looked like somebody had run it over and tried to fix it. The blue paint was chipped and brown splotches of corrosion bloomed on its face, but what was clear was a small rendering of what was meant to be a lighthouse and at the very top—an elongated oval shape with a white circle in the center.

"The Great Eye," Circe said in a whisper.

CHAPTER 15

Whatever this town—which was actually more like a village— had been, it had long since lost its luster. The few buildings we passed were mostly boarded up or left to the elements. I didn't see a single person. Abana had been alive and bustling, but this place was dead.

As we navigated the single narrow street that ran through the center of town and emerged onto a gravel turnaround, the nighttime sky fell down around us and met with something darker and more foreboding. In the gloom, the Black Sea looked like a giant void in the earth, like I could step off the edge of the wind-battered bluff and fall into nothingness. The only break in the blue-black night was the thing we'd been looking for—the lighthouse.

It sat at the farthest edge of the bluff, a beacon to ships sailing that great black void. It was a solid four stories high, painted ivory, and shaped like an octagon at its base. At the top was a white light spinning in a slow circle like a small sun.

I didn't see a car or any other signs that someone was actually there. We walked through a small opening at the center of the rusted gate that surrounded the entire structure. As we approached, a rounded wooden door creaked open and a shadowy figure appeared in the doorway.

"Sorry to bother you so late," Circe called out.

"Have you reached your destination or are you just passing through?" he asked in a deep, raspy voice.

I glanced at Circe.

"A little of both," she replied.

"You with that other group?"

"We're not with anyone," Circe said.

The man stepped out of the doorway and straightened up. He held some kind of lantern in his hand that lit half his face. We were still a good ways away from him, but even from where I was, I could tell he was abnormally tall. Persephone pushed forward a little but I stayed put.

"Spidey sense tingling?" Marie whispered.

I nodded.

"Me too," she said.

The man waved us closer, and I hesitantly followed Persephone and Circe, clinging to Marie's hand.

As we stood in front of the man I realized he was taller than Persephone by at least a foot, maybe more. He held up his lantern and let his gaze wander to each of us. When he looked at me the hair on the back of my neck stood straight up.

He had an untrimmed salt-and-pepper beard and wore a wide-brimmed hat. His skin was wind chapped, like deep brown leather. His brown eyes were piercing and narrow, and his long shawl-like coat hung down so far it scraped across the ground as he shifted his weight from one foot to the other.

"What can I do for you?" he asked.

"We need to charter a boat," Persephone said quickly. She skipped mentioning the Great Eye, and I just had to trust that it was for a reason. "The people in Abana said you might have one we could borrow."

"Is that so?" he asked. His mouth turned up and the skin around his eyes wrinkled. "Another group of people came here asking the very same thing."

"Did you help them?" Persephone asked.

The man smiled. "No. I turned them away, but it seems they found someone else to accommodate them. They sailed into the heart of the Black Sea without knowing fully what they might find. Pity."

"Why pity?" Circe asked.

He glanced out over the bluff, then back to us. "Those waters are dangerous. They always have been." He ducked through the door and called back to us, "Come in."

Persephone started to follow him and I grabbed her by the sleeve.

"We're just gonna follow him in? Y'all didn't have a weird feeling at all?"

"Oh, I did," Persephone said. "That's exactly why I'm going in."

"That makes no sense," I said.

She disappeared inside and Circe followed her. Marie and I went in but stayed near the door in case we needed to make a quick escape.

The inside wasn't what I thought it would be. I'd never actually been inside a lighthouse so I didn't have much to compare it to. It was dimly lit by dancing firelight and so warm I'd already begun to sweat. There was a big open space in the center, a neatly made bed near the back, and a small kitchen with a table and chairs. Narrow windows were cut into the stone walls and were covered in blue-green glass. In the corner sat a large staff carved with two intertwined snakes running its length. A thick, sweet smell lingered in the air, and I pinpointed its origin in the dozens of potted plants the lighthouse caretaker had scattered around the interior. They were all *Crocus sativus*, bright purple blooms with crimson stigmas.

The man stirred the logs in the woodstove and gestured for us to sit at the table. A pulsing white light filtered down from the glowing orb high above our heads, and it lit up the space like daylight every few seconds.

Circe sat and rested her elbows on her knees. "We have come a very long way," she began. "And we don't have a lot of time but—"

"Who are you?" Marie jumped in. "And is this the Great Eyeball or what?"

Circe rolled her eyes and let her arms flop at her sides. Persephone scowled at Marie but the man grinned.

"Was there a younger guy with the group that came here before?" I asked, hoping he'd forgive Marie's little outburst. "He would have been injured. His jaw was broken, I think."

"In fact, there was," said the man. "He looked like he'd seen better days." He lowered his lanky frame into a rocker by the woodstove. His long coat caught on the runner and for a split second I thought I saw a flash of something gold on his foot. He quickly readjusted himself. "He was here along with three others. They have not been back since and I don't expect they ever will be."

"You said they were sailing the Black Sea," Circe said. "Do you know why?"

The man cocked his head to the side. "I can see that you are already aware of what they were looking for. You're looking for the same thing. I have yet to figure out why or if you even realize how pointless it is."

Circe stared at the man and something in her expression changed. Her eyes went wide. Her mouth turned down at the corners and she pressed her hand into the top of the table.

The man stared into the fire. "What is it you seek on the island?"

Persephone clasped her hands together in front of her. "Who said anything about an island?"

"It's the only reason anyone would travel to the center of the Black Sea."

"We never said that's where we were going," I said.

He glanced at me. "But it is where you are going, isn't it? Didn't you come here looking for a way to get there?" He laughed, and the deep, throaty sound echoed off the walls. "I don't much care for games. For trickery."

"We're not trying to trick you," Circe said. "We need answers and time is not on our side."

"Of course it isn't," he said dismissively. "You're mortal."

The way he said mortal made it clear that he himself was not.

"Can you help us?" I asked. If he could help, I didn't care what he was.

"My advice would be this—don't go. I don't know why you or that other group have taken such interest in that place, but they aren't coming back and neither will you if you press on. I'm doing you a favor. Believe me."

"What do you think happened to them?" I asked.

"The waters are treacherous, vengeful. They're probably at the bottom of the sea by now."

"What if they made it to the island?" I asked.

He chuckled. "I hope they drowned. It's a much kinder fate."

Persephone rose from her chair and slowly approached the man. "The Great Eye is said to reveal all. We came here hoping it would point us in the direction of the island."

"And so it seems you've failed before you've even begun," he said. "The Great Eye does indeed see much—but not all. That place is one thing it cannot show you."

My heart sank. "Why not? Why can't it show us how to get there?"

"Because magic was worked on the place. A kind of magic that no longer exists in this world. It is beyond the reach of men."

"And gods?" Persephone asked. "What about them?"

The man was suddenly out of his chair, gripping Persephone's left wrist. Circe scrambled to her feet, lunging at the man, who immediately sidestepped her. Marie's eyes turned black as she launched herself at him. He still held tight to Persephone's wrist but somehow managed to catch Marie by the front of her jacket with his opposite hand and toss her against the rocker. He reached into the folds of his cloak and pulled out a gleaming golden sword the length of my arm.

Warmth flooded my palms and I spread my fingers out. From under the door, tendrils of thorned vines slithered toward us like a mass of writhing snakes. The violet plants broke free from their planters and intertwined with one another, creating thick ropes. I envisioned them taking hold of the man, and they coiled around his ankles, pulling themselves up his legs. He blinked repeatedly, then in one quick motion drew the golden blade across Persephone's forearm. A cut opened in her skin and she winced. The vines gripped the man's arm and wrenched it back.

Persephone broke from his grasp and clutched her wound. Blood trickled out, but as she clenched her jaw, stifling a groan, the wound sealed itself up.

The man stepped back and holstered his sword as Circe and Marie scrambled to their feet. He didn't move, but the look on his face was thoughtful.

"What was that?" Marie asked, her eyes still darkened, her hands curled into claws. She was ready to tear this dude's throat out.

He took two sweeping steps and grabbed the carved staff resting in the corner. Marie moved toward him and he tapped the staff hard on the floor. Marie wobbled on her feet, then collapsed in a heap.

I rushed to her side and turned her over. She was breathing steadily but was completely unconscious.

"What did you do?" I screamed. "If you hurt her I'll—"

"She'll have a peaceful rest," he said quickly. "Leave her be and explain yourselves."

The vines doubled and tripled their number as my heart galloped in my chest. They began to wrap around the man's waist.

"Where does this power come from?" he asked, staring at Persephone and then at Marie's limp body. "Who gave it to you?"

"We are the descendants of Medea," Circe said.

The man looked to me. "The plants?" He seemed confused, and then his face relaxed. "I see. But immortality? What power is that?"

"The Absyrtus Heart," Circe said quietly. "They were transformed by it."

"The Heart?" The man's face fell. "It still exists?"

Marie stirred and her eyes fluttered open. The man shook the vines free from his arms and legs and retook his seat. The offshoots retreated to my side and curled protectively around me.

"You know about the Heart?" Persephone asked. "How?"

The man didn't answer immediately. He leaned back in the chair and stretched out his legs in front of him. His cloak came up and revealed that the flash of gold I'd seen earlier had been an ornament on a pair of elaborately constructed sandals. They shone in the dancing light of the woodstove. Each sandal had a pair of intricate gold wings protruding from either side. An image pushed its way to the front of my mind—the wide-brimmed hat, the carved staff in the corner, the winged sandals—I inhaled sharply. It was the figure from the pottery shard.

"Hermes."

The man ran his fingers through his beard. "In the flesh," he said, staring off to the side. "You have my name, now I would have yours."

Persephone stepped back, her face blank. Circe cupped her hands over her mouth and Marie pulled herself up to a sitting position in a daze. No one spoke but I was entranced. The strange sense of unease I'd had when we first saw him was familiar—it was the same feeling I had when Hecate revealed herself to me and when we visited Dr. Kent. It was the same creeping dread, like the tendrils of a poisonous vine, snaking its way around me, telling me that I was in the presence of something way beyond my understanding.

"I'm Briseis," I offered since no one else seemed able to speak. "That's Circe, Persephone, and Marie."

He glanced at them. "Such familiar names, but unfamiliar faces."

I tried my hardest to gather myself. "The boy who came here, he was my friend—or at least he pretended to be." I swallowed my rage as the vines clung to my legs. "He is a descendant of Jason, and that means he's related to you."

"A thousandth great-grandson?" He laughed. "It would be ridiculous for him to assume that should mean something to me."

"His mother thought it would." I moved closer. Marie reached for me but I shrugged away from her. "She said she'd found hints of your existence. She wanted to use the Heart to be one of you."

Hermes laughed and leaned his head back to look up at the light twirling in the top of the lighthouse. "Immortality makes you godlike. No one will disagree with that. But my father was Zeus himself." He scoffed as he said the word. "My mother was the daughter of Atlas, of Pleione. Her blood was the blood of the makers of the universe."

"As is ours," said Persephone.

Hermes's brow arched up. "Medea was talented, a student of the original Circe, but she was not a goddess."

"Her mother was Hecate," I said.

He leveled his eyes and seemed to take in everything about me in one sweeping glance. "Impossible." Hermes tented his fingers under his chin, his posture suddenly rigid.

"It's not," I said. "She was the mother of Medea and Absyrtus. She's been watching over our family from the beginning with the help of the Fates."

Hermes was struck silent. "I thought the power of the Heart was due to the great Circe's involvement. She was a goddess, daughter of Helios himself. But I never thought . . ." He trailed off, his eyes glassy, his thoughts somewhere far away.

"I've seen Hecate with my own eyes," I said.

Hermes turned to look at me, his jaw slung open. "It isn't—it cannot be. If she were still in existence, she would be the oldest among us by more eons than you can possibly fathom. She was born from the night itself." He fell into a contemplative silence.

"The last piece of the Heart is on Aeaea," Circe said. "We have to get to it before Karter and the others. Did you—did you tell him who you are? Does he know?"

Hermes shook his head. "I told them nothing."

Persephone stood at Circe's side. "We need a vessel," she said. "And we need any information you can tell us about Aeaea. If the Great Eye can't lead us to it, then we have to figure out another way to get there."

Hermes rolled his head back and sighed. "I've been there many times. When Circe was in exile there, when Odysseus and his men came upon her and she turned them to swine. But the sirens guard it now."

"So you can help us?" I asked again. "You can show us how to get there?"

"Why should I?" he asked. "I don't dabble in the lives of mortals. It's forbidden. There was a time when gods and men were intertwined, but that time has long since passed."

"Mrs. Redmond—Karter's mother—your descendant— killed my mom," I said. "Hecate said I could bring her back if I could reunite the pieces of the Heart. I need the piece that's on the island to do that."

"She said this to you?" He was dumbstruck. "Why?"

"You don't have anybody in your life that you love, do you?" I asked.

Persephone gasped. "Briseis—"

I faced Hermes. Fear settled in the pit of my stomach, but I had something to say and this man—this god—whatever he was—was not going to stop me. "You're not concerned with the lives of regular people like me and my family. Fine. But I care. Hecate cares."

"Then where has she been?" he asked. "Seems she could have helped you at some earlier junction. She's let you travel across the world and offered you no help. This is what you fail to understand. Those of us who remain are so far removed from mortals. We do not burden ourselves with your troubles. We can't."

I hated that he had a valid point. Hecate hadn't intervened in all this time. But something had changed. Something had driven her to step in and offer me this chance to get my mom back, and I wasn't going to allow this dude to pretend like that didn't matter.

"You sleep in that bed," I said, measuring my words carefully. "You got this fire goin'. You live in a lighthouse and the people in a few towns over think your name is Mr. Herman." I almost laughed. "You're doing all of this, putting up this front— for what? You don't seem to mind if people around here think you're just the caretaker. I'm pretty sure you don't need a fireplace to keep you warm or a bed to sleep in. You're a god. You could be or do anything, and what you chose is to act like a regular person. If you're so disinterested in mortal life, why do you do it?"

Hermes sighed, and I braced myself for his reaction.

"Because I am numb, Briseis." He removed his hat and set it on the arm of his chair. He ran his hand over the top of his head, a gesture that struck me as uniquely human. "The lives of mortals begin and end in a breath for me. But you love and grieve and suffer and are joyous. Your lives burn so bright and yet so brief. You burn with the light of a million feelings, longing and angst, elation . . . love. What I have is despair. Unending hopelessness."

Persephone shifted where she stood.

Hermes glanced at her. "You have only begun to taste what eternity will offer you—a bitter fruit."

"Not tryna be disrespectful, but you sound a little jaded," I said.

"I am," Hermes said. "There is no shame in admitting that."

"We find purpose in the way we help others," Persephone said. "I've been helping my mortal family for generations. There is meaning in that. I think that's what Briseis means when she asks you if you have someone to love, someone to care for." She nodded at me. "You have so much time and you spend it hidden away? Doing—what?"

"I should find love?" Hermes huffed. "So that it can be snatched away from me in the blink of an eye? So that their presence can fade from my memory like they never existed to begin with?" Hermes raised an eyebrow. "Come find me when you've wandered the earth for eons, after everyone you've ever known or loved or cared for is in the underworld. Tell me how much purpose you find in that."

"Are you gonna cry about it?" Marie asked suddenly. She was fully awake and fully over listening to Hermes.

Hermes angled his head to look at her, too.

She marched up to him with no hint of hesitation. "I don't appreciate you hypnotizing me or whatever it was you did. Keep that staff out my face. Got it, Jafar?"

A smile crept across Hermes's lips. He was either about to snatch Marie out of her skin or he understood her *Aladdin* reference. I wasn't sure which was more terrifying.

"We need a boat," Marie said. "And some help figuring out which way to sail it. That would be helpful for what we're tryna do right now. You've been around forever, you're sad about it.

Got it. Completely understandable. Have you tried therapy in the last couple hundred years? It might help."

Persephone tilted her head back and looked up at the strobing light. "He's going to kill us all."

Hermes flicked his hand at her dismissively. "I'll do no such thing. You'll have a boat." He stood and marched up the spiral staircase until I couldn't see him anymore. "Sleep. Set sail in the morning," he called from somewhere above.

Circe rushed to Persephone's side and examined her arm. Marie was suddenly standing next to me.

"You were scared, huh?" she asked.

"Are you serious right now? I thought he was gonna end us. So yeah, I was scared."

"Sorry," Marie said. "But we don't have time for his pouting. We needed to know if he was going to help us or not so we could figure out what to do next." She shook her head. "I don't get it. All these gods do is sit around and be angry and jealous. Like damn. You could do something useful. Cure cancer or something. Instead, he's in here doing what? Playing lighthouse keeper?"

"You're not wrong," I said. "But they're playing by rules we don't know anything about. And honestly? I don't even care. He says he'll get us a boat. That's enough for now."

Marie sighed. "You're right, but I really wanna know where he got those fancy sandals. Where do you get gold sandals with wings?"

I laughed. "You were talking to him like he's not the god of—what does he do again?"

"Messenger god," Circe said. "Guardian of travelers. Did you see that sword?"

Persephone held up her arm. "I got a good look at it."

Circe winced. "No—I know it's just—remember the story, Seph."

Persephone went very still suddenly.

"Y'all are gonna have to clue me in," I said.

We huddled around the small table.

"That sword? Hermes lent it to Perseus to slay Medusa," Circe said. "The shoes, too." She squeezed her eyes shut and took off her glasses. "I'm losing my mind here. Is this really happening?" She was so knowledgeable, but it was one thing to know the stories and another to have their participants standing right in front of you. "We just have to keep it together. He said he'll get a boat in the morning, and we're just going to have to go with that because we don't have a choice."

I pulled Circe's moon clock out of my pocket and flipped it open. "We have five days left. Is that enough time?"

"We're close," Marie said, trying to reassure me. "We'll leave in the morning. We'll do what we came here to do and then we'll go home."

"Did you give her the information?" Persephone asked.

I looked to Marie. "What information?"

"It's just a backup plan," Marie said. "In case something happens I got all the paperwork together. All you have to do is show up at the airstrip at the time and date I tell you and you'll be able to get home. Alec will have something for you, too. Just check in with him. And Nyx will stay with you as long as you want her to."

I looked at each of them, waiting for someone to explain. "Y'all are planning for me to go home . . . alone?"

Circe avoided my gaze. "We have to plan for the worst even if we're hoping for the best. If something should happen, if you find yourself alone, you have to get home to Mo. I left very clear instructions with Khadijah. You'll have everything you need."

"Excuse me, but what am I missing?" I asked.

"It's just in case," Marie said.

Persephone turned and walked toward the fireplace. "We need to rest," she said. "Circe and Bri can take the bed, me and Marie will keep watch. I don't trust Hermes to take our safety into consideration. He's a little too reckless for me, and we don't know where Karter and the people he's with actually are or what they're capable of."

Marie put her hand over mine and kissed me gently on the cheek before nodding to Persephone. They went out the front door, and Circe began to pull the covers back from the bed.

Above me, I heard Hermes's heavy footsteps pacing the floor. He said we would have a ship, and I assumed that meant he was going to help us know which way to go. I couldn't help but picture us boarding a boat and Hermes taking off on his little golden sandals, laughing at how dumb we all were. I didn't want to take that chance. As Circe slipped into the bathroom, I quickly climbed the stairs.

The room at the top of the lighthouse was made entirely of glass. Hermes stood against the panes opposite me, and the light that guided ships to port spun in a slow circle between us. I didn't know how it was supposed to work, but I was pretty sure electric lights needed some kind of bulb or fixture and they definitely needed a power source. There wasn't a glass housing or wires or even a supporting structure of any kind. The light beamed from a free-floating orb that undulated in the center of the upper room.

"Magnificent, isn't it?" Hermes asked.

"I—I guess. I'm not really sure what I'm looking at, though."

"The Great Eye," he said.

"And I'm guessing it's more than just a light to help ships sail in from the sea."

Hermes nodded. "So much more, but that's a very convenient cover story."

I stared into the light and for a moment thought I saw something moving inside it—the hazy image of a figure. I blinked and it was gone. I took a step back. "It can't show us how to get to Aeaea but you've been there, so are you gonna show us the way?"

He set his hands on the railing that surrounded the light. "Yes. But if I'm being honest, I don't expect any of you to survive the journey."

A vise closed around my chest and a scratching at the window drew my attention to a gathering of roots, caked in dirt, that had climbed the outer wall and were trying desperately to make their way inside.

"Briseis?" Circe called from below us. "You good?"

"I'm fine," I said. "Be right down." I turned back to Hermes. "Don't worry about whether we'll make it or not. I just need to know you're going to put us on the right path."

He pulled his bottom lip between his teeth and rubbed his temple. "Why do it if you know you can't possibly survive? I see it so often in mortals—this drive to run headlong into the most perilous situations imaginable with no regard for the outcome."

"I care about the outcome," I said. "I want to get my mom and go home. I want to get back what was taken from me."

"You think you'll make it home?"

There was a part of me that knew the odds weren't good, but it didn't matter. "I have to try."

He thought for a moment and then looked to the light. "The Great Eye sees what has been and what is; it cannot see what will be. That is what the young man wanted."

"Karter?" I asked.

"He wanted to know the location of the island, but more than that he wished to know how this would end for him—and for you. But that is beyond the scope of my power. The future is something the Fates might have some grasp on. Perhaps he should have gone to seek them out instead."

I didn't want to think about the Fates spinning our lives out of golden thread in that dank grotto under the museum. I stared into Hermes's eyes. "Karter wanted to know what would happen to me? If you didn't tell him who you were, why would he share that with you?"

"He didn't. I plucked it from his head." He glanced at his staff, which was leaning against the glass. "I guard the Great Eye, but it is not the only power at my disposal. When I sent your friend to sleep down there, her last thoughts were of you."

My face flushed hot.

"But when I looked into the boy's head, he wanted to know a great many things—the location of the island, the ultimate fate of his mother, and what would become of the bond you and he shared if the two of you should survive this."

I turned away. It didn't matter. What he'd done was unforgivable.

Hermes fixed his gaze on me. "If you could look into the Great Eye and see something, anything, what would it be?"

I stared at the light. "Hecate has my mom. Can I—see her?"

Hermes extended his hand. Vines scratched at the windows and grew long thorns that screeched as they drug across the glass. I put my hand in his and he guided me close to the rail. He reached out and set his other hand on the orb.

My vision blurred, then went completely black. I stumbled back but felt a hand on my shoulder steadying me. When my head cleared I stood in a garden overflowing with black flowers. The sky above me was a pale purple, and there were no stars, no clouds, no moon or sun. The garden wasn't walled; the black foliage simply spilled across a rolling landscape in waves. A heavy, smoky scent filled my mouth and nose. My eyes stung and began to water. As I wiped at them with my hand, a low rumbling mixed with what sounded like rushing water drowned out the furious pounding of my own heart. On a rise, in the distance stood a woman in a tattered, flowing dress. She gazed up at the sky, her hands pressed against her own chest.

Mom.

I tried to move my legs but I was stuck to the spot where I stood.

"Mom!" I screamed.

Her head tilted to the side for a moment and then she turned her face back to the sky.

I pumped my legs and clawed at the air as I tried desperately to run to her, but I couldn't move. The entire landscape shifted. The sky became the ground and then all of it faded away. The last thing I saw before it went dark was Mom turning and walking away.

When I regained my focus I was back at the lighthouse, staring into the light, Hermes's hand on my shoulder.

"Where was she?" I asked through a torrent of tears. "What was that place?"

"I could not see it." He sounded troubled by that. "It may be a place meant to be hidden from prying eyes. You said Hecate gave you a full cycle of the moon to retrieve your mother?"

I nodded.

Hermes sighed. "Perhaps that's all she could offer. Even in her power she cannot hide a mortal soul from the one god who has dominion over the underworld for very long."

"And that would be who?"

"Hades," Hermes said with a deep, mournful sigh. "Be thankful you haven't run afoul of him. Pray you never do. He is the worst of my father's brothers, and time has managed to make a monster of him."

I could only picture cartoon images of the god of the underworld. Hermes seemed to be implying that Hades was still around, that he still existed, and worse yet, was vying with Hecate for Mom's soul.

"Your companions are waiting," Hermes said. "You should rejoin them and rest."

I turned and went downstairs as Hermes retook his spot at the window.

"Everything okay?" Circe asked as I fell into the bed next to her.

"No."

She fished around in her bag and pulled out a pack of tissues and handed it to me.

She fluffed the pillows under her head as I wiped my face.

"Look at us," Circe said. "We're laid up in Hermes's bed like it's no big deal. Even with everything I've seen, everything I know to be true, I never would have imagined this."

"There are about a thousand things I never could have imagined, and they've all happened to me in, like, two months." I sighed and lay back, staring up into the latticework of crossbeams over my head.

"You've been through a lot," she said, giving me a little half smile. "Too much, if we're being honest."

I rolled up onto my elbow. "Can I ask you something?"

She nodded.

"All that stuff you and Marie and Persephone were talking about, the what-ifs—you really don't think we'll get out of this in one piece, do you?"

She hesitated. "I don't want to scare you but, no. I don't. But I know we have to go. Not just for your mom, even though I'd still do it if that was the only goal, but also because maybe if we bring the pieces together, we can be rid of them." She settled into the blankets and sighed. "I used to feel selfish for wanting that. I was raised knowing the Heart was my responsibility, but over the years it's become such a heavy burden that I don't feel selfish for wanting to set that burden down. Look at what it has cost us. The Heart doesn't define who we are or what we're capable of. Without it, we still have our gifts and we still have each other. That's enough for me."

"Me too," I said.

Circe may not have had confidence that we would get through this, but I decided that I was going to do whatever I needed to do to keep us whole.

CHAPTER 16

When I awoke the next morning it took me a minute to remember where I was. The smell of coffee and the sound of hushed voices brought everything back. Circe and Marie sat at the table.

"Morning," Circe said.

Marie glanced at me, and I was struck by how sad she looked. Her eyes were red, like she'd been crying. I quickly got up and joined them at the table.

"What's wrong?" I asked, pulling a chair up next to her.

"Nothing," Marie said.

"Doesn't look like nothing," I said, closing my hand over hers. "Were you crying?"

She straightened up. "I don't know if you noticed, but Hermes is a dick."

"Oh," I said. "Yeah. What happened? He said something that upset you?"

"Keep in mind," Circe said. "He was right when he told us the gods are disconnected from regular people. Who knows how long he's been out here by himself, and I just think he hasn't had anyone actually speak to him in any meaningful way in a long time. He's . . . abrasive."

Marie huffed.

I pushed my chair back. "Where is he?"

Marie looked me over, and the sadness was washed away by her wide smile. "You gonna cuss out an actual god over me?"

"Yeah," I said.

"I'm flattered," Marie said. "But I don't think you need to worry. He's getting us a boat. We'll be out of here soon, and hopefully I'll never have to see him or his ugly little sandals ever again."

I'd let it go until I saw him, then I'd probably cuss him out anyway. I pictured him slicing me up with that gold sword he had on him the night before and shuddered. Even still, seeing Marie upset bothered me.

I went to the small bathroom and brushed my teeth, splashed my face with water, and put my hair in a puff high on top of my head. In my rush to pack I'd neglected to bring a bonnet. I laughed to myself. I still needed to take care of my hair even if I was on a collision course with a bunch of gods and possibly killer mermaids. When I came out Marie was waiting right outside the door. She slung her arm around my shoulder and kissed me gently on the cheek.

Circe picked up her bag. "We already loaded everything onto the boat. I brought your bag in case you wanted to change. I thought you'd want to get moving." She handed me my backpack.

"Thanks," I said. "So we got the boat, then? That's good."

"'Boat' is kind of the wrong word, don't you think?" Marie

asked, glancing at Circe, who only shrugged. "C'mon," said Marie. "Wait till you see this."

I tossed my bag on the table and followed Marie and Circe up the staircase to the top of the lighthouse. The Great Eye was dim and it hovered in the center of the glass-enclosed upper room. I looked out over the bluff and caught sight of the boat. Marie was right. "Boat" wasn't exactly the right word.

A sailing vessel rocked lazily in the water. Black sails flapped in the stiff breeze as Hermes and Persephone stood on the deck talking amongst themselves.

I turned to Circe and Marie. "I don't know who we think we are but this is some *Pirates-of-the-Caribbean*-level stuff."

"Who's gonna handle that thing?" Marie asked, grinning. "Because I'm low-key interested in being Captain Hook. I know some sea shanties."

"And why do you know pirate songs?" I asked.

"Long story," Marie said. "My favorite one goes like this." She cleared her throat and puffed out her chest like she was about to belt out an entire song at the top of her lungs.

"Do not start," Circe said. "I will kick you off the ship if you start singing."

Marie grinned devilishly. "You mean, make me walk the plank?"

Circe rolled her eyes.

Persephone waved as she caught sight of us from the ship's deck.

"We'll be ready to go in fifteen minutes," Circe said. "Persephone has some sailing experience. We should be able to manage it." She started back down the stairs, then paused. "Marie, could you pull the car around the side of the lighthouse? I'll make sure we didn't leave anything behind and meet y'all out there."

Marie squeezed my hand, and she and Circe left. I lingered for a minute, looking out over the water as it broke against the ship's belly. There was nothing for as far as I could see. I began to think of Mom in that far-off place. She'd been looking at the sky, too, and I hoped she knew that I was coming for her, that no matter what I had to do or what I had to face, I would find her and bring her home—or die trying. I quickly turned and went back downstairs.

I tossed my bag over my shoulder, readjusted my glasses, and stepped toward the door when suddenly, my ears popped like they had when we'd taken off from the airport in Red Hook. Hermes was seated in the chair by the fireplace like he'd been there all along. My heart almost jumped out of my chest.

He stared into the hearth. "You said you were friends with the boy. Karter."

I held on to the wall to steady myself. "Yeah. I—I was."

"Do you believe he is beyond redemption?" He didn't look at me as he spoke.

"He set me up," I said. "He helped his mom manipulate me and my parents. He knew what she was doing and he let it happen."

"That's not what I asked." Hermes finally turned to look at me. His brown eyes, wide and searching, held none of the smugness or indifference he'd shown the night before. "Do you think he can be forgiven?"

"I—I don't think—" I stopped. "Why does it matter to you?"

219

He stood and closed the gap between us in two steps. My pulse shot up. Towering over me I realized how much he had in common with Hecate. The tall frame, the large hands, the long arms. And somehow, he was smaller than she had been.

He rested his hand on my shoulder, and the weight of it almost made my knees buckle. He drew it back. "I sometimes forget how fragile mortals are. Forgive me." He straightened up. "You have a perilous journey ahead of you. I do wish you the best."

It was a hollow gesture. *He* didn't believe we'd make it, so wishing us the best was kind of ridiculous. "What did you say to Marie?" I asked. "She was really upset."

"I was under the impression that she'd accepted her fate."

"Her fate? What's that supposed to mean?"

He was quiet for a moment before answering. "I think it's best not to say." He moved toward the stairs. "The sirens do not take prisoners," he said, changing the subject. "They do not compromise. They will lure you to the water's edge and drag you to a watery grave without hesitation."

"Um. Okay," I said, a little confused. "I was kind of hoping you'd have something else for me. Circe said something about a lyre. Do you know where I can get one by any chance?"

Hermes raised one bushy brow. He glanced around the room. "I'm sorry to say I haven't been in possession of that particular object in a thousand years. I suppose you'll have to use Odysseus's method."

"Remind me of what that was," I said.

"Tie yourselves to the mast and hope for the best."

I blinked and caught a glimpse of his gold sandals as he ascended the staircase and disappeared.

Outside, a narrow stone pathway snaked around to the bluff, and a rickety staircase made from weathered wood and rusted metal rails led down to the shore. I descended the steps and stood among the rocks slicked with green moss and sea silt as Circe and Marie climbed into a small dinghy tethered at the water's edge.

"Ready?" Marie called.

I climbed in beside them, and Marie rowed us out to the ship. We scrambled up a ladder and onto the deck.

I'd never been on a boat bigger than the ferries that criss-crossed the East River. The ship Hermes secured for us looked like Blackbeard was gonna pop out at any moment and tell us to swab the deck. I heard the unmistakable beating of the Absyrtus Heart coming from somewhere below me.

"Here ya go, Marie," Circe said. "You wanted to be Captain Hook? Have at it."

Marie grinned. She looked around the ship and scrunched her nose up. "Everybody gotta say the word 'matey.' That's the rule. Ahoy, matey!"

"Nobody ever actually said that," Persephone said as she emerged from a small room at the front of the ship.

"You'd know," Circe said.

"Wait," said Marie, glancing back and forth between Circe and Persephone. "I have at least seven questions."

I laughed despite the sense of dread that had been growing in the pit of my stomach since we got there.

"When were you a pirate?" Marie clasped her hands together in front of her and stared Persephone right in the face. "You weren't gonna tell me that? You know how much I love pirates."

"That's why I didn't tell you. You'd never shut up about it."

Marie crossed her arms over her chest. "Rude. We're gonna talk about that, but right now, I wanna know where Hermes got this boat. Because it looks like he stole it from Jack Sparrow. What is happening here?"

"Seriously," I said. "Shouldn't we use something more—I don't know—modern?"

"Something with an engine?" Marie chimed in.

Persephone huffed. "Modern doesn't necessarily mean better. Hermes knows these waters. He has assured me that this kind of vessel is much better suited for what we're attempting."

"So he told you where to go?" I asked.

Persephone nodded. "The Great Eye can't see Aeaea, but it can see the rocky outcroppings where the sirens dwell. When we approach, we have to let the wind carry us in as quietly as possible. A modern ship is too loud."

"So, what's the timeline here?" I asked. "How long will it take us to get there?"

"We should reach the *Sirenum scopuli* by nightfall," said Circe. "If we can get on to the island around that same time we should make camp and wait till morning to go any farther."

"We've got provisions for several days, and we have backup in case that runs out," Persephone said. She glanced toward the stack of our belongings. Circe's traveling apothecary was tucked away there. I realized she meant we could grow some food if we needed to, and honestly, I was embarrassed that I hadn't considered using my power for something like that. I was too focused on getting a few tendrils of Devil's Pet around Karter's neck.

Persephone got to work uncoiling ropes and inspecting the wide swaths of sail while I helped move the rest of our belongings into the room at the front of the ship. Inside, there was a single bed set into an alcove and a small table. The windows were made of green and blue stained glass, and as the sun slanted through, it washed the room in a dappled, emerald light. I imagined a captain and her shipmates sitting around counting their treasure, plotting their next adventure. We weren't sailors or pirates. We were two people with the ability to control plants and an immunity to poison and two immortals, one of whom was my girlfriend. There was a lot of strange and wonderful power between the four of us, but I still wasn't confident it would be enough.

I finished loading our stuff and rejoined Persephone on deck. She'd drawn up the sails, but as she stared at them they barely moved. The breeze that had kicked up earlier that morning was completely gone.

"What now?" Marie asked.

Circe went to the captain's quarters and came back clutching a small vial with a cork stopper, something from her miniature apothecary. She held it between her fingers and gave it a shake.

"*Cytisus scoparius*," she said, tossing it to me.

I held it up and peered inside. "Common name, broom." I'd come across the description in the big book where Selene had illustrated a thousand poison plants in vivid detail. I handed it back to her. "What are you going to do with it?"

223

"Broom can raise the winds. If you have enough of it you can raise hurricane-force gales. Usually it's used for purification rituals or protection spells." She uncorked the bottle and sprinkled a few minuscule pieces of the dried plant into the palm of her hand. "But in this freshly grown form it can be used to stir the air around you. It's helpful for sailing on a windless day."

She breathed deep and the pieces sprouted yellow and orange blooms and angled grass-green stems. Circe quickly snapped off the petals and tossed them high into the air above her head, where they blew apart and rained down on us like confetti. A breeze gusted across the deck, scattering the broken petals to the water. A gale, with enough force to violently rock the boat, descended on us. I grabbed ahold of Marie to steady myself as the sails billowed and snapped and the ship lurched forward.

Persephone set a heading and we sailed away from the bluff in the bright light of the morning sun. I watched the lighthouse shrink, but even at a distance, I could see Hermes standing in the upper room. Messenger god, protector of travelers. I wondered if he'd done all he could do for us.

The novelty of being on a wannabe pirate ship wore off as soon as the nausea set in. The sway of the boat was gentle but the way my stomach flip-flopped around inside me was not. I stayed close to the rail in case I needed to throw up, gripping it until my hands ached. The moist air in my face helped, but the sick feeling continued to roll over me in waves.

Marie stood beside me, her hand on the small of my back. "You get seasick?"

I shrugged. "I guess? I've never been on a boat like this."

Persephone joined us and slipped the slender finger of a freshly skinned ginger root into my hand. "Powdered is better, but you look like you could use some relief sooner than later. Bite off a chunk. It'll be a little bitter, but the fastest way to get it into your system is just to chew it."

I bit into the pale yellow flesh and chewed it as fast as I could. The stringy pieces stuck between my teeth, but almost as soon as I'd finished the first chunk I started to feel a little better. I bit off another, wincing as the bitter taste stung my tongue. I didn't care if it burned out my entire throat, I needed the relief.

Persephone patted me on the shoulder and went back to staring off into the distance from the front of the ship through a pair of binoculars. Circe sat on the short steps that led to the area belowdecks. It was empty down there except for the cages containing the Absyrtus Heart in two of its many forms. I could hear the rhythmic beating even as the constant rush of wind battered the billowing sails.

In the early afternoon, everyone ate but I still couldn't stomach anything heavier than some fruit and bottled water. Persephone produced four pairs of noise-canceling headphones she'd purchased before we left New York.

"These are the best ones money can buy," she said, handing us each a set. "Nothing gets in. Try it."

I slipped them over my ears and immediately the world went silent. I could see Marie's mouth moving but heard absolutely nothing. I pulled one of the earpieces away from the side of my head and the sound came rushing in like a wave.

"As soon as the rocks come into view, we should put them

on," said Circe. "Persephone will let us know when she sees them."

I nodded. "What do we do if the sirens try to come onto the ship?" All I could picture was the pottery shard and the figures being pulled overboard.

Circe and Persephone exchanged glances.

"We just have to try and get as close to the shore as possible and in silence," Circe said.

"Seems like a solid plan," Marie said, sarcasm dripping from every word. "Just be real quiet. Cool. Why didn't anybody else think of that?"

"I know being a smart-ass is just your way, but it's not helpful right now." Circe seemed annoyed. "If you have a better idea, I'd love to hear it. If not, I don't know, you could always just be quiet."

Marie stayed quiet but she wasn't happy about it. She pressed her lips together and let her gaze wander to the deck under her feet. The stress of this journey was testing our patience.

I gently nudged Marie. "I have an idea, but I don't know if it'll work."

"Let's hear it," Persephone said, shooting Marie a quick glance.

"Auntie—" I stopped short. It had just slipped out. Auntie. A title I didn't know if Circe wanted or needed or deserved. Not because she wasn't all the things an auntie should be: concerned with my safety but not in a way that kept her from letting me do things I probably shouldn't, kind to a fault. But she'd been all those things to me in a little less than a month. It was enough time for me to understand that I cared about her and she cared about me, too. I thought of my auntie Leti and what she might have done in this situation. Circe reminded me of her in a way. Maybe that's why I'd slipped up. Or maybe it wasn't a slipup at all.

I looked up and met Circe's gaze. Her eyes were glassy with tears, her bottom lip pulled between her teeth. She was trying her hardest not to cry.

"I'm sorry," I said quickly, heat rising in my face.

"Don't be," she said quietly.

I could almost hear Mo's voice in my head. I didn't have to choose. I could have both. "Auntie, do you have Devil's Pet in that case you brought?"

She scrambled to her feet and rushed off to get it, batting at her eyes. When she returned, she held a single bloodred thorn. She set it in my hand and I walked to the rail closest to us. As I breathed deep and let the warmth flow through my fingertips, the Devil's Pet burst to life. An entire gathering of the poisonous vines materialized from the single thorn. They writhed in my palm like the tentacles of some monstrous sea creature, doubling in length and thickness with every breath I took. When they were too heavy to hold, I set them on the deck and they branched out like arms, like fingers. Grasping at the rails they hauled themselves up and over. They covered the outside of the hull in hundreds of thick offshoots, sprouting crimson thorns the size of icicles and serrated purple leaves tipped in deadly poison.

"Why didn't we think of this?" Persephone asked, staring at Circe, who just grinned.

I let the Devil's Pet form a protective armor of deadly thorns that encased the entire ship, slithering across the decks and covering nearly every square inch of the exterior.

"If sirens do come up the side, they won't be happy," I said.

"They sure won't," said Marie. "And I thought I was cold blooded. You got me beat."

Persephone returned to her perch on the upper deck, and as the afternoon faded and the sky turned fiery, she called down to us.

"We're approaching something in the water."

I rushed up the short flight of stairs and she handed me the binoculars. I peered through and spotted in the distance three distinct rocky outcroppings and beyond them, more sea.

"I see the rocks, but isn't the island supposed to be right behind them? I don't see anything out there." I lowered the binoculars. "I know it's cloaked, but shouldn't we see . . . something?"

"Look again," Persephone said as Circe and Marie joined us on the upper deck.

I took another look, and this time I spotted something strange beyond the rocks. The air was blurry. The way it looks when the sun is beaming off the concrete in the hottest part of the summer, like the air had been turned to shimmering liquid.

"What is that?" I asked, passing the binoculars to Circe.

As she peered through she gasped. "That, my beautiful niece, is Aeaea."

"You sure?" I asked.

Circe handed the binoculars to Marie and turned to Persephone. "It's cloaked. Just like we thought, but it's there. I can feel it."

I stared into the distance as the sun sank lower on the horizon.

"It's nearly sunset and we're almost to the point of no return," Persephone said. "Let's get our headphones on and prepare for the worst—"

"But hope for the best," Circe said quickly.

The mood had shifted. There was a renewed sense of hope. We were so close.

"We'll have to steer directly through the outcroppings," Persephone said. "Circe, we need a big gust and then you need to call down the broom so we can keep the sails as still as we can. Once we're clear, send them up again and get us to shore as quickly as possible."

Circe nodded, set her headphones over her ears, and went to the deck to do as she was asked.

"Stay together, stay quiet." Persephone adjusted her own headphones and went to take her place at the wheel.

Marie gripped my hand and led me to the main deck, where we watched as Circe brought in a gale-force wind, then called down the broom, letting it drift silently to the deck. The sails deflated as we glided closer to the rocks. The sun dipped below the horizon, and within a few minutes the fiery sky had turned almost purple. I touched the plastic cups of the headphones, hoping they would do their job.

Without the wind pushing it forward the ship slowed to a crawl. The hazy mirage of rippled air moved like a hulking, shadowy beast just beyond the rocks. My heart thudded in my ears and stirred a sense of terror in me. I looked down at my feet—at the boards of the deck. In my headphones I could hear my own heart, but anyone else within earshot would have heard the beating of another. When I raised my head, Circe was staring straight at me as if she'd come to the same sickening realization.

The Heart was beating like a drum—announcing our presence to whatever creatures prowled the Black Sea.

From the corner of my eye, Persephone's flailing arms caught my attention. She motioned frantically to the water, and as I raced to the ship's rail, I caught a glimpse of long fishlike tails, streaked with green and blue bioluminescent markings, cutting through the water at impossible speeds. I blinked, and a dozen more appeared just beneath the surface—heading straight for us.

CHAPTER 17

Something impacted the hull below the waterline and the ship shuddered under me. I struggled to see in the encroaching dark, but as more tails joined the swarm gathering at the side of the ship the black waters lit up, casting a hazy glow all around us.

The sirens darted through the water and the ship began to rock from side to side. Marie grabbed my arm and yanked me away from the rail, her terrified eyes wide and black. She pushed me against the center mast, and I gripped it to keep from sliding across the tilting deck.

Persephone came scrambling down as Circe grew another stalk of broom in the palm of her hand. She was going to try and get us moving again. No sense in trying to stay quiet anymore. We'd already been noticed. Circe plucked off the blooms and prepared to launch them into the sky when the ship listed violently to the side. Her legs twisted under her and she tumbled across the deck. Marie was at her side in an instant, catching her around the waist and helping her steady herself.

"We're gonna tip over!" I shouted.

Marie didn't even glance at me. She couldn't hear me as

I screamed at her to grab onto something. None of them could hear me. I focused on the tendrils of Devil's Pet laced through the rails. I willed them to grow. They writhed around the ship, their red thorns jutting out, ready to impale anything that might have tried to climb up.

Circe gathered another handful of broom and got it up in the air, calling down the wind, but it wasn't as strong as it had been before. The breeze puffed out the sails and we lurched forward, but it was at a fraction of the speed. Circe's gaze darted from the rail to me and back again. She was absolutely terrified.

Persephone wrestled with the wheel as she struggled to keep the ship in line. Suddenly, something slammed into me from behind. A sharp pain rocketed through my right hip as I hit the deck with a thud. I instinctively touched my back where the pain was the worst and my hand came away wet. Blood? I struggled to see clearly, examining my hand. Not blood. Water.

Circe stood to my left, but she didn't move. She wasn't looking at me. She was staring ahead, and as I followed her gaze, I let out a scream that only I could hear. A siren had made its way to the main deck.

It drug itself along the wooden boards, its webbed hands slapping at the deck. It stopped and coiled its long, narrow tail under itself so that it could raise its torso into an upright position and stare at us.

I scrambled back as far as the confines of the ship would allow. The siren's tail flexed like a muscle covered in slick evergreen scales, the wide fin pressed into the deck, allowing the creature to steady itself. Its upper torso was humanlike, but this creature was not some fairy tale sea-princess. Slits between the flesh of its ribs opened and closed as it heaved. Its webbed fingers ended in sharp bony protrusions. A clear membrane closed over the eyes as it blinked, and a scant layer of thin dark hair covered its head in patches. This was the creature all the stories said sailors feared, and I understood why.

Marie moved in front of me, and the siren's head snapped up. It crouched down, set one hand on the deck, and launched itself toward Marie, who in turn propelled herself forward. They collided and tumbled to the floor. In the chaos of limbs and thrashing tail, something bounced out and landed in front of me—a pair of black headphones.

I searched for Marie's face in the tangle of tail and clawed hands. The siren suddenly drew back, panting, gills opening and closing like a dozen mouths on both sides of its chest, but this time its mouth also opened and closed slowly. Was it speaking?

"Marie!" I screamed.

She glanced back at me, the veins in her neck bulging, as if she were straining, fighting against something with every ounce of strength she had. I frantically looked to see if the siren was hurting her, but it had retreated, its mouth still moving. It tilted its head and caught my gaze. It bared two rows of jagged teeth in a hideous smile. And then, without warning, it propelled itself over the edge of the ship and to my horror, Marie dove in after it.

I scrambled to my feet and rushed to the rail. Marie's hair, white as snow, disappeared under the surface. I ripped off my glasses, put my foot on the rail, and launched myself over the side of the ship without a second thought.

Every muscle in my body spasmed as I hit the water feetfirst. The cold was numbing and I had to fight to keep myself from instinctively inhaling the murky water. I gripped the headphones to keep them in place as I kicked in the inky blackness. My vision without my glasses was bad enough on its own, but trying to see through the water was nearly impossible. Flashes of light darted around me. I kicked hard, pushing myself above the water where I gasped, sucking in a chestful of air. The hull of the ship loomed high over my head and the latticework of Devil's Pet reached toward me, gripping my waist. I stuck my head below the water and caught a glimpse of Marie—in the embrace of the same siren who'd been on the deck. It was pulling her deeper into the water. She didn't fight back.

I filled my lungs with air and dipped below the surface. I swam toward them and realized suddenly that the Devil's Pet was pushing me along, faster than I could have managed on my own.

Another siren came careening toward me in a streak of yellow. I flicked my wrist, and a new offshoot of Devil's Pet branched off and caught her just above her fin. It sliced through the scales, filling the water with the creature's blood. Its mouth twisted into a hideous scowl and it turned to try and disentangle itself. I kicked toward Marie, my lungs burning, my movements stifled by the cold. I thrust out my hand, hoping it was enough of a signal to the Devil's Pet. It was. A new offshoot sliced through the water and wrapped itself around Marie, yanking her away from one of the sirens. When she was close enough I grabbed hold of her and the vines reeled us in like fish on a line.

As we broke the water's surface, I coughed and gasped. Marie clawed at the vines, trying desperately to break free.

"Marie, stop!" I screamed, holding her tight. "Please!"

There was a sudden splash to my immediate right, and my head was yanked to the side. Where there had been only silence, now there was a cacophony of sound. Circe and Persephone screaming from somewhere over my head, the splashing of water, the groan of the ship as it listed in the choppy sea, Marie's frantic breathing, the thudding of the Heart in the belly of the ship, and the siren song.

The stories didn't describe it fully. There's no way they could have. The sound was like a familiar song being hummed in unison by a hundred voices, a downpour of rain, and an almost electrical buzzing all rolled into one. There were no words, just sound, and suddenly the only thing I wanted was to be below the waves in the cold embrace of the sea.

My mind went blank. There was nothing but relief. Everything faded away.

Circe's voice cut through the silence and the dark. "Briseis, give me your hand! Please, baby! Reach for me!"

I opened my eyes to see Circe leaning over the rail as I was being hauled up. I reached out and the Devil's Pet pushed me the rest of the way. She grabbed me and pulled me onto the deck, where my legs went out from under me. I shivered uncontrollably as Circe cradled me in her arms.

"Marie," I said. "Where is she?"

"We got her," Persephone said from somewhere. "She's okay."

"What's happening?" I asked. My vision was still hazy and my teeth chattered together as I tried to sit up.

"The sirens are retreating," Circe said. She helped me to my feet as Marie sat in a daze. I went to her and put my arm around her shoulder.

A sound still lingered in the air. Not the siren sound, not the thudding of the Absyrtus Heart, but something else entirely. Persephone had removed her headphones and was listening intently.

"What is that sound?" I asked.

"Look," Persephone said.

I cautiously walked to the rail to see that the sirens hadn't just decided to leave, they'd been drawn off by something. They retreated to the rocks and sat atop them in all their scaly, slimy hideousness. Our ship was now moving slowly past them, to the shore of an island that had appeared out of nowhere. The sandy shoreline of a small cove came into view. Beyond it, a thick, almost tropical-looking forest, and on the shore, in the breaking water, stood a woman playing a stringed instrument—the origin of the mysterious new sound.

"The sirens fled when she started playing," Circe said.

"Who is she?" I asked.

Persephone shrugged. "I don't know."

The ship glided into the cove, and Persephone dropped the anchor and secured the sails. "I'll take the dinghy to shore first. Stay here until I get back."

"What?" Circe said. "No. I'm going with you."

"No," Persephone said firmly. There wouldn't be any further discussion. Persephone went to the side of the ship and lowered the dinghy into the water, then descended the ladder and rowed to shore.

Marie joined me at the rail and tossed a blanket around me. She handed me my glasses and I slipped them back on.

"Thanks," I said. "Are you okay?"

She nodded. "I'm so sorry. My headphones came off and it was like I didn't have control of myself. All I wanted to do was go into the water."

"The same thing happened to me. I guess the stories were true. Siren songs are no joke."

"Mermaids are not to be messed with," Marie said softly. She turned to me. "You saved me."

"I couldn't let these mer-hos just take you away," I said. "I don't wanna have to tell people you left me for a fish."

Marie smiled and held my hand to her lips, kissing it gently and pulling me close. We watched as Persephone made the short trip to shore. Circe crossed her arms over her chest and tapped her foot anxiously.

Persephone allowed the dinghy to come to rest on the shore. As she got out and approached the woman, she stopped in her tracks, her entire body rigid. It could only have been in response to the woman's immense height. Persephone herself was tall, but like Hecate, like Hermes, like the Fates, this woman towered over her by what I guessed was at least two feet.

"What is happening?" Circe mumbled.

Persephone and the woman spoke for several minutes, then Persephone motioned to the ship. The woman glanced toward us and nodded. Persephone got in the small boat and rowed back to us.

"Come on," she called from the bottom of the ladder. "Leave our belongings. We'll come back out for them."

We climbed down and piled into the boat. Persephone rowed us to shore without saying a word. As we reached the shore and climbed out the woman approached us and extended her hand to me. I hesitantly allowed her to help me out of the dinghy. My hand looked comically small tucked inside hers, and she didn't help me out as much as she lifted me like a baby doll and set me in the sand. After I was out, she pulled the dinghy onto the shore in one smooth motion, like it was made of paper.

We stood in front of her, and as I stared into her face I knew she was not mortal. She was not like me or Circe, but she was not like Marie or Persephone either. Her golden brown skin glowed from within. Her hair was black as the night sky, and her eyes . . . her eyes were the color of fall, all shades of brown and gold at once. She wore a gown that dusted the ground at her feet, its hem singed. She held a stringed instrument, like a small harp, in her left hand.

"How did you get the sirens to leave us alone?" I asked.

The woman sighed. "They cannot stand the sound of music more beautiful than their own." She plucked at the strings of the instrument. "They have forgotten who they were before. Forgive them."

I wouldn't be doing that, but I wasn't gonna say that to her.

"I was asked to make sure you arrived safely," said the woman. "But I'm afraid I can offer no further assistance."

Circe glanced at Persephone.

"Hecate asked her to come," Persephone said. "She possesses Orpheus's lyre. The only thing that can keep the sirens at bay."

Circe's mouth fell open. Marie took a step back. I stared at the instrument she held.

"Hecate is the mother of us all, in a way," said the woman. "Not as literally as it applies to your family, but she is the oldest among us to still exist. I owe her an incalculable debt. When I was taken she was the first to know. No one is free from her watchful eye, not even Hades himself."

Hades.

Another name I had become all too familiar with.

"You—you're—I can't believe it," Circe stammered.

Circe, who was normally so sure of herself, was at a complete loss.

Now was not the time to remind everyone, once again, that I wasn't up to speed on the relevant mythology, but I felt like I should've known who this woman was supposed to be. Marie pressed her mouth to my ear and murmured the answer.

"Persephone."

Not our Persephone, but the original Persephone. Her story was one I was familiar with. She was the woman who'd become the object of Hades's obsession, the woman he'd kidnapped and kept in the underworld for half the year.

She smiled and set the lyre in the sand. "Come. Make your camp on the beach."

"We can't," I said. "We have to keep moving. There are other people coming here. They'll go after the Heart and we have to get to it first. We can't stop."

"They made landfall on the other side of the island," the woman said.

My heart sank into the pit of my stomach. They were already so far ahead of us. Did they already have the last piece? Was that possible?

"They landed on the other side of the island?" Marie asked. "Are there sirens over there, too?"

"No," the goddess Persephone said. "But there is something equally dangerous. I watched it smash their ship on the rocks. Four survivors came ashore, though I'm uncertain if there were others aboard. Three adults and a young man. They haven't left. I assume they are dead."

I struggled to reconcile the sudden dull ache of loss with the anger that coursed through me like poison. If Karter had been on that ship he could be dead now and it didn't sit right with me. I thought that's what I wanted—to see him pay for his part in what happened to Mom, but I didn't feel relief at the possibility that his body could be floating in these cursed waters. I felt only sadness. But if he'd been one of the four who made it to shore he might still be out there, which meant there was still time to find him and make him answer the only question I had—how could he have hurt me and my family like that after everything we'd shared? I didn't just want revenge, I wanted answers.

The woman gazed back at the tree line. "This place was once barren. Nothing grew here until the original Circe was exiled to this land. What she created was meant for her alone. The only people who have thrived here were people like her, people like Medea and her children. The rest fell victim to the nature of this place. Poison lingers in the air, in the foliage, in the very soil at your feet." She looked us over. "This will not be a problem for you, but make no mistake—the path is treacherous in ways that no poison could ever measure up to in its ability to change you."

"So Medea *was* here," I said. "She lived here?"

"She did. And she remains here still," said Persephone. "Her grave is at the very center of the island."

A hush fell over us and we all turned our gaze to the trees. The gravity of the situation wrapped itself around us like the embrace of wayward vines—our foremother's remains rested in this place. This was hallowed ground.

"We should get our bags from the ship," said Circe. "Maybe make a fire?"

I glanced out at the water. "Is it safe for us to be going back and forth? The sirens are still out there."

"They will stay where they are until morning," the goddess said. "I'd make sure to retrieve your things well before then." She turned her back to us and began to walk away.

"Wait," I said. "You're leaving? How will we get past them when we leave?"

She turned and glanced over her shoulder. "*If* you make it back here, I'll be sure to meet you." She gave the lyre a little shake and continued on her path until she melded with the shadows at the farthest end of the beach and disappeared.

"They really don't care about us at all," I said. "They can just walk away whenever they want and pretend it's because of some ancient rules. Maybe they just don't give a shit."

"She saved us from the sirens," Circe offered.

"They could do more," I said. "They're gods. They can't help us get where we need to go?"

"I don't know if they can or if they think what they've done already is enough, but all we can really depend on in this moment is one another." Circe gave me a tight smile. "I think that's enough."

Circe and our Persephone made two trips back to the ship to bring ashore our things and the two cages. As Circe set them in the sand the Heart's pulse ticked up.

Marie made a fire and we spread out blankets in the dry sand above the tide line. The trees behind me groaned and creaked as they leaned toward us. Snakelike offshoots of vines the color of blood slithered out. I reached out to them and they encircled my wrist. A tingling sensation revealed them to be poisonous—deadly. It was somewhere between the toxicity of belladonna and oleander, judging by the amount of cold on my skin. As I recalled the toxic effect of the oleander, images of my mom's terrified face blazed bright in my head. I shut my eyes, disentangled myself from the vines, and tried to push the thoughts away, but they replayed on a nightmarish loop. A hand rested gently on my shoulder, and I turned to find Marie kneeling at my side.

"I know you're not okay, so I won't ask you that," she said. "But is there anything I can do for you right now? You hungry?"

"A little," I said. "And I'm still cold."

Circe and Persephone joined us on the blanket as Marie stoked the flames and the warmth engulfed me. Circe opened a cooler we'd brought along and handed me a water and a sandwich she must have picked up the day before at one of our stops along the coast.

"It's lamb on rye," she said. She tossed me a bag of chips.

Marie took one bite, rewrapped it, and tossed it back in the cooler.

"Not up to your high standards?" Persephone teased.

"Taste it," she said. "Tastes like ass."

I laughed. "Can't be that bad." I took a bite and was immediately proven wrong. "I think it got wet." The bread was soggy, and the meat had a pinkish tinge that made my stomach turn over.

"Here," Circe said. She handed me a small vial that contained the shriveled remnants of some kind of leaf. "See what you can do with that."

I uncorked it and dumped the pieces into my hand. I concentrated as hard as I could, and from my palm sprouted a tangle of pale roots and then the pencil-thin trunk of a small tree. I set it in the sand, knowing it wasn't the right soil for it to flourish, but it would have to work for now. It pushed up to the night sky, and I sank my fingertips into the sand beneath the short wiry tree with green fruit that darkened the longer I kept my hand near its root. *Persea americana.* Avocado.

We ate until we were stuffed and sleepy. The terrible events of the journey to the island began to fade. Persephone took first watch, and I curled up next to Marie as I waited for sleep to find me.

CHAPTER 18

We don't have a dog.

That was my first thought when I heard the noise, before my eyes fluttered open, before I remembered that we weren't at home, and that of course we didn't have a dog because Mom was deathly allergic. Mom wasn't there at all because . . .

I opened my eyes.

A furry, snorting snout, wet and wriggling, was just inches from my face. The musty smell of dirt invaded my nose, and I yelped as I scrambled to my feet. Persephone caught me by the arm and slipped her hand over my mouth.

"Be quiet," she whispered. "Do not make any sudden moves."

The boar rooting around our camp was the size of a small car. Its stubby legs sat atop jagged hooves, and a pair of razor-sharp tusks curled out of its upper lip. Its beady black eyes focused on the ground in front of it where it was turning up the dirt.

Marie still slept soundly on the blanket. Circe stirred, and Persephone slowly reached for her ankle. As her eyes opened she rolled to a sitting position and looked around.

"What the—"

"Shhh!" Persephone chided. She roughly pressed her index finger to her lips in a plea for silence.

Circe reached over and shook Marie, who woke up, saw the creature, and got up so quickly all I saw was her terrified face, and then she was standing behind me.

"What the hell is this?" Marie looked around frantically. "A pig?"

"A boar, and they are aggressive," Persephone said. "Very, very aggressive. We need to get moving anyway."

Circe slowly moved to her case of poisons and pocketed several vials. She picked up the two cages and handed one to Persephone. We slowly packed up everything that could fit in two backpacks—one for me and one for Marie—and left the rest on the beach. We backed away to the tree line as the giant boar continued to sniff around.

"I knew we were going to come across some strange stuff, but hairy pigs wasn't on my bingo card of weird things we might run into," I said. Mermaids and living gods hadn't been on that list either, but there we were. Suddenly, giant wild pigs didn't seem so strange.

"The original Circe turned Odysseus's men into boars," Persephone said. "She supposedly changed them back, but now I wonder . . ." She trailed off, lost in her thoughts.

I took out the moon clock from the side pocket of my bag. The waxing gibbous phase was almost over, and the full moon was set to rise. We only had a day and a half left.

I took the vial of Living Elixir and the invisibility potion from my bag and put them in my pocket for safekeeping. Doubt crept in and seeded itself in my gut once more. We weren't even a 100 percent sure the last piece of the Heart was on the island. Everything had led to this, but the other pieces had made their way to the ends of the earth—why should this last piece be any different? If it wasn't there, we had no time to make other plans. It was all or nothing.

Persephone looked at the sky through the canopy of leaves high above us, then back at the shoreline before it disappeared from view.

"We'll keep a steady heading," she said. "We don't have a map, so we might have to come back across the island in a kind of grid. Just pay attention to the trees. If they start to thin we're probably heading to the coast, not the center of the island."

We all nodded in silent agreement and started our trek into the forest in search of the last piece of the Absyrtus Heart.

The forest on Aeaea was unlike anything I'd ever seen. The tightly packed trees at the Ravine back in Brooklyn, even the vast forest behind the house in Rhinebeck, were nothing compared to this place. It was full of foliage that didn't belong on the same continent much less crowded together on an island in the middle of the Black Sea.

Ancient olive trees stood like sentries, their twisted, gnarled trunks a testament to their age. They'd almost certainly been there when Circe and Medea roamed these woods, and now they were watching us follow paths that no mortal had seen in thousands of years. Alongside the olive groves were massive Antarctic beech trees draped in damp moss, towering cannonball trunks with fruited bark, and haunting skeletal cypress. I knew them all, but the island sheltered species of trees and flowers that weren't as easy for me to identify.

Ivy, Dutchman's-Pipe, towering willow trees shrouded in curtains of Spanish moss, grew intertwined with short flowering bushes dotted with apricot-colored leaves, magenta blossoms, and long quill-like darts grouped at the center. There were trees running with sapphire-blue sap that smelled faintly of mint but that stung my nose and back of my throat so bad I almost coughed up a lung. A fallen tree trunk was festooned with something that looked almost identical to the *Dioscorea dodecaneura*, a rare plant with heart-shaped leaves, only these had clusters of cerulean florets protruding from their stems. They yawned open to reveal tiny gatherings of garnet-colored spines.

The sun was still slanting through the canopy as we made a slow march toward what we thought would be the center of the island, but the light was slowly dying. After what felt like hours, a familiar sound filtered through the trees. Circe heard it, too, and stopped abruptly, shoving her hand down on her hip.

"This cannot be happening," she said angrily. She stomped ahead, and as the trees thinned, we found ourselves on the beach again, this time on the opposite side of the island.

Marie let out a string of choice words while Persephone simply looked up at the sky and closed her eyes.

"Well, obviously this isn't it," I said. "Let's turn around and go back in at another angle."

I clenched my jaw and tried to quiet the voice in my head that reminded me this was yet another setback, another waste of our precious time.

Persephone walked the length of the beach, looking up and down the shore. I wasn't gonna throw a fit, but I felt like screaming, like crying. The frustration was so overwhelming it made my chest ache. I kicked the sand with the tip of my sneaker and struck something solid. A chunk of wood stuck up out of the ground. I grabbed it and dusted it off, then scanned the beach to discover that it was littered with chunks of similar debris. I wondered how many ships had sunk off these hidden shores and how many of the pieces now scattered there belonged to the ship Karter was on.

As we prepared to head back into the woods, I glanced behind me for a moment and wondered what could be lurking in the water on that side of the island that was powerful enough to not just sink a ship, but reduce it to pieces small enough to fit in my hand. I half expected to see some kind of tentacled beast lumber up onto the shore. Remembering that this was not out of the realm of possibility, I quickly turned and followed Circe back into the forest.

We kept a good pace, making sure to watch for signs that anyone else had been there recently. Four people had made it to shore, and I was certain Karter was one of them. If they weren't dead, they were on the island somewhere. Marie stayed close to me, and the plants that surrounded us stayed ready, shifting and rustling in the shadows.

"Stop," Persephone said. She'd gone ahead of us and now stood motionless in the shadow of a towering oak.

I stopped, midstep, and tried not to breathe.

"There's something up ahead," she said. She set down the

cage and stalked closer, keeping to the shadows. She disappeared over a small rise and returned a few moments later.

"It's a house," she said, picking up the cage. "It's empty."

"We should have a look inside," Circe said.

"Should we?" I asked. I already felt like we weren't moving fast enough, like we weren't covering enough ground. I didn't want to stop.

"We might be able to find something that'll put us on a more direct path," Circe said.

Marie took my hand and pulled me forward.

The house was a sprawling stone building set among the bracken that had almost completely overtaken it. It sat in a shallow dip in the landscape. The remnants of some kind of fence or animal pen lay broken all around it, completely overtaken with vines. A broken and crumbling pathway of cut stones led to the threshold of the main building, where a large door might have once stood. It wasn't a structure that was built at any time in the recent past. It reminded me of the ruins we'd passed on our way to the Great Eye.

Persephone ducked inside and I followed her. The building was remarkably well preserved. A hearth sat to one side of the main room and the stone floor was intact, arranged in a herringbone pattern. Several large clay pots stood against the wall, and the pieces of what must have been wood furniture were scattered throughout. The roof was thatched but was so overgrown with vines that the tendrils had pushed through and spread themselves across the stone walls.

Off the main room was a long hallway with two more rooms,

also in good shape for as long as they must have been there. Near the rear of the building, I found myself standing in an apothecary. Circe and Persephone joined me as Marie lingered in the front room.

Stone shelves ran floor to ceiling and clay jars still sat arranged on them, covered in dust, moss, and errant tendrils of star jasmine that had pushed their way through cracks in the outer wall. To the right stood an altar with the crumbling remains of a cloth decaying on top of it. On the wall directly above it, painted in faded hues, was the unmistakable image of the Colchis family crest—Hecate and her three faces, the key, the torches, the crown of poison.

Persephone put her hand on Circe's back to steady her. As I met her gaze her eyes misted over and I slipped my hand in hers.

"They were here," Circe said, clasping my hand between hers. "Right here, Medea and the original Circe. They stood here and—" She stopped suddenly, her voice choked with emotion.

I understood what it was like to come face-to-face with a part of your past. To feel like you were sharing space with the people who had come before and wondering what they wanted or needed you to do.

"And now we're here," I said.

Circe nodded as she stared at the image.

A sudden yelp drew my attention up. Marie walked into the room—backward.

I let go of Circe's hand and took a step toward her. "What are you doing?"

She stumbled, lost her balance, and fell straight back. She didn't even try to catch herself. Her head hit the floor with a sickening thud and my heart leaped into my throat.

"Marie?" I quickly knelt at her side. Her eyes rolled backward until only the whites showed under her half-closed lids.

Shouting from the hall cut through the air. Persephone and Circe both buckled at the knees. Circe fell into a heap as Persephone grabbed the stone shelf to try and hold herself up. Jars tumbled down and broke against the floor, scattering their contents all around.

A short man in a tattered T-shirt and jeans rushed in. He pointed at Persephone. "She's still up. Hit her again!"

Persephone moved toward the man and caught his outstretched hand in her own. The bones popped as she crushed it. The man howled in agony, clutching his mangled hand to his chest. A woman barreled into the room and stepped closer to Persephone.

"Sleep," said the woman through gritted teeth.

Persephone immediately collapsed.

I willed a length of vine to wrap itself around the strange woman, but before I could order it to choke the life out of her, she looked me dead in the eye.

"Sleep."

CHAPTER 19

I heard the retching first and then I felt the pain. As my mind found its way back to the confines of my skull, my senses awoke one by one. My entire body ached, like I'd fallen asleep in the most awkward position on the most unforgiving surface.

More retching and then a sour smell that made the muscles under my tongue seize up. I wanted to puke. I tried to roll over but the ache in my bones kept me pinned to the floor. At least, I thought it had to be the floor. I forced my eyes open and the light was like a knife cutting into my brain. I groaned.

So did someone else nearby.

I reached to touch my face and found that my hands rose up together. I focused on my wrists and saw that they were bound with zip ties.

"She's up," a voice said.

Footsteps rushed over and hands roughly pulled me into a sitting position. My head pounded, the room spun, and my stomach turned over again. I found my glasses dangling from the chain around my neck and slipped them onto my face. The lens was cracked over my right eye and the frame was bent, but as my eyes adjusted, the remains of a small stone building came into focus around me. This one didn't have a roof and only three of its four walls were still standing. Leaves, dirt, and broken branches littered the ground. A man sat on the edge of a wooden bench, clutching his stomach as he vomited onto the stone floor.

I turned away to keep myself from doing the same thing. I tried not to breathe. How did I get there? I didn't remember walking out of the other building or anything after the strange woman had told me to sleep and my body obeyed without question.

The same woman now took me by the shoulders and violently shook me. My head felt like it was going to come off my neck.

"Wake up. Get it together." She slapped me hard on the side of my face, knocking my glasses sideways. The sting of her palm sent slivers of light through my gaze. My eyes involuntarily teared.

I gritted my teeth. "Don't touch me."

"Or what?" the woman asked. "What are you gonna do?"

"Viv, don't antagonize her," said another man who had been standing behind me. He went around and patted his incapacitated friend on the back then sauntered over to me. "Just relax. We won't hurt you if you just do what we ask."

"The hell we won't," said the woman. "She's the reason Katrina is dead, Dre. I should kill her right now."

"How are we gonna get the last piece, then?" the man called Dre shouted back at her. "Look at Calvin. He's—he's not in good shape. We can't even get close to the wall."

They knew about the Heart.

They'd tried to get there and clearly, judging by the thick yellow vomit Calvin was spewing onto the floor, had run into something they couldn't get past without severe consequences. And they knew Katrina Valek—Mrs. Redmond.

"We don't need her!" Viv shouted. "We'll figure out another way."

"We *do* need her," said Dre. "And there isn't another way. Katrina had the right idea but you know how she was. She never wanted to wait too long for anything. She should have kept up the front a little longer and then maybe we wouldn't have to be in this position." He turned to me and scowled. "Katrina's our sister. Or at least she was. She's dead now, thanks to you."

I adjusted my glasses and stared back and forth between them. I could see the resemblance. I could also see the resemblance to someone else—Hermes. I wondered if they even realized how close their immortal ancestor was or how repelled he'd been by them to not even care what happened to them on the island.

I suddenly wondered if these were the people Phillip had encountered when he tried to sell the counterfeit pottery shard. It would explain why he couldn't get his story straight. The woman, Viv, was able to knock me out without laying a finger on me. She'd probably done the same thing to him.

There were three of them, but the goddess Persephone said four people had come ashore. Karter had to have been the young man she mentioned.

"Karter was with you, wasn't he?" I asked. "Where is he now?"

Viv scoffed. "Probably dead."

I was annoyed that a part of me wondered how she could be so callous toward her own nephew, but I was quickly reminded of how his own mother had treated him the very same way. I pushed aside the pity I felt for Karter. He'd stood by and watched my mother be poisoned to death and kept me from helping her. I hated him more and more with each vivid, terrible flashback.

"This island is a curse," Dre said. He walked back over to the man they'd called Calvin, who seemed to have emptied the entirety of his guts onto the floor. He sat shakily on the bench, his eyes glassy. Open sores tore across his skin. The flesh on his fingers was black from rot. One of his hands was folded awkwardly. He had my Persephone to thank for that.

"We got too close to the wall," Dre said as he followed my gaze.

I looked at him, puzzled. "Wall?"

"A stone wall, three stories high," Dre said. "Right at the center of this island. Built in a sort of rectangle. Big silver gate at the opening."

"It's not even locked," Calvin croaked.

"Doesn't need to be." Viv smirked. "Look what it did before you even got close enough to touch it."

"It?" I asked. "What are y'all even saying?"

Viv shoved her knee into my shoulder as she went by.

"Where are the people I was with?" I asked.

"Probably right where they fell," Viv snapped. "Don't know why you're worried. You know at least two of them can't die."

I straightened up. Karter must have told them everything. Anger bubbled up in me and some of the rotted leaves surrounding my legs turned an obscene shade of emerald green. I closed my eyes and willed the plants outside the ruined building to come in, to tear the place apart, to catch these people and crush them in their deadly grip. Rustling and cracking split the air. I opened my eyes to find all three of my kidnappers staring at me. Viv smiled. Dre and Calvin only looked on.

"You think you're the only one with abilities, sweetie?" Viv asked. She stepped toward me and caught my chin in her sweaty palm. She squeezed my jaw until I felt like it would pop out of place. Her dark brown eyes looked on me with all the malice and contempt she could muster.

"Sleep."

I awoke with a start, sitting straight up, my head swimming with confusion. The light had dimmed and shadows stretched across the floor. My throat was bone dry, my lips rough and peeling. The pain in my neck was like a raging fire.

Viv and Dre sat next to each other on the bench while Calvin lay balled up on a pile of leaves on the floor. His breaths came in slow rasping draws. Dre glanced up and scowled at me as he reached into his pocket and retrieved something—two small glass vials.

The Living Elixir and the invisibility serum.

My hands flew to my right pants pocket only to find it flat—empty.

"What are these?" Dre asked.

I said nothing. My mind went in circles. It was clear he wasn't sure what they were. I needed all six pieces of the Heart to bring my mom back and he was being way too careless as he rolled the vials between his fingers.

"Is one of them the Living Elixir?" Viv asked.

I looked away.

"It is," she said giddily. She snatched the vials away from Dre and held them close to her face. The silvery liquid of the invisibility serum coated the glass as she examined it. The crimson Living Elixir shimmered in the light. "Which one is it?"

I stayed silent.

She uncorked the bottle of Living Elixir and held it to her lips. It took everything in me not to allow the horror I felt to show on my face or in my movements. Viv watched me intently. She recorked the vial and opened the invisibility elixir. I allowed my eyebrows to push together just slightly and I pressed my hand into the floor, letting the dried leaves crackle underneath it.

Viv grinned and brought the vial to her mouth.

"Stop," Dre said, gently touching her arm. "She didn't say yes."

"She doesn't need to," Viv said. "Look at her. She knows this is the one."

Dre sighed. "Try to think about who she is, what she can do. It could be anything."

"But it's not just anything," Viv said. "Look at her face! She knows what it is and she thinks she can keep it for herself."

She tipped up the glass bottle of invisibility serum and drank it in one gulp.

I blinked back my utter astonishment.

Dre's face twisted into a mask of confusion. Something told me he was under the impression that *he* was the only one who was going to reap the benefits of the Heart. But he kept his mouth shut. Neither one of them appeared to give a single thought to Calvin, who lay gasping on the floor.

Viv held out her hands in front of her. "Do I look different? Do you notice anything?"

"No," Dre said flatly.

Viv suddenly clutched at her throat, then fell forward onto her hands and knees. The cry she let out was the sound of a woman in pain but it sounded like music to me. Served her right.

"What's happening to her?" Dre asked.

He tried to comfort her but she knocked him back as her chest and head took on a hazy quality. She lifted up her shirt and screamed at the sight of her nearly transparent torso.

"What is it?" Viv screamed. "What did you do to me?"

"It's an invisibility elixir, and I don't think you're supposed to drink it," I said.

She gripped her belly, which flickered in and out of view as Dre looked on in horror. Viv stumbled to her feet and lunged toward me, but Dre caught her and pushed her back.

"Don't," he said. "Not now."

"The other vial has to be the Living Elixir," she said. Her teeth were showing through her half-transparent cheek. She slid the second vial into her pocket and turned to Dre. "When we get to the last piece, we can make her transfigure it and we can both take it. I won't have to be the only one who gets to live forever."

She doubled over again and lowered herself onto the floor. The invisibility serum pushed its way through her, rendering different parts of her body invisible every few seconds. She groaned into the rotted leaves littering the floor.

"Keep that vial safe," Dre said to her.

I shifted around on the floor. Every joint in my body ached. I brushed the dead leaves from my shirt and they turned from brown to yellow and then green.

"Try anything and I'll have you asleep for a week," Viv snapped. Despite her precarious state of existence she hadn't given up on being an asshole. "I'll put you in a sleep that makes you forget to eat, to piss. You'll die before you ever get a chance to wake up. Keep it cute and we won't have a problem."

My head swam and a wave of dizziness washed over me. My arms and legs were stiff. "What did you do to me anyway? You can just make people pass out?"

"Viv has the blood of Hermes in her veins," Dre said. "He was known to put people in a trancelike state so that he could pass messages to them and make them think it was a dream."

They knew their own histories the way Circe and Persephone knew ours. I'd seen Hermes put Marie into a state of unconsciousness with barely any effort. Apparently they, or at least Viv, could do the same thing even though it took much more of an effort.

"We are favored," Viv said.

I glanced up at her. I wondered if she could see the shock on my face as I registered that her arms were completely invisible.

"We're special," she said through gritted teeth. "The old gods are dead. Katrina wanted to believe they weren't but that was just wishful thinking. It's better for us if they're gone.

We will be the new gods and we will take back everything that was stolen from us."

"You sound just like her," I said angrily. "She wanted to take her place among the gods, too." I almost laughed. "That woman couldn't even take care of her own kid. She couldn't get into a locked garden. Who lied to her and told her she was anything more than a bad mother, a thief, and a murderer?"

Dre's eyes widened in shock. "Watch your mouth. You might piss off Viv here, and maybe I won't stop her from getting to you this time."

Viv looked like she was ready to bum-rush me at any moment.

"She's probably going to die," I snapped. "You know what the main ingredient in that invisibility mixture is? Wolfsbane. It's deadly. And you just downed enough to kill a bunch of people. How did it taste?"

Viv tried to get to her feet but was stopped by another surge of pain.

"You're angry," said Dre, speaking to me like I was a little kid. "But it's only because you don't understand the bigger picture. Katrina was driven. She knew we deserved more, that we could *be* more. Maybe if your family hadn't been so selfish, you'd get it. Your line has been hoarding the Heart. If you had just done what she wanted we wouldn't even be here like this."

I rolled my eyes and turned away from him. "She wanted to be immortal and she didn't care how many people she had to hurt or kill in the process."

Dre shook his head. "We will do things differently." He

narrowed his eyes at me. "Help us get to the last piece. I know you can. Karter told us everything. Your abilities are remarkable. You can help us and nobody else has to get hurt."

"I would rather die," I said.

Viv huffed. "That can be arranged."

Dre kept his hand firmly on her knee even as it disappeared. "No. You'll come with us and help us get inside. Just like you did for Katrina in your garden. Get us in and out safely and we'll let you go. We won't need to worry about you once we've taken our rightful place. You'll be nothing to us and you can live your life—inconsequential as it is—in peace." He said it so casually, like he hadn't just insulted and threatened me at the same time. This dude and his family were the most selfish, self-obsessed people I'd ever met in my life.

"Y'all really think the gods are dead?" I asked.

Dre's eyebrows arched up. I wondered if Karter had, perhaps, left out the most important part of what had gone down in Rhinebeck—that a literal goddess had shown herself and brought her wrath down on Katrina.

"We know they are," Viv said. "Katrina tried to convince you otherwise, huh?" She shook her head. "Stupid. She was ridiculous." She stood up on shaky legs. "Let's go. It's early. We can get there in a few hours if we leave now."

Early.

I looked up through the trees that stretched high above the ruins of the building. The sun hadn't been fading after Viv had sent me to sleep. It was rising. It's why I felt like I'd been hit by a bus. I'd been in a deep sleep on a stone floor for hours. I'd lost an entire afternoon. A full night. It was morning and it was day twenty-eight. The last day to reach the Heart if I had any hope of getting my mom back. I struggled to stand up.

"I'll help you," I said as I got my feet under me. "But we have to go now."

Viv smiled. "See, Dre? She just needed a little convincing." She came over and shoved me with invisible hands out into the overgrown foliage. "Keep it cute," she repeated. "I'll have you in a coma if you try anything. Got it?"

I nodded, but it took everything in me not to envision ropes of Devil's Pet wrapping her up. They'd do it if I called to them and then she might put me back to sleep. I had to get to the center of the island, so I kept my head down as we began our journey.

CHAPTER 20

A tug in the pit of my stomach led me forward. It was the same feeling I'd had just before I found the Poison Garden back home. A sense that something was calling out to me, beckoning me. I tripped along behind Viv. With each passing moment she looked sicker; her brown skin was almost gray as the flickering invisibility of her various parts began to subside. But the poison in the wolfsbane—that would not subside. That would usher her to her grave.

She cursed at me and threatened me every five minutes that she'd put me to sleep if a single blade of grass so much as moved in her direction. I had to explain to her that there were some things I could control and some things I couldn't. I wasn't calling the plants, but they reacted to me nonetheless. Thick tendrils of Devil's Pet slithered along the ground on either side of us. The trees groaned as their boughs arched overhead. They were waiting for me to give a signal.

Behind me, Dre kept his arm around Calvin's waist as they shuffled along, trying to keep pace. Calvin's condition, like Viv's, worsened as we moved toward the heart of the island.

He struggled to keep his feet under him, and Dre kept yelling at him to get it together. I didn't know how somebody was supposed to just get it together after being poisoned by some toxic plant. These people were irrational, and that made them dangerous to me and to one another.

My throat burned with every breath I took. My lips were starting to crack, and I realized it was probably because I hadn't had anything to drink in hours.

I stopped. "I need water."

"Shut up," Viv said. She shoved me forward and I lost my balance, falling face-first into the dirt.

I was too exhausted to move, too wrecked to pay attention to the pain that bloomed in my cheek. As I lay there, a sprig of trumpet-shaped blooms stretched toward me. One of them tipped itself up and spilled a mouthful of dew across my lips. The water stung my chapped skin and brought with it an unexpected chill. Another bloom tipped over and gave me another little drink. My glasses were off again, but even then, I could make out the cream-colored blooms of the thornapple.

Viv grabbed me by the back of my T-shirt and yanked me up to my feet. "No cheating, sweetie." She kicked at the flowers and some of them broke off under her shoe. A ripple of anger coursed through me as she laughed. "On second thought," she said, "I am a little thirsty."

She reached down and grabbed one of the other blooms that was still brimming with dew and put it to her lips. Dre leaped forward and smacked it out of her hand.

"It's poisonous!" he shouted. "Angel's trumpet—I think."

I shook my head. "Wrong."

"It's not toxic, then?" Viv asked.

I could see the desperation in her wide eyes and pinched mouth. She was dying of thirst.

Drink it, I thought. *Every last drop.* I overdramatically wet my lips. The poison in the thornapple was enough to kill her. Paired with the wolfsbane in the invisibility mixture, I was hoping it would be enough to finish her off.

"It's poison," Dre said, glowering at me. "And you've had your fill of that already. Keep moving."

Viv shoved me forward and we pressed on. I looked between the trees as we went, hoping to catch a glimpse of Marie or Persephone. I kept hoping Circe's voice would ring out in the encroaching dark, but there was nothing. They might still be sleeping. Viv could have put them so far under they'd forgotten to breathe. Terrible thoughts invaded every corner of my mind until I found myself gasping for breath, sweating but not from the heat. I wrestled the panic into submission. A branch broke somewhere to my right. We all stopped midstep and Viv glared at me.

"I didn't do it," I said quickly.

She peered into the tree line, then turned back around. "Keep moving."

We continued on, but somewhere in the shadows there was a flash of something between the trunks. A person. I kept my head down and my mouth shut.

The trees began to thin and a rush of panic washed over me. I thought we were approaching another shoreline, but all of that faded away as we pushed into a large clearing littered with *Tacca chantieri*. The black bat flower. Exactly the same species as the ones in the glade outside the garden back home. The difference here was the sheer volume of them. They were so tightly packed I couldn't see the grass beneath them, and as I walked into the glade, they all turned their whiskered faces toward me.

Across the clearing stood a stone enclosure. Dre had said it was three stories high but I think he was off by a lot. The top of the wall was at least twice the height of the house in Rhinebeck, maybe a full five stories. It rose up from the surrounding land like it was born from it. A constellation of star moss bloomed at its base and swirled up the sides like thick green galaxies, catching each slick slate-gray stone in its orbit. Dre put his hand on my shoulder and I shrugged away from him.

"See the entrance?" he asked.

The gleaming metal gate was festooned with vine-like structures I didn't recognize. They were a deep cobalt blue with thorns the color of rust and blooms a shade of peachy coral.

"What is that vine?" Dre asked.

"I—I don't know. I've never seen anything like it before."

Dre tilted his head back. "One of those thorns barely nicked Calvin and now he's dying."

"Shut up!" Viv snapped at her brother. "You don't know that." She pushed past me and knelt next to Calvin, who had collapsed into a heap among the black bat flowers. "You're gonna be fine. As soon as I'm stronger, I'll bring you back."

"That's not how it works," I said.

Viv glared at me. "It'll work the way I say it does."

A snapping of branches drew my attention up just as Circe and Persephone emerged from the tree line on the other side of

266

the clearing near the towering enclosure. Circe set down the two cages.

I began to sob. I was so relieved they were safe. Circe's face twisted into a mask of anger as she looked me over. She curled her hands into fists and a rumble shook the ground under my feet.

Viv clamped her hand down on my shoulder and squeezed as hard as she could. "You better tell them something. Don't let them come any closer or I'll put you in a coma."

I held up my still zip-tied hands in front of me. "Stop! Just—just stay there!"

"Everybody calm down," Dre said.

Circe still marched toward us. Viv inhaled sharply and a wave of sleepiness washed over me. My knees buckled and I almost fell. Circe stopped.

"She's one of them, one of Jason's descendants," I said through a yawn. My arms and legs felt heavy. I struggled to keep my eyes open. "She can put you to sleep, just like Hermes could."

"Hermes?" Viv asked in confusion. "Why are you talking about him like you know him?"

Circe narrowed her eyes at me—no—past me. Behind me.

Something slammed into me from the side and I tumbled to the ground. A growl like a wild animal cut through the air. Viv broke for the tree line. Persephone was on her in the blink of an eye. She caught her by the throat and lifted her up.

"Hold her!" Circe yelled.

Viv twisted around in Persephone's grip and locked eyes

with Circe, who suddenly gasped and fell straight back into the sea of black flowers.

Hands looped under my arms and pulled me back into the brush. I kicked and screamed, trying to break the person's grip. I reached up and grabbed at their shirt, tearing it, clawing at their face. A face I knew.

Karter.

He pulled out a pocketknife and slipped it between the zip tie and my wrist, cutting the plastic. As soon as my hands were free, I hauled off and socked him as hard as I could, catching him somewhere close to his nose, judging by the amount of blood that began to leak from his face. I pummeled him with closed fists. I screamed at him until my throat hurt.

"Get away from me!" I screamed through a torrent of tears.

"I'm helping you!" he yelled back as he attempted to catch me by my wrists. "Briseis, please! I'm so sorry! Please!" Tears streamed down his face.

I scrambled to my feet and darted back out into the clearing. Viv lay still and silent, her neck bent at an angle that told me she was dead. Marie was crouched over Circe, cradling her head. Persephone had Dre by his neck, his feet dangling off the ground.

I ran up to Marie. "Is she—is she hurt?"

"That woman did something to her." Marie's voice was changed, as were the color of her eyes. "I can't wake her up."

Circe's chest rose and fell so slowly, with a pause so long in between, that for a second I thought I had watched her take her last breath. When she drew in another, I realized Viv had put her into one of those sleeps that she wouldn't wake up from.

I frantically searched Circe's pockets to see if there was

anything I could use to revive her. The vials from her stash of apothecary plants were all mixed up, and in my panic I didn't know which one was which. I tried to think. I needed smelling salts, ammonia. I scanned the glade and found what I was looking for near the walled enclosure. Clover.

I sprinted over and plucked several out of the ground. Scooping up a handful of soil I pressed the clover into the dirt and tried to do something I hadn't attempted before. I could make plants grow by pushing my power outward, focusing on the plant. But I needed to do the opposite. I needed the nitrogen-rich clover to rot—and quick. I concentrated on reversing the flow of energy, drawing it back up and into myself, taking from the plant instead of giving. The clover wilted and crumbled into the mound of soil in my palm. Stirring it with my finger, the overpowering scent of ammonia wafted into my nose.

I rushed back to Circe's side and held the dirt by her face.

"Bri, what in the hell is that?" Marie asked, covering her nose and mouth with her sleeve.

Circe flinched, coughed, then sat bolt upright. I tossed the dirt away and brushed off my hands.

"Are you okay?"

"What happened?" she asked groggily.

"Viv put you to sleep again," I said. "She did the same thing to me last night."

Circe picked herself up and stood next to Persephone, who still had Dre held up in front of her.

"Look," Persephone said. She lifted her other arm, revealing the handle of a knife protruding from between her ribs.

"Oh my god!" I shouted.

269

"Somebody shanked you!" Marie said.

Persephone clenched her teeth. "It's not gonna kill me but it still hurts! Pull it out!"

Marie walked up and yanked the knife out in one quick motion. Persephone winced.

I leaned over and put my hands on my knees. "I'm gonna be sick."

"You gotta be kidding me," Marie said angrily.

"C'mon," I said. "Give me a break."

"No. Look." Marie pointed, and I followed the gesture to see Karter walking slowly toward us. Marie was gone from my side in the blink of an eye. She snatched Karter up and brought him over to me. "Look who decided to crawl out of the brush like the rat he is."

"Please don't kill me!" Karter pleaded.

"Us!" Dre shouted from Persephone's grip. "Don't kill us! Please!"

"I can't think of one single reason why I shouldn't," Marie said. The growl of her voice made Karter's eyes grow wide. "It looks like somebody already whooped your behind."

Karter's gaze flitted to me, and Marie smirked.

"I've been trying to help you!" Karter wailed. "Bri, I called you! I told you where we were going!"

"Are you kidding me?" I was so angry I wanted to scream. "You think that you're helping me? You saw what happened to my mom! You were right there! You let it happen!"

"My mom would've killed me, too!" he shouted. Marie gripped his arm and he lowered his tone. "You have no idea what she was really capable of."

I put my face so close to his I could smell the blood smeared across his face and I could feel the warmth of his strained breathing. "I don't know what she was capable of? I know better than anyone."

"She killed my dad!" Karter shouted as another rush of tears traced their way down his face. "She didn't even pretend like she didn't do it. He was in her way, and she cut him down like she does to every single person who stood up to her. She would have killed me, too, if she didn't think I could have helped her get to you."

I didn't have a reply. I was shocked into silence.

"Your father was weak," Dre mumbled. "She never should have—"

Persephone closed her hand around Dre's neck, and his lips turned so purple they were almost black.

"You're all related?" Circe asked.

"Uncle Dre. Auntie Viv. And—" he stopped short. He glanced over to where Calvin lay. He too was unnaturally still. "He was a cousin, but they were close."

Persephone set Dre's feet on the ground but kept her hand at his neck. He sputtered as he fought to catch his breath.

"You cut her loose?" Dre asked, eyeing my hands and then staring at Karter. "You would turn your back on your family?"

"Family?" Karter stared at the man with so much contempt I could almost feel it rolling off him. "Is that what we are? Family?"

He stepped toward Dre and Marie put her hands on his chest to stop him.

"Maybe your mother was right to try and get you out of the

picture," Dre said. "You're weak, like your father. You don't deserve the kind of power we're about to possess."

"You don't deserve it and neither do I!" Karter shouted. "I don't want it anyway. I never did." He looked down at the ground. "I just wanted my mom to be proud of me."

"She wasn't," Dre said. "I hope you know that."

Marie eased her grip on Karter and he turned away from his uncle.

Persephone pushed Dre back. "You're done talking."

Dre raised an eyebrow. He was incredulous. "You think you can tell me what to do?" He drew his lips together and spit directly into Persephone's face. She broke his neck and tossed his lifeless body into the forest so hard it splintered the bough of an elm tree as it crashed through.

Persephone stood panting, her teeth bared, eyes wide.

"Seph," Circe started, but Persephone shook her head and stomped away from us.

Circe sighed and bit her lip. "Look what these people have become." She nodded toward Karter. "Look what they're willing to sacrifice to get to the Heart."

"Y'all aren't any better, are you?" Karter asked through a mask of pain. "How many family members have you sacrificed for that thing?"

"Shut up," Marie said angrily. "You don't know what you're talking about. They're not hunting people down and murdering them."

"They're still dead," Karter said. "And all for what? For nothing."

"He's right," Circe said.

Marie and I both whipped our heads around to look at her. She looked up, the full moon blazing in the nighttime sky. "We've lost too many. But no more. This is never going to be over if we don't get in there and get the last piece. We have to end this."

I searched Karter's face for some trace of the guy I'd shared so much with, the person I'd trusted and laughed with and confided in. To my astonishment, I found something of the person I had found a strange and beautiful friendship with. Right there in his big brown eyes was the bumbling, awkward guy who loved horror movies and couldn't do much in the garden besides rake and sip lemonade. He was still in there.

He turned to me, his eyes pleading. "Bri—"

"I—I can't forgive you," I said before he could finish. "I just can't."

His tears cut paths through the smears of blood on his cheeks. "I know. I'm still sorry. I just need you to know that."

In that moment all I could think of were the Fates. They'd insinuated that we were all fated to follow a certain path. If that was true, then it meant Karter was meant to be there on Aeaea as the last members of his family treated him like he was expendable and left him alone in the world. It struck me as uniquely cruel.

"I'm so sorry, Bri," Karter said again.

I held my hands up and willed a cage of vines, none of them poisonous, to bind him. Coiling tendrils and wide leaves encapsulated every part of him until I could only see his eyes through the tangle of foliage.

"He's not going anywhere," I said. "And we have something more important to do right now."

Circe nodded in agreement and retrieved the two cages as Persephone gazed toward the walled enclosure. Something dark and unreadable passed over her face.

I went to Viv's body and took the vial of Living Elixir from her pocket, grasped Marie's hand, and approached the gate.

CHAPTER 21

If the gate guarding the entrance to the Poison Garden back home was a wicked grin, this one was an insidious smirk. The bars weren't straight up and down anymore but instead, tilted to the left and right like jagged broken teeth. The gaps were big enough to walk through. Maybe that had been what Dre and the others attempted to do. But how they hadn't managed to worry about the blue vines creeping their way across the bars didn't make sense. The audacity of the coral blooms paired with the blue trunks of the vines screamed danger. As we approached, my suspicions were confirmed as the air spilling down my throat turned icy. It took my breath away. Circe and Persephone both began to cough. Marie sucked in a breath and held it.

I angled my body to slide through a gap in the gate, and as I passed through, a coil of the deadly vine encircled my ankle and climbed up my leg, turning around my calf and gripping my thigh. The thorns drug across my jeans, then laid themselves flat.

"What is this?" I asked.

Circe ran her hand over her forehead. "I think it's called Beast of Burden. I've never actually seen it in person."

I let out a breath and pushed forward, helping Circe transfer the two cages into the interior of the walled structure. Marie came in after her and then Persephone. We stayed close to one another as we navigated a narrow pathway that followed the right angles of the interior wall. When we emerged into the inner space, we all stopped. I was dumbstruck. This garden was like the Poison Garden on steroids.

There were no mundane herbs, no quiet plants. The inner sanctum of the giant walled garden was in full bloom. There were no partitions there, only a big open space where the most poisonous plants I knew of grew straight from the ground. The air was made of ice—of poison. Devil's Pet with offshoots the size of tree trunks slithered among the bushes of crimson brush. More tangles of Beast of Burden crowded the overgrown pathways between the earthen plots. Black hellebore, bloodroot, clusters of euphorbia, hemlock bushes the size of boulders, mandrake whose roots rose from beneath the rich soil like the appendages of a corpse. Poison ivy clung to every brick, and all of them seemed to wake from their long slumber as we entered.

In the nearest corner of the garden a tangle of black hellebore as far across as I was tall bloomed, showing us their bright canary-yellow centers. The entire gathering of plants twisted back on itself, revealing a waist-high rectangular stone structure.

A box.

Persephone slowly examined it and a moment later called out to us. "You won't believe what this is."

As I approached the structure the hellebore pulled back to reveal a single word etched into the stone wall above the box.

Medea.

No one said a single word. The box was a sarcophagus, and in it were the remains of the woman whose story had defined the Colchis family.

"Who put her here?" Marie asked.

Circe shook her head. "I—I don't know." She pulled out the moon clock and held it in her trembling hand. Its ticking fell in time with the beating of the caged piece of the Heart. "We don't have much time left."

As we moved away from the grave, the hellebore fell over it like a shroud, hiding it from view. But as Medea's final resting place was hidden, something else was revealed.

As if on command, the deadly foliage shifted in the moonlight, revealing a mound in the very center of the garden. At its peak stood what could only be the thing we had gone there to find—the Mother. The last piece of the Absyrtus Heart.

It stood like a petrified monument to Medea's slain brother, Hecate's only son—Absyrtus. It was triple the size of the pieces we'd seen that still retained their anatomical shape. It sat atop an onyx stalk as thick around as my leg. The roots laced through the earth, breaking the surface like the tentacles of a sea creature every few feet and extending all the way to the wall.

"Do you know where we are?" Circe whispered. "Gods . . ."

My breath caught in my throat. It wasn't that we were in the presence of this rare and deadly plant, it was that we now stood in the spot where Medea had laid her brother to rest. Where she had, no doubt, wept over his grave, where she had spilled her own blood to keep these shattered pieces alive. We were again sharing space with Medea across the centuries.

"Any idea what we're supposed to do now?" I asked. We'd

done the impossible. We'd gathered the pieces of the Heart together in the same spot, but what now? I took the vial of the Living Elixir out of my pocket and rolled it between my fingers. "Maybe we pour it on top of the Mother?"

Persephone quickly moved to one of the cages and opened the metal door. She retrieved the intact piece of the Heart and set it in the dirt beside the Mother near the top of the mound. The roots immediately anchored themselves in the ground, and while the beating of the Heart had dwindled to once or twice a minute, it stood tall, like it knew it belonged there.

Everything around us was steeped in shadows. The dense foliage made voids of corners, and the abyss of fading purple above us made night-lights of the stars. We had no time left. We had to figure out how to combine the pieces of the Heart and hope that Marie and Persephone's presence was enough to count as bringing them together.

Circe unlocked the other cage and took out the flat red stone. She handed it to Persephone, who buried it in the mound near the foot of the Mother. Circe made a sound. Like a short quick gasp—a sob. But as I turned to look at her, Marie swept in and turned my face to hers. Persephone walked behind me and took Circe by the arm, pulling her away.

"What's going on?" I asked.

Marie slipped her hand around my waist and pulled me close. "Have I told you how much I care about you today?"

I stared into her big brown eyes as she let her gaze move over the contours of my face like she was trying to memorize every part of it. A sinking feeling settled over me. "What's wrong?"

Marie shook her head and gently pressed her lips to mine.

She tasted like honey. Her breath was warm and sweet, and she held me like this embrace would never ever be enough. Normally, I would have been swept up in being with her like this, but this was different. There was an urgency in that moment that made me uncomfortable. When she pulled away, I readjusted my glasses. I thought she'd be smiling at me, happy we'd finally come to the end of our journey, but the expression that met me wasn't that at all. She was on the verge of tears.

A gasping sob sounded from behind me, and I turned to Circe and Persephone. They were caught in an embrace, their faces buried in each other's shoulders. Circe's tearstained face twisted into a mask of sorrow, of anguish.

"What is it?" I gave Marie's hand a squeeze and went to stand with them. I put my hand on Persephone's arm. "You guys okay? What did I miss?"

Circe didn't move to wipe her face or let go of Persephone. She simply exhaled a shaky breath as another torrent of tears cascaded down her cheeks.

"We knew what we were getting into," Persephone said.

Circe huffed. "Did we?"

"Maybe not fully, but we're here now and I think I finally understand what needs to be done and you do too." She kissed the top of Circe's head as her own eyes misted over. "I've had my suspicions. You know this. I think it's clear now—we must recombine the pieces. We have to give up what was given to us in order to make it whole again."

I didn't understand.

"We know who we do it for," Persephone said. "I've lived my fair share of lifetimes. I'm ready, Circe." Persephone broke

Circe's grip and stood in front of me, her hands resting on my shoulders. "How far are you willing to go for the people you love, Briseis?" She smiled warmly. I was completely lost. "You've crossed an ocean," she continued. "You've braved the sea and this wild island, and now you're here, to save your mom. Gods, what a remarkable person you are. To be loved by a person like you is the most any of us could ever hope for. I would go to the ends of the earth to make sure the people I care about most could be free from their burdens, from their fears. Let me do this for you and for Circe and for those who may come after. Let me do my part to unburden you."

She leaned in and hugged me tight, then moved to the mound and climbed atop it. She stared into the dark, and it took me a second to realize she was staring at Marie.

A wave of confusion and then the clarity of understanding broke over me like the crashing of a wave. Persephone was a piece of the Heart now, and we had to reunite them. She was saying goodbye to Circe and to me, and now she was waiting for Marie to join her.

"When we were in the Grotto with the Fates, I saw something I couldn't share with you," Marie whispered.

"I—I don't understand," I said.

She grasped my hand. "We gotta get your mom back. And if I have to give something up to make that happen, I will."

My mind went in circles. "Wait. What—what are you talking about? We're here. All the pieces are here and—"

"The pieces have to be put back together," Marie said softly. "Like a puzzle."

She stepped away from me but I cut off her path. I pressed

my hands into her chest. "What are you doing? Stop talking to me like you're not gonna be here when all this is over." As I said the words I understood fully how this had to work. The Heart flowed in Marie's blood, in Persephone's, too. It gave them their immortality, and if the pieces were to be reunited, they had to give that up. Not just their power but also their lives. The very lives granted to them by the Heart. It was the fear that had lived in the back of my head from the beginning of this journey. It was always there, but I hoped that we could find something, anything, that would give us another option. But we were out of time. This was the only path forward.

"No," I said. "No. Marie, please. You can't—"

"I can. And I will." The tears flowed from us both. "I knew it might be like this before we left Rhinebeck. I just—I couldn't tell you that. I didn't know how. The Fates, they cut my thread."

I couldn't speak. Marie and Circe had seen what would happen. Clotho, Atropos, and Lachesis had shown them.

Marie took my face in her hands and I wound my arms around her neck. "I've stolen more moments than I can count," she said. "But these past few weeks with you were the best of them." She gently slipped the vial of Living Elixir from my hand.

Circe moved to my side and put her arm around me.

"Tell your mom I said hi." She kissed me and then was standing opposite Persephone before I could blink.

Circe held me tight as I struggled against her. "Marie! Please! This is what the Fates showed you?" I turned to Circe. "We have to find another way!" She simply shook her head and tightened her grip on me.

Marie uncorked the vial and deposited the contents of the Living Elixir in the soil next to the Mother. Persephone took a glinting object from her pocket and drug it across her palm. She handed the knife to Marie, who repeated the action, and as they held their hands over the Mother, Marie locked eyes with me. She smiled the way she had when we'd first met. Like I was the only thing she could see, like I was the only thing that mattered.

Marie and Persephone allowed their blood to flow onto the surface of the Heart, and in the light of the full moon, in a garden of poison on an island that wasn't supposed to exist, the Mother—the original piece of the Absyrtus Heart—began to beat.

CHAPTER 22

The pulse rocked the ground under my feet, and I clung to Circe as we struggled to keep our footing. The sound reverberated through the enclosure and in my bones. I stumbled back and fell hard on the ground. The Mother shifted on its stalk, and as the fresh infusion of blood moved through it, it sprouted a hundred new tendrils that latched onto Marie and Persephone.

I scrambled to my feet, but the roots of the Heart had risen out of the ground and wriggled on the surface like serpents. I tried to find a path through to Marie, but they cut me off at each turn. I frantically searched for her in the dark and found her standing rigid next to the Mother. Curling, nearly transparent vines had sprouted from the upper chambers of the Heart and attached themselves to Marie's arms and legs. She didn't fight them. She just stood there, her eyes wide and black. The tendrils penetrated her skin like needles, and something flowed away from her through the tubelike structures. Something viscous and crimson—blood. The Heart was draining Marie and Persephone.

I kicked aside a tangle of writhing roots and pushed my way

up the side of the mound. The ripple of heartbeats shook the soil loose beneath me and my feet sank into the nearly liquified dirt. I fought my way through and reached Marie just as her legs gave out. She fell into my arms and we both tumbled to the ground. Cradling her as best I could I pulled her to my chest. Her eyes were open but she wasn't looking at me or anything else. Her breaths came in ragged tears. I put my face in her hair, breathed her in. Her fingers twitched at her sides as the life drained out of her.

I pressed my lips to the cool skin of her forehead. She sighed. And then she was still.

The vampiric vines detached themselves from her and from Persephone, who lay lifeless in Circe's lap. Circe had managed to make her way up the opposite side of the mound and into the same state of shock and sadness that I was in.

The tendrils retreated, and the Heart itself began to sink into the top of the mound, like it was being pulled inside by an unseen hand. I scrambled back, pulling Marie's lifeless body along with me.

As the Heart disappeared in the dirt, the beating became muffled and distant, but the shock of each pulse still rippled through the ground. The mound collapsed in on itself, and then suddenly, everything went eerily still. The beating stopped. The network of roots retreated beneath the ground, and the other plants settled until the only noise I could hear was Circe's gasping sobs and my own heart, not just beating, but breaking.

I gazed around the garden in a state of hazy grief. Circe rocked back and forth, cradling Persephone in her arms. The moon had risen high above us and its dappled silvery light now flooded the enclosure.

Marie was gone.

Persephone was gone.

And I didn't have my mom back.

I'd failed everyone I loved, and I didn't know how I was going to face Mo when I went home. I promised her I was going to bring Mom back, and I hadn't been able to do it. And I'd have to tell Alec and Nyx I couldn't save Marie. I'd have to live with that, myself.

"What did we do wrong?" I sobbed.

Circe turned to me. "I—I don't know."

I rested my hand on Marie's chest and stared down at her face. She looked like she was sleeping. I leaned down, buried my face in her hair, and cried until there were no tears left.

"Briseis." Circe's voice cut through the night and reached me in the depths of my unbearable sadness.

Something was wrong.

I looked up to see movement in the dark. The roots of the Heart had retreated below the surface of the soil and went still, but something was still moving under the dirt. The ground bubbled up like it was being displaced from somewhere below. It took me only a second longer to realize that something was rising from beneath the place where the mound had been.

Suddenly, the beating of the Heart picked up, strong and steady. I gripped Marie's shirt and held my breath.

A hand—covered in tattered, broken flesh—clawed its way out of the dirt.

I opened my mouth to call to Circe but no sound came out. Fear had stolen any rational thoughts I might have had in that moment. All I could do was watch as the hand, connected to an arm, attached to a torso, emerged from the earth.

I'd backed up as far as I could. Unable to carry Marie with me any farther and unable to leave her, I resigned myself to the fact that I wasn't going to be able to get away from whatever this creature was that was slowly pulling itself from the ground.

In the pitch-black night, with only the moon and the bioluminescent glow of foxfire lighting the space around us, I watched in a state of utter shock as a broad-shouldered man emerged from the remnants of the mound and pulled himself up to a standing position.

His bones were visible through swaths of ragged skin that knitted themselves together at his shoulders, hips, and neck. The man's chest heaved as his body mended itself. He tipped his head back, breathed deep, then leveled his eyes and stared directly at me.

"Where am I?" he asked.

My hands flew to my ears, an involuntary reflex in response to the sound of his voice. It was like Hecate's, a chorus of voices all in one, wrapped in an echo and impossibly loud.

The man pressed his fingertips to his lips. He shifted where he stood. "Where is my sister?" He stretched his arms and looked at them as if they didn't belong to him.

"Who are you?" Circe asked. Her voice sounded small and hollow compared to his. How she'd found the courage to speak was beyond me, but the man turned to her and spoke gently.

"Absyrtus."

Circe's eyes widened in the dark. We hadn't failed after all.

We did the thing that had never been done. We had resurrected Medea's beloved brother, Absyrtus, and he stood before us.

"My sister," he said. Something like fear invaded his voice. He looked around the enclosure as if he expected to see someone there.

It was my turn to find a way to suspend my own disbelief about what was happening. "Medea," I said quietly.

The man took two halting steps and then, finding his balance, swept over and crouched in front of me. He rivaled Hecate in height, and his hands seemed massive compared to hers. His eyes were kind as they stared down at me.

"Yes," he said. He reached out and grasped my arm, and it took everything I had not to scream. His hand was big enough for his thumb to loop over my shoulder while his little finger cradled the crook of my elbow. He stared into my face. "Where is she?"

I glanced to the place where we'd found Medea's grave. Absyrtus rose and walked to the spot, where he fell to his knees and held his face in his hands.

"She's been gone a very long time?" he asked without turning around.

"Yes," I managed to say.

He heaved a sigh, and his shoulders rolled forward. "She has returned to the dirt and I am risen from it." He looked at the stars twinkling against the midnight sky. "Mother."

The ground shook with the violence of an earthquake. The stone wall behind me split right up the middle, and pebbles rained down on me as I covered Marie's body with my own.

A tangle of Devil's Pet covered me like a blanket, shielding me from the rain of rocks and debris.

A low hum emanated from the far end of the garden. A great black abyss grew out of the darkness, like the widening of a hideous mouth, and from it stepped a giant black dog. Its yellow eyes glinted in the darkness as it stalked out of the hole that now danced with the light of a roaring fire.

A familiar figure emerged from the void.

Hecate. The mother of us all.

Her gaze swept over me. A small smile danced across her lips but faded as she eyed Marie. She looked to Circe who, despite her grief, seemed to be in a state of utter shock at seeing Hecate in the flesh.

Absyrtus walked toward his mother as if he were wading through water, like he couldn't get his body to work in the way he needed it to. She approached him just as slowly, with caution, a look of disbelief stretched over her perfect face. As they met in the middle of the garden she reached out and, cupping the back of his head, brought his face to her chest. He wrapped his arms around her, and they held each other, murmuring private things into the night air. When they broke free from each other, Hecate removed her outer cloak and wrapped it around her son before approaching me.

Her face was damp with tears as she loomed over me. "You've come to do this impossible task. Something I myself could not have done, and you have succeeded."

"Have I?" I asked as I gazed down at Marie.

Absyrtus stood at his mother's side. "You have," he said gently. "I dwelled in the nothingness so long I thought I had become a part of it for all time." He crouched down and touched Marie's forehead.

She took a breath.

A ragged cry, made of sorrow and hope, broke from my chest.

"Marie." I couldn't find any more words to say. Her eyes remained closed, but she stirred, and relief flooded through me. "Wait," I said. "What about Persephone?"

Absyrtus followed my gaze. Hecate put her hand on his arm. They exchanged glances and he nodded. He walked to Persephone and picked her up, cradling her against his chest.

I gently transferred Marie's weight to a bed of black ivy that had bloomed around us and stood in front of Hecate. "You can let her come back, too?" I looked to Absyrtus. "You can bring Persephone back, can't you?"

Hecate cupped my face in her hands. "She came to this sacrifice willingly."

Circe stumbled over to me and fell to her knees in front of Hecate.

"Please," Circe said. "Please don't take her."

"You are unaware of the rules," Hecate said. "If there is to be an exchange, it must be a soul for a soul, and Persephone made her choice, in words whispered to me over offerings and black flames—things that will remain between her and me for eternity. She would not allow it to be anyone else. Not you, not Briseis. Just her."

I recalled the tail end of the ritual Circe and I had walked in on Persephone performing, how angry Circe had been.

"She has always been with us," Circe sobbed. "My great-great-grandmother knew her and her mother before her." Circe sat back, resigned to the understanding that Persephone would not be coming home with us. "I don't know how to live without her."

Circe was right all along. We would not come out of this unbroken. We would not be whole.

Hecate studied my face and smiled warmly. "Marie is granted another chance. Persephone wanted it to be no one but her who kept the balance." She took a long, deep breath. "And because you have returned my son to me, he can make his journey to the underworld. That, too, is an exchange. One that requires an equally meaningful return."

Hecate glanced at Absyrtus, who nodded and motioned for me to follow his gaze toward the void. Someone else was emerging from the darkness. As her face came into view I broke into a run. The poison garden cleared a path for me as I sprinted forward. I felt like I was moving in slow motion, my legs pumping under me but not fast enough. Nowhere near fast enough.

I leaped into her arms before she'd had a chance to fully emerge from the void. The heat beat against my face and the drop-off below me looked a mile deep, but I didn't care. Nothing mattered in that moment because I was finally, after all we'd been through, in my mom's arms.

"Mom! Mom! Mom!"

She locked her arms around me and pulled us out of the gaping void to where the cool night air swirled around us. The moonlight danced against her skin, and she pressed her face to my hair and whispered my name over and over again like a prayer, like a plea, like a thank-you, like I love you.

CHAPTER 23

I don't know how long I held on. Minutes, hours. I never wanted to let go. Mom turned my face to hers and I took her in all over again.

"Is this real?" I asked. With everything I'd seen I was worried this was some illusion, some trick.

"Yes, baby," she said to me. "It's real."

Her voice was like a song, and I never wanted it to end.

Absyrtus approached us, cradling Persephone in his arms. We stepped aside, and after giving me a nod, he descended into the void and disappeared. Circe came up, supporting Marie's weight as Marie hobbled along beside her. Hecate loomed in the darkness behind them with her dog at her side. Marie breathed deep, like it hurt. She held her hand up in front of her, opened and closed her fist.

"Something's wrong," Marie croaked.

"She's mortal," Hecate said as she brushed by us.

I looked Marie over. She was changed in a way I couldn't fully explain, but she smiled at me and reached for my hand, which I took and held tight. Mom looked back and forth between me and Circe. There was so much she needed to be filled in on, I didn't know where to start.

"Mom," I said. "This is my auntie Circe."

My heart sputtered as I realized that we were standing in the center of the deadliest place on earth and now that Marie was mortal and Mom was back, we couldn't stay there.

All around me the deadly foliage pulled back. Blooms closed and thorns retreated. The air was suddenly warm and sweet instead of icy. Mom and Marie would be all right.

Mom smiled and pulled Circe and Marie close to us. We clung to one another for a long time, crying, smiling, feeling grateful and grief stricken and full of wonder, all at the same time.

Hecate moved around us and stood at the opening to the void. I caught her eye and she sighed.

"We will meet again, my dear Briseis. Of that you can be absolutely sure."

With that, she turned and the void swallowed her and her familiar once again.

Circe helped Marie limp out of the poison garden as I trailed behind with my mom. I stopped and plucked a sprig of hellebore and willed it to bloom until it twisted itself into a wreath of the deadly black flowers. I paused to set it atop Medea's grave.

I ushered my mom through the gate and found Marie standing outside the tangle of vines holding Karter captive.

"What's goin' on here?" Mom asked.

"Karter's in there," I said.

Her eyes grew wide and she stepped toward him. "Make the vines go away, Bri. I want to whoop his behind myself."

"You're alive?" Karter asked. "I'm really happy about that. Please don't kill me."

Mom crossed her arms over her chest and glowered at him.

"Wait," I said. "I'm not saying he doesn't deserve it, but I have a different idea."

"Beating him to death sounds like a good idea to me," Marie said.

I was happy to see that while her immortality had been stripped away, her personality remained intact.

"What do we do with him?" Circe asked. "If we leave him here, he's dead."

"I see no issues with that," Marie huffed.

I shook my head. "No. We take him to Hermes. That dude needs a pet project, and Karter needs . . ." I trailed off. I didn't know what he needed exactly. A mentor? A parental figure? A friend?

I willed the vines to release him and he fell into the sea of black bat flowers, panting.

"C'mon," I said to him, taking my mom's hand again. "Let's go home."

The trek through the forest was hours long. Little was said. All I wanted to do was curl up with my mom and listen to the beat of her heart. She, too, was somehow different. There was a stillness about her that felt like she was just doing her best to hold it together. She'd spent a month in the underworld and couldn't have known for sure that we could find a way to get her back. She said we'd have time to talk about it later and so I tried to let it go. All she wanted was to take me home and I was okay with that.

When we reached the shore we piled into the dinghy and began to row out to the ship. Bioluminescent streaks under the water's surface sent my heart into a frantic gallop, but as the sirens appeared, so did two other figures.

On the sandy shoreline, Persephone, queen of the underworld, stood bathed in moonlight and with her was her namesake, our Persephone.

"They're together now," Circe said. "Her and everyone who has come before. She'll always be with us."

Our Persephone now carried the lyre and played it so beautifully Circe began to weep. The sirens retreated, and we boarded the ship and sailed away from Aeaea on Circe's conjured winds. Persephone stayed on the shore waving to us, and we stayed at the rail until the island disappeared behind the veil of invisibility that had guarded it since time immemorial.

I spent the early morning hours curled up beside my mom. She managed to find a way to sleep, but I couldn't. I was afraid I'd wake up and find that everything we'd done was just a dream. I was scared to death that Mom wouldn't be there when I woke up, so I just didn't sleep. As Circe guided us to port at the foot of the Great Eye, Hermes met us on the rocky beach and Circe went to talk to him.

"Who is that guy?" Karter asked.

"Your thousandth great-granddaddy," Marie said.

Karter looked confused.

"It's Hermes," I said, wondering what that might mean to him. I studied his face as he took in the information.

"He didn't tell us that's who he was when we first met him," Karter said.

"He's kind of a dick," I said.

Marie stared at Karter. "I guess it runs in the family."

Karter eyed her and Marie squared her shoulders. She may not have retained her strength after her transformation, but I had no doubt she'd beat Karter's ass if he so much as looked at her sideways. He didn't test her.

Mom walked up and put her hand on my shoulder. Karter looked back and forth between us.

"I'm sorry," Karter said, keeping his eyes on the deck. "I'm never going to be able to tell you how sorry I am. My mom—" He sighed, shaking his head. "Everything you saw her do, everything you learned, it was terrible."

"Terrible?" I asked. "She killed my mom. She killed my birth mom. You said she killed your own father. 'Terrible' is the understatement of the century."

Mom's grip tightened on my shoulder.

Karter nodded. "Yeah. I just—now that you know all of that, would you believe me if I told you that those three things alone weren't even the most evil, awful things she'd ever done?"

I stared into his face. He was on the verge of tears. I imagined what it must have been like to be in his shoes, to know that this person who was hurting everyone around her was the only person in the world he had to depend on.

"What do you want me to say?" I inched closer to him, and honestly, I didn't know if I wanted to punch him, or hug him, or cuss him out. "You said you were my friend and I trusted you."

"I know." Tears streaked down his face. "I know and I hate myself. I didn't know what to do."

"You could have told me what your mom was doing sooner. You could have said something. Were you ever really my friend?" Now it was my turn to let the tears fall. "All that time we spent together in the garden, after everything I shared with you . . ." The knot in my throat made me feel like I couldn't breathe.

"Mo's cooking," Karter said. "Watching you make those plants grow, being right there with you when we were pulling weeds and talking about school. I was your friend, and I didn't know how much I wanted that until I met you. My mom liked for me to be alone. It was better for her that way." He set his jaw and winced. He angrily wiped his face. "I was your friend and I still want to be."

"I can't just pretend that none of this ever happened." I looked at my mom. I had her back, but I'd never forget how it felt to watch her die or the million times I thought I'd never see her face again. I'd never be able to get Mo's grief-stricken face or the sound of her wailing as she held my mom's lifeless body out of my head. It didn't matter that he felt bad, that he regretted it. He couldn't take it back.

"I just want you to know that I'm going to regret what I did forever and I'll try to make it right," Karter said. "Even if you don't ever forgive me."

I turned away from him and gazed out over the water as it broke against the rocky shore. Mom looped her arm around me and pulled me close. I wrapped my arms around her waist and only let go when Circe gestured for us to join her.

We went down to the shore and followed Circe and Hermes into the lighthouse. Hermes sat in the chair by the fireplace. He appeared to be thinking very hard about something, his dark eyes troubled. Karter stayed close to the door as I pulled out a chair at the table and guided Marie to it. Hermes glanced up and looked her over.

"You've been stripped of immortality," he said. "And still I sense an air of relief about you. Why?"

The look on his face caught me off guard. His eyebrows bunched together, his head tilted—he looked like a kid who'd just asked a very important question, something he couldn't fully comprehend.

Marie stared right back him. "I *am* relieved. I'm lucky to even be alive."

"It's this fragility that excites you?" he asked.

"I have lived my share of lifetimes." Marie sighed as she echoed Persephone's words. "But I don't know if I've ever really *lived*." She glanced at me. "But that's what I plan to do now, so yeah. I'm happy to have a chance to do that."

Heat rose in my face. It was the wrong time to feel so moved by her words, but it was clear they were directed at me and I couldn't help but smile.

"And you," Hermes said, turning to Mom. "You've come back from the underworld. Do you understand what a feat that is?"

"I do," Mom answered.

"Only a handful of mortals have ever been able to return from that place," he said.

Mom nodded. She hadn't gone into detail about what she'd been through, but there'd be time for that later.

Hermes stood and crossed the room to tower over Karter, who tried desperately to press himself into the wall behind him.

"And what will you do?" Hermes asked. "You're alone in this world."

"He's not," Circe said. "Remember what Persephone—" She stopped short and swallowed whatever sob or grief-stricken howl had clawed its way up her throat. "Remember what she said. She found purpose with us, with her family. Maybe you have a chance to do the same thing." She looked to Karter. "He's looking for redemption, but he's not gonna find it with Bri or her mom or anyone else here. Maybe you can help redeem him . . . for himself, for his own benefit."

Hermes returned to his seat and motioned for Karter to follow him, which he did on unsteady legs. He sat down in a chair across from Hermes, and they stared at each other for a moment before Karter looked away.

"You'll stay," Hermes said to him. "We'll see what redemption there is to be had."

Hermes kept Karter busy unloading our things from the ship and transferring them into the trunk of our rental, but between rowing the dinghy out to the ship and lugging our stuff up the rickety steps, Hermes had taken Karter aside and said something to him that sent Karter into his own thoughts. He avoided eye contact with me and didn't try to speak to me at all. I was a little surprised by how much that stung.

Finally, when we'd loaded our things, Mom helped Marie into the back seat of the car as Circe and I said goodbye to Hermes. Karter stood in his shadow, staring down at the ground.

"You know where to find me should you need my assistance," Hermes said.

"I thought you didn't get involved with mortals," I said.

He eyed me carefully, and I decided not to press him. He'd clearly had a change of heart, and whether that was due to Persephone's intervention or Karter's sudden need of him didn't really matter. He could use his power to help somebody other than himself, and that was really all we'd been asking of him anyway.

As Circe turned to head to the car, Karter slipped a folded piece of paper into my hand and pressed my fingers closed around it. His hand lingered on mine for just a second longer than it needed to.

"Bye, Bri," he said.

I pulled away from him, tucked the paper into the back pocket of my jeans, and walked to the car without looking back. As we drove away from the Great Eye, I breathed deep, let the cool air from the cracked window fill my chest. We'd taken our own hero's journey, and we'd emerged with wins that meant more to me than anything, and losses so profound I thought there was a good chance we hadn't been able to fully process them yet. Circe reached over and patted my shoulder, and when I looked in the rearview mirror, Mom smiled at me the way she did when I'd done something she was proud of.

Nyx met us at the airport outside Red Hook when we landed the next day. She and Circe shared a new round of tears, and what I hadn't fully realized was that Persephone had her mind made up long before we left Rhinebeck, much the same way Marie had.

Nyx had left Mo at the house with Dr. Grant keeping watch.

"And Roscoe, of course," Nyx said as she peered down at our pile of belongings. "No cages with strange plants growing inside them?"

"No," Circe said. "Never again."

Nyx went to Marie and ran her hands over her face. They pressed their foreheads together and cried tears of relief.

"Be careful," Marie said. "I'm fragile now."

Nyx huffed. "You? Fragile? I don't care what transformation you've undergone. Nothing could take away that spark. Try to remember that."

The door to Marie's sedan popped open, and Alec climbed out. He wrung his hands together in front of himself as he approached Marie.

"Welcome home," he said.

Marie studied his face. "Were you crying?"

He dabbed at his eyes. "Absolutely not."

"Liar," Marie said.

He reached for her, and she pulled him into a tight embrace. Alec closed his eyes as he rested his head on her shoulder.

"I love you," he said.

"I love you, too, old man," said Marie. "Please don't get your snot bubbles on me."

We all piled into the car and made the drive to Rhinebeck. I thought the ride would be relaxing, a relief to be so close to home, but the anticipation was palpable. I couldn't wait to get to Mo, but I also couldn't put the thoughts of Karter and his new life with Hermes aside. I suddenly remembered that I still had the note he'd slipped me in my back pocket. I pulled it out and read it.

I'm sorry, Bri. I'm so sorry. You deserve so much, and I let you down. You don't have any reason to forgive me, and I don't even think I should ask you to do that. Please just know that if you ever need me, I'll be here.
Karter

P.S. Also, if I turn up missing, Hermes did it, because this man is on some other shit.

"What are you grinning about?" Marie asked gently.

I handed her the paper and she smiled, too. "I hope Hermes two-pieces him with that staff of his. He deserves it."

As we pulled into the driveway, Mom was out of the car before it came to a full stop and Mo was pulling open the front door as the tangle of vines that had encapsulated the entire outer facade broke open.

Mom rushed forward and Mo caught her around the waist and pulled her close. Relief and joy poured out of them both like water from a broken dam and it spilled out over all of us. Marie began to weep and Nyx embraced her as I made a break for Mom and Mo.

Mo caught me up and pulled me between them. As they clung to me, I caught a glimpse of Circe. She hung back, dabbing at her eyes. I stuck my hand out and motioned for her to join us. She hesitated, and then Mom and Mo both reached for her, bringing her in close.

The tendrils of vines that had encircled the house snaked across the ground and wound themselves around my ankles. Circe laughed and kissed me gently on the top of my head. I leaned my head on her shoulder as hundreds of pale yellow peonies burst to life around us.

It was the reality I never knew I wanted, but that Mom and Mo had somehow been able to prepare me for, a blending of the past, the present, and the future. Not a choice between any of them but the combined joys and sorrows of each in their own way. I was the seed set in the soil, nurtured by the love of my family, and allowed to grow, to stretch, to reach for the sun.

CHAPTER 24

SIX MONTHS LATER

"Ma'am, we don't do that here," Marie said into the phone. She clicked her freshly painted nails on the counter and hung up without another word. "I'm real sick of people asking us if we do readings. That's Mama Lucille's business and they know that."

"Give people a little bit of a break," Mom said, patting Marie on the shoulder, as she grabbed her keys and picked up her bag.

"You know Marie has zero customer service skills," I said. "She told Dr. Grant's dad to put some baby powder on the top of his head."

Mom whipped her head around and looked at Marie.

Marie grimaced. "Hold on. Every time he comes in here the light bounces right off the top of his dome, and last time it caught me right in the eye and I couldn't see for several minutes."

Mom rolled her eyes. "You're off phone duty, but you can stock up the glass and stoppers for the tinctures. Bri and Circe got a batch of something brewin'."

"It'll be ready soon," I said.

Circe came into the apothecary carrying a basket full of honeysuckle. "You leaving?"

Mom gave her a quick hug and readjusted her bag. "Yeah. I'll be home by three. The painters finished up last night, so today, I'm measuring for the new coolers."

"Exciting!" Circe said, beaming.

The revenue from the apothecary was enough to hire on some folks for the shop back in Brooklyn and open a new one right here in Rhinebeck on Market Street. Mom was having way too much fun picking paint colors and ordering new supplies.

Circe was still technically dead, and while rumors swirled that another of the Colchis women had returned to the area, she was fine leaving it up to conjecture. Anyone who knew the truth—Mama Lucille, Dr. Grant, Isaac, Alec—was fine with allowing the gossip to fade away.

Other things were not as easy to let go of. Sometimes I'd find Circe standing outside the door at the back of the Poison Garden, palming the key. She thought it would be easy to let her lifelong job of guarding the Heart go, but it turned out to be more of a challenge than she'd anticipated. She went her whole life believing that the protection of the Heart was the most important thing in her life. I couldn't blame her as she struggled to put that burden down. To help, we filled the underground chamber where the Absyrtus Heart had been housed with rocks and dirt and sealed the door shut. I offered to get rid of the key, but she insisted on hanging on to it a little while longer.

Circe turned her attention to the care and running of the apothecary, and together, we fixed it up and got back to work. We brewed vats of essential oils and distilled flower essence. We grew our poison and black flowers for the goddess, restocked the everyday plants, and even set up an online shop. We spoke often of Persephone, of Hecate, and less often of the Heart.

Mom headed out, and Mo poked her head into the apothecary.

"Y'all good in here?" she asked.

"I have something for you to try," Circe said.

Mo tried to sneak away, but Circe caught her by the arm and pulled her in. "You keep putting this off, but I gotta put my foot down. You insist on using that natural deodorant, and I respect that, but—"

"It's chemical free," Mo said. "Aluminum free. No weird stuff I can't pronounce. It's not that bad."

"I thought somebody was roasting onions the other morning," Circe said.

Mo stared blankly at her.

Circe grinned. "And when I came downstairs, do you remember what you were doing?"

Mo crossed her arms. "I just came back from a walk with Roscoe. I was sweaty. What was I supposed to do?"

"No more natural deodorant, Mo!" Marie said. "Please! They don't sell new nostrils anywhere around here, and I'm scared the ones I got now are permanently damaged."

Mo turned to me. "Tell me the truth, love. Is it that bad?"

I nodded. "Is the natural stuff onion scented? Maybe that's the issue."

Marie laughed until tears streamed from the corners of her eyes.

Circe handed Mo a small round container. "I don't know where you got the one you're using, but please burn it and use this instead."

Mo huffed. "I'm tryna be healthy, and y'all worried about some funk?" She pretended to be mad, but she put the container directly in her pocket. She knew it was the truth.

Circe's phone rang in her pocket and she answered it. The smile on her face told me it was Dr. Grant.

"Don't forget we have a date tonight," Circe said into the phone. "Dinner and a movie. I'm paying."

Marie walked to the door and gave me a little nod. I glanced at Circe, who waved me out the door, letting me know it was cool to take a break.

I took Marie's hand, and she led me outside and around the side of the house. She pulled me close and kissed me. I kissed her back. Everything about her was exactly the same as it had been before, but she *was* changed in some way. I'd watched her cut her hand on a piece of broken glass when we were fixing up the apothecary, and her frustration at having to wait days for it to heal was hard to watch. Her mortality made her vulnerable in a way she hadn't been in more years than she could remember. Watching her navigate this new way of existing was both heartening and scary. I worried about her safety more than I'd needed to before, but she hadn't lost a single bit of her attitude and seemed to be finding a rhythm that worked for her.

We held each other under the vines and blooming roses for a long time. She murmured things against my ear that affirmed what I already knew—I was in love for the very first time. The thought sent a little shiver of excitement through me. We would be mortal and fragile together and there was something beautiful about that. As we returned to the house, I thought I'd like to spend all my free time kissing her under the shade of the foliage.

We had this one precious life and what we did with it was entirely up to us. I wanted to use it to love and be loved in return.

ACKNOWLEDGMENTS

What I meant to write was a story about a girl who got to embark on a magical, fantastical adventure. What I ended up with was a story about the heavy burden of generational trauma, the toll grief takes on the mind and body, and ultimately how the bonds that connect us can span time, space, and even death. I think that's the wonderful thing about storytelling—it has the power to help us along. In my case, there was healing to be done. I'm so grateful that I get to write these stories.

Big shoutout to my agent, Jamie Vankirk, and my editor, Mary Kate Castellani. Thank you to Ksenia Winnicki, Beth Eller, Emily Marples, Lily Yengle, Lucy Mackay-Sim, Noella James, Erica Barmash, Mattea Barnes, and the entire team at Bloomsbury.

To Raymond Sebastien, thank you so much for your work on the covers for both *This Poison Heart* and *This Wicked Fate*. Your work brought these characters to life.

As always, a big thank-you to my family—Mike, Amya, Ny, Elijah, and Lyla. Love you all so much! To my brother Spencer, love you and thank you for always being there.

And of course, to my readers—I don't get to be here without your support, so let me take a moment to tell you that I appreciate you all. From your TikToks and BookTube videos to your character art and Instagram posts, it's all so wonderful, and on days when I feel like I should hang it up, you remind me exactly who I do this for. Thank you from the bottom of my heart.